Shielded Mates Volume 3

A Guardians of Chaos Duet

C.D. Gorri

Shielded Mates Volume 3
A Guardians of Chaos Duet

Featuring:
Witch Shield
Vampire Shield

Guardians of Chaos Books 3 & 4
by C.D. Gorri
Edited by BookNookNuts
Copyright 2021, 2022 C.D. Gorri, NJ

To the loyal readers of LLS,
You are the best! <3
Xoxo,
C.D.

STOP! Before you go, sign up for my newsletter and get the latest on
my releases, giveaways, freebies and more:
https://www.cdgorri.com/newsletter

DEDICATION

To the seekers, the defiant ones, the ones who know they are special and rock out to their own beat.
We knew the second we saw you; you were unique, and we love you for it...
xoxo, C.D. Gorri

Witch Shield

Guardians of Chaos

BLURB

She's on a mission to prove magic exists. He has to change her mind.

What happens when a Witch falls for a feisty normal bent on outing the single most vital secret in the known universe?

Egros must convince Elena's mate's sister to stop her investigation into the supernatural world. The cunning female is too smart to bespell. He'll just have to try the old fashioned way.

Margo Wells has done the unthinkable. The human woman has tracked her brother all the way to the Guardians of Chaos' Keep, and she's not leaving without proof magic exists. All her life, Margo was different. With this revelation, she's finally found vindication.

Will Egros put a stop to the infuriatingly beautiful woman's investigation, or will he lose his heart instead?

Guardians of Chaos Pledge

I am the watcher in the storm.
I am the sword who strikes true.
I am the iron shield.
I protect against those who seek to control the wild nature
of magic.
I am the guardian of chaos.
To thrive, we must be free.
From chaos comes creation.

Prologue

any years ago...

Egros closed his eyes, not even bothering to block the blows from the other children in the yard. He hadn't done anything to deserve it, but he took it all the same.

This wasn't the regular school recess bullying that he'd seen on after school specials when his father was not home to scold him for watching *normal* television. Witches weren't normals, even if they could pass more easily in society than other supes. Some even went to regular schools and universities.

But not Egros. The Pyke Coven heir did not attend any ordinary school, and the boys who were alternately kicking and punching him while calling him all manner of crude names were not ordinary children.

Oh, they hated him the same way normals hated their peers. With complete and absolute prejudice, and with no one particular reason. He felt their scorn rain down on him with every blow and curse word.

Maybe it was simple jealousy. Maybe they felt threatened by his family name. Or perhaps, it was just sheer stupidity. He contemplated all possibilities while doing his best to protect his nose and teeth from sustaining permanent injury.

The boys ranged in age from Egros' own thirteen years to sixteen and maybe older. Perhaps they could have been friends in some other reality. But not in this. Not where Egros Pyke was smarter, richer, and more powerful than any one of them.

Quiet and studious, he did not ready to anger the way the other boys did. His magic was too great for him to give in to typical hormone induced aggression. Egros knew better. Had been taught better by his now gone mother.

No, he could not lash out, even if he wanted to. Egros Pyke had to maintain control above all else. Even revenge.

The truth was, if you combined the students currently stomping on him, Egros would still outdo them all when it came to money, through no fault of his, brains, which his extensive reading could take credit for, and power, some of which he was born with, the rest he'd inherited, as all Witches do.

All Witches were taught the basics when they were very young. The first lesson number learned was that magic was finite.

There was a limited supply of magic in this plane of reality. It could be reused, recycled, and willed to another. A practice that Witches in particular knew how to do. Passing one's own store of magic to another not of their line was rare, but possible.

The most common way for a Witch to gain his or her magic was to inherit magical stores from an ancestor, usually a parent. Then he or she would continue the tradition of passing it on from one generation to the next.

Magic could theoretically be bartered, sold, or given away to another. But those cases were extremely rare. Some Witches were greedy and grasping, just like normals. They wanted more magic than their lot and sought ways to procure it.

The best way to ensure more power was to marry into a Witch family renowned for their strength. Just like his father had done when he'd married Egros' mother.

An opportunistic Witch, Bartholomew Pyke had taken lead of their Coven from his father before him, but leaders needed power. The Pyke family had nearly depleted their own magical stores years ago.

Bartholomew was not satisfied with what he had, and so, he'd found a young, trusting Witch to be his bride. Egros' mother had been in the area visiting family. Young, naïve, and trusting, she'd been seduced by Bartholomew into a loveless marriage that had been the death of her. Literally.

Igraine Renaldo had been barely twenty, sweet and pliable. She'd used her incredible magic primarily to grow things. Plants, trees, and flowers native to the New Jersey forests were her specialty. Herbs however, were her favorite.

She'd taught Egros the importance of balance when he was barely old enough to walk in the back of their always cold house. No matter how high she'd set the thermostat, Egros always found it bitterly cold inside the Pyke house. Her herb garden was the only place he'd ever felt warm.

Bartholomew Pyke was not known for warmth or feelings of any kind. Especially not towards his awkward son. After his mother's death, things had only gotten worse.

He supposed he should thank his dear old dad

for the way he could take the beating he was currently receiving without a single flinch. His present abusers were only kids, after all. Just like Egros, but not. Of course, everyone had their differences.

Most Witches dressed like normals in jeans and t-shirts touting their favorite teams or bands, but not Egros. His dress was too somber, too plain to fit in.

He wore all black from head to toe. Had done so ever since his mother had died. It was his own rebellion against his father. The only way to get back at Bartholomew Pyke through his own constant mourning for the mother who'd loved him. She'd been the only parent who had ever shown him any affection at all.

Also, unlike his peers, Egros did not flout rules. He had nothing to prove by going against authority figures with gags and pranks. His own rebellious plans were too serious, too important for such triviality.

"Why won't you cry?" One of his assailants shouted, kicking him harder.

But Egros was beyond pain at the moment. He'd managed to close off that part of his brain, losing himself in thought. He could blast them all with a single twitch of his finger, but he wouldn't. Magic was not allowed to be performed outside of class until a

Witch had reached the legal age of sixteen years as set forth by the Council of Covens.

No. Underage magic was simply not allowed. There was a simple reason, and that was young Witches were not able to control their spells. Magic was notoriously untrustworthy in someone with no strength to confine it.

So no, Egros did not use magic to stop their kicks and punches, though he could have.

Easily.

The boys didn't see his restraint. Did not understand that he was protecting them by not lashing out. They wouldn't thank him for it either. In fact, he was pretty sure his silence made them hit harder.

Rolling onto his stomach to protect his face, he closed his eyes and waited for the kicks and stomps to end. Egros could take a beating. Had done so for years at the hands of his father.

Imagine what they would say if they knew the head Witch of the Coven Pyke regularly beat his only son and heir. Thoughts of his father filled his head as Tom Riley spit on his back while pummeling his stomach with the hard rubber toe of his sneaker clad foot.

"You gonna just take it, runt?"

"Mommy can't help you, can she? I heard she was a drunk who went and fell out of a window, is that right?"

"Nah, I heard she killed herself because she was ashamed of having this emo fuck for a son!"

"Oooh! Yes! I think he is gonna cry!"

They were wrong, though. Egros never cried. Not even at his mother's funeral. Bartholomew Pyke would not tolerate a son who wept. There was not much the old man did abide. His son, least of all.

The bell rang, signaling the end of the school day, and Egros exhaled. He knew the boys would finally stop tormenting him now that they were free to leave school. One last mouthful of phlegm hit him in the back of the head before they snickered and walked away.

He barely even cared. This petty torment was so much better than what waited for him back home. Egros lay there a moment, reaching out with his preternatural senses to connect with the trees and plants surrounding the courtyard. He always felt better when he connected with nature.

It was soothing somehow, communing with the trees the way his mother showed him when he was very young. Trees were so often overlooked in today's world. But they were the watchers outliving most people, standing strong and true. Trees were the first record keepers. Sentinels, all of them, standing guard, protecting those under their purview.

Egros often talked to the trees. It was how he knew where to walk, when to stop, when to hide under their shade when his father was rampaging back home. Trees had an excellent system of communication. They could pass knowledge from one to the other through their roots. A little known fact even among the supernatural.

"Egros?" Mr. Bellamy, their teacher, found him curled in a ball on the ground.

Egros sat up slowly, wincing at the pain in his ribs. He looked at the older Witch and waited for the inevitable questions that he knew would come.

"Happened again, didn't it? Why don't you fight back?"

"Nothing happened, sir. May I go to the restroom," he winced as he stood up.

"The bell rang. School's over. Go home Mr. Pyke."

"Thank you, sir."

The bruises would hurt worse tomorrow. He knew this from experience, and yet that was the least of his worries. Egros swatted at the dirt the boys' shoes had left all over him. He hated having dirt on him.

School was over for the day. He walked home through the secret path in the woods only he seemed to know about. Unsurprising, since the other students who attended the private school open only to magical folk, mainly Witches from his Coven, tended to steer clear of the Pyke family heir.

To normals, it was a private school for troubled children with a fiercely steep tuition. That alone kept most people from applying, though there were one or two every now and then. Witches were taught to control their magic at St. Barnabas' School.

But Egros already knew all about control. He had to. Both his parents' lineages were long and powerful. The Pyke Witches had squandered their magic, while the Renaldo family had only grown theirs.

Rumors spread through the coven like wildfire after the unlikely match had been made between his mother, who had been twenty years his father's junior. Though her death, years earlier, had been ruled accidental, Egros always suspected that was not the case.

She had been a victim of his father as well, and shame filled him at his own weakness and inability to protect her. Igraine Renaldo had tried to protect her child, but she'd been no match for Bartholomew Pyke.

His coldness would have been enough to kill her soul, but it was his rage after she'd refused his demands to hand over her magic that had killed her.

After that, Bartholomew had been on the hunt to

locate the Renaldo family magic. But Igraine had hidden it well. It was the one secret she'd made Egros keep, and he would until his dying day.

"What is mine is yours, my son. Our secret, okay? He must never have it, promise me?"

"I promise Mother."

"When the time comes, you will know how to unleash your power. Just believe in yourself, my precious boy."

It was the last time he'd spoken to her before going on an overnight retreat with his class. The next day, he'd returned to find her dead and his father angrily demanding him to hand over anything his wife had given to her only child.

"Mom is gone? She's dead?" Egros asked, tears pouring from his eyes. Fear and disbelief had made him ask questions he knew his father would hate him for.

"Stop sniveling, boy," his father had sneered, and struck him across the face.

"Now, tell me where she hid her magic."

"I don't know, sir."

"Useless brat. Just like her. Get out of my sight!"

He'd raged for hours until neighbors came to take Egros for the night so Bartholomew could mourn privately.

Mourn. Yeah, right.

Egros knew then what no one else would admit. The head Witch of the Coven Pyke had killed his wife, and no one was going to do a thing about it. Egros was alone. One day, he would pay the man back for what he'd done. He was going to leave the Coven, and when Egros was strong enough, he would return to make his father face justice for his crimes.

It had become Egros' sole motivation for being the best Witch he could be. Over the years, his father had grown more displeased with his son. Even worse, the old man grew enraged and bitter as he remained unable to locate his wife's powers.

So yeah, Egros took his beatings. Suffered them in silence, just biding his time. He knew where his mother's magic was all along. Even now, his fingers brushed against the uncut amethyst pendant that he always wore around his neck.

The stone was suspended by magic inside a round silver circle and hung from a strand of leather made from dragon skin hundreds of years ago. Not the Shifter kind, but the wild ones who used to roam the earth before knights and crusaders wiped them out.

The pendant was an old family relic on his mother's side. It was also the key to unlocking the Renaldo magic, his rightful inheritance by birth and his mother's wishes. All he had to do was whisper the words his mother had told him over and over again since he'd been a baby.

But Egros knew better than to try that now. If his father knew he held the key to Igraine Renaldo's magic, he would force the boy to hand it over. And that was something Egros would never do. Not willingly.

"Not ever," he whispered fiercely.

Egros' eyes narrowed as he came into the small dried up patch of land behind his father's house. It was his mother's old garden, planted when Egros was just a baby. It was dead now. Just like her.

"Where is it, eh? Useless boy thinks he can hide it from me. It's mine!"

Egros heard his father's mad mutterings from outside the open window. The old man was in his room again, tossing his belongings around. Always searching for the thing that would never be his.

Egros turned around and walked back into the woods. He would sit and wait till his father's madness passed, or exhaustion took him into one of his deep slumbers. Either one would be preferable to what would happen should he enter the house just then.

He sat against the gnarled bark of a beech tree and waited, eyes closed, until the still of the night cloaked him in its protective covering. Some magic was just natural, and the woods had always welcomed the Pyke boy.

When he opened his eyes, sensing his father's quiet, Egros saw a black Wolf lying beside him. A Shifter, not a wild beast. One he knew well.

He smiled at Storm and patted his head. Egros was all alone in the world except for this Wolf Shifter. He'd befriended him one day in these same woods not too long ago. Storm had been injured and Egros had healed him.

Now and then he showed up, just to check in. He always seemed to know when Egros had had a bad day. Like today. The Wolf's name was Hudson Stormwolfe. He was a friend and sort of a protector too, waiting to intervene should his own father prove too rough.

"I'm fine. It was school bullies, nothing else," he told the Wolf.

The beast whined, and Egros looked down and grinned. A brown paper bag was by his leg. Inside, he found a sandwich, apple, and carton of iced tea.

"Thank you, Storm."

Then he ate. Together they stayed in the woods, boy and Wolf, until the sun broke through the trees. Something told Egros not to go home that night.

Good thing too. The next day, he'd returned home to discover his father gone. The Enforcers, that was what they called their own magical police force, were already there. They investigated, questioned Egros, but he remained silent.

A few hours later, Kingston Baldric, leader of Storm's group of Guardians, had come to fetch him. Egros had not said a word while the adults negotiated custody of him. He was still an underaged Witch.

"He has no family, no friends, and no one else who wants him," the Dragon Shifter stated without inflection.

"Fine. But he has a future here," one of the Coven elders said.

"He will decide his future. Until then, he will stay with us where he will be protected."

That was how Egros Pyke wound up in the Keep of the Guardians of Chaos. The building was old and large, full of hidden power and secrets. Egros could sense magic and mystery.

Power had a unique smell. It gave him a tingling feeling he couldn't quite explain. But he knew he was safe there, and with that revelation, the boy finally exhaled.

"Welcome Egros," Kingston Baldric, Alpha Dragon Shifter, and leader of that group of the Guardians of Chaos said in a kind and even voice.

"Thank you, sir."

"You understand what we do here?'

"Yes."

"And you wish to join us?"

"I do."

"Might I ask why?"

"Because magic needs me. And I will protect it, with my life if necessary."

"Alright," Kingston said, nodding at him. "First, you will train. Then, when you are a man, and if you still want to, you may make your vow to the Guardians."

"Agreed," Egros said, and shook his hand.

This was his destiny. He felt it in his bones and in the pendant pulsing gently around his neck. Egros was finally right where he belonged.

ONE

"Margo Wells?"

"Hmm?" Margo's head swiveled right once she'd heard her name.

"Letter for you."

"Oh," she replied. "Thanks."

One of the several uniformed security officers working in the nondescript government building stopped in front of her desk. He checked Margo's badge before nodding, then he dropped the large manilla envelope with the word classified stamped across it in bright red ink on the plain wood surface.

Margo stared at the envelope and shivered once. Her office was always a brisk 64 degrees. She should have worn a sweater, she thought before turning her complete attention to the plain missive the guard had brought her.

She blinked, cleared her throat, and perused the ominous looking package before touching it. It was big, 10 by 13 inches from her estimation. Seemed way too large for the desk she was currently using while working this temporary assignment. It practically dwarfed the small rectangular keyboard on her private laptop.

Margo never used anyone else's hardware. Simply didn't trust it. Besides, she had higher security clearances than most agents could ever dream of. It was easy enough to disguise the super powered laptop to look like the part of the standard Lenovo ThinkPad everyone else used. Was only a matter of stickers, really.

Still, Margo frowned before reaching out to touch the envelope. A sharp pain went through her head, gone before it even registered, and she waited for the brief flash of intuition that usually followed such an occurrence.

For years, she'd had *feelings* when something big was about to happen. Usually, something life-altering. She didn't call them premonitions, though that was as close to the truth as she would allow. Never cared for the word psychic, either. Rang too close to 900 numbers and infomercials for her liking.

Still, these little tidbits of knowledge that some-times crept into her conscious mind from the great beyond, the ether, or some other such place, were not always good. Some considered them a burden, but she was too cautious to label them that.

Truth was, it had been a long time since she'd shared them with anyone. It just wasn't worth it. How often had she been called crazy by someone she knew after she'd shared a glimpse of their future? Even worse, were the horrified stares and wide berths they'd walk around her if her predictions came to pass, as they always did.

It was a difficult lesson, but Margo had learned to keep her visions to herself very early in life. Oftentimes, she simply ignored them. Like that one recurring dream she'd been having ever since she was a child.

In that dream, Margo was either sleeping or hurt, she could not tell which. But that wasn't why it was so odd. It was the fact she was being carried by a fair-skinned stranger with purple flames engulfing them both that freaked her the fuck out. That strange violet hue matched the ethereal glow that seemed to come from the handsome stranger's eyes.

She could not see his entire face, just that hypnotic, inhuman stare of his. Secretly, she thought it was hot, but that was something she only ever admitted to herself. Didn't matter, anyway. He was a figment of her imagination. A guy that hot simply had to be.

Margo did not know who he was, only his eyes were visible. The rest of his face was hidden by her own poofy crown of curls. She couldn't tell if he was nuzzling her or what.

Whatever.

She did get the feeling he was taking her to safety. That she was, in fact, safer with him than anyone else on the planet. Her own knight in shining, *er*, leather. He wore a black leather jacket. In fact, his entire outfit was black.

Margo had kept that particular vision to herself for almost thirty years. It was just too private to share, and she couldn't be sure if it was only her imagination. Some childish dream of prince charming coming to rescue her or something like it. Besides, Margo didn't need rescuing. She was a kickass woman who was more than capable of saving herself, *fuck you very much* to all the naysayers.

That morning though, she'd seen something else. Over her usual steaming mug of coffee, prepared with one cream, no sugar. Margo had caught a glimpse of this same envelope. Large and plain, sitting on her desk.

Her visions were like that sometimes. Like snapshots someone had just airdropped straight into her brain. Still images. No context.

Frustrating? More often than not. But the years had taught her patience. So, she'd accepted the image, committed it to memory, waited a bit, and *bam*, there it was.

Like magic.

The very same thick manilla sleeve, printed label with her name in bold, no return address, from her vision. There was only one clue as to where it came from. The small stamp at the top left corner portraying a hand holding the world told her all she needed to know.

The envelope had come from Mother.

Not Mother, as in the woman who gave birth to her, but *Mother*, as in her boss. The code name was for the five foot ten inch, three-hundred pound, half-Chinese, half-African American male who ran her department.

Mother made even the stoutest of agents cry with only the slightest hint of his disapproval in the curl of his upper lip. How he got the moniker, she had no idea, and she wasn't interested in asking. The last guy who did got his head put through a wall. So yeah, she was good with not knowing.

He was even scarier than some of the creatures she

tracked for him. Assessing the situation, Margo could only come to one conclusion. This was classified. She looked around to gauge her level of privacy before even attempting to open the missive.

Nope. The place was hopping with agents. She rolled her eyes, impatient as always. She could practically hear Logan in her head.

Just chill out, Gogo.

That's what he would say in this instance. Her brother had dubbed her *Gogo* years ago because she was always in a rush and unable to get the words 'Logan go' out of her mouth fast enough. So, it was always '*go go*' until she became *Gogo* herself.

Sigh.

It could be worse. She had a coworker dubbed Head because of the size of his noggin.

Not her fault, she was always looking for what came next. Especially when she could often see the outcome as clearly as if it had happened already. Like the time she'd shoved Logan across the street, saving him from a car that had made a wild turn at the corner where they'd been eating popsicles on a hot July day.

There was no logical reason the then eleven-year-old Margo would have known the car was coming at that precise moment. But she had, and thankfully, that vision had saved her brother's life.

Margo was always getting *feelings* like that. She still listened to the warnings her sixth sense sent her. Even if she'd stopped sharing them long ago.

Who needed another psych eval in their file, anyway? Not this chick.

To the other employees that afternoon at the busy downtown Newark NSA building, Margo was just another law consultant. Just another temporary to fill in on whatever case needed her.

It wasn't unusual to get deliveries at work. Cases overlapped, new materials came in, evidence, dossiers, *etc.* Mail was delivered and sent out all the time. So no, not unusual. Especially when so few lawyers worked in this particular office.

Margo liked her job for that reason. The hiding in plain sight aspect was appealing and thrilling on several levels. But that was her, a complicated mess of conflicting likes and dislikes.

She liked rules, though she flouted them. Adored court but avoided it. Liked to read but had no time to indulge, and she absolutely abhorred audiobooks. Loved musicals but hated listening to show tunes in the car or anywhere other than while watching a movie or show.

Then there was her greatest love, the unknown, or as she preferred to think of it, the *unrevealed*. Margo had a seriously complex love hate relationship with mysteries. In fiction, they were fine, but in real life, not so much. She'd made it her life's work to uncover the truth about the biggest mystery of all.

Magic.

Yep. Margo Wells, hard ass lawyer and government agent, was hunting for proof that magic actually existed in the world.

Her peers thought her crazy. Hard to believe, since they were all part of the same unit assigned to watch supernatural creatures. Yes, they were real. No, she did not have ready or deliverable proof. It was classified, of course.

Ever since she'd taken up her job with the DPCA, also known as the *Department of Paranormal Creatures and Activity*, she'd come to learn that some of the most widely accepted mysteries and legends of all time were real.

The world might only believe in what they could see, but for Margo, who could see beyond the norm, she believed in something more. What was known as the truth and the actual truth were distant cousins in her world. To think, there was still so much they had to discover, and even more, they had to keep hidden.

If the general public knew how many secret branches of the government actually existed, they'd shit a collective brick. Margo was sure of it. Hell, even the most intuitive conspiracy theorists couldn't fathom the level of deception at work on the daily. But that was life, she supposed. Hadn't she accepted that long ago?

It didn't really matter to her. Lies for the common good were all that held society together sometimes. Margo tended to just accept it for what it was before she moved on.

Her one truth was this: secret government agencies did, in fact, exist, and Margo Wells worked for one of them. That was her reality.

Mother, her boss at the DPCA, had assigned Margo to this NSA office to investigate some of their new cases, searching for any hint of the paranormal. Many of them skated dangerously close to revealing the secrets her agency worked so hard to keep.

She meticulously searched, found, and quietly sent those cases to her agency. The DPCA would step in to handle them covertly. Other cases she found and recognized were sent to secret agents she knew from the other various government agencies of the same ilk.

Yes, they too existed.

Some of them dealt with natural disasters. Others with critical planetary emergencies. And others still handled communications and skirmishes between

Earth and beings from other realms, planets, and even solar systems.

Then there was her organization. The Department of Paranormal Creatures and Activity, or the *DPCA,* as they were called. So yes, she sat there disguised as a simple NSA legal consultant in order to do her job. Even as she crept around her desk, strode down the hall, and closed herself inside the closet ripe with janitorial supplies in order to open the strangely ominous envelope, she had to admit she loved it all. The mystery, the action, and the magic.

Especially the magic.

Two

O kay, so Margo had a vested interest in the findings of her agency. A former US Marine, esteemed lawyer, and all around badass, Margo was not only in the top 1% of her graduating class at Harvard Law. She also excelled in combat and had earned medals for her sharpshooting skills.

Her extreme intelligence and affinity for language had seen her graduate from college three years early and pass the bar exam with only one year of law school under her belt. So, despite appearances, Margo was a Wells through and through.

Neither the color of her skin, nor the fact that her mother was not married to her biological father at the time of conception, birth, or at all, for that matter, could change that. Her parents had simply fallen in lust and bed, in that order, and she was the byproduct.

Her father's family had all but refused to acknowledge her existence at first, even going so far as to try and have her mother moved to a different hospital since she and Logan did, in fact, share the same birthday.

Cassidy Green wasn't much of a mother. She'd worked in law enforcement until her untimely death, leaving little room for her child. No, it was Margo's Aunt who'd taken her home from the hospital. And she was the one who had raised her when Cassidy was killed five years later on assignment.

Both she and Logan's mother, a truly lovely human being, were responsible for her and her brother's meeting. Those two women had been tougher than nails and made damn sure the siblings had ample visitation with one another.

Was that weird?

Maybe. On paper, for sure. But Margo had never felt anything but acceptance and love from either of them or from her twin brother. Hell, if it wasn't for Logan, she could not fathom where she would be right now. Okay, technically, he was not her twin, but the second he'd found out about his sister, he'd demanded time with her. Even after his mother had died, and he'd been barely old enough to form sentences, Logan made sure Grandfather Wells included her in all their family plans and events.

Logan Wells might be her half-brother on paper, as it was true, they shared the same father and had different mothers, but he was her whole brother in her heart.

He was a genius scientist, physician, and a kickass bass player. They'd been born the same day, just minutes apart, and in the same hospital. His poor sweet mother had put up with the knowledge of not only Margo's birth, but she'd made her feel welcomed and loved too. Even agreed to call her his twin, to her secret delight.

But regardless of her mother and his father's infidelity, Auntie Beth, Lily Wells, and Logan were the best parts of her childhood. Margo's own mother was never one to stick around and she'd left her only child in the care of her sweet Auntie Beth more often than not even when she'd been alive.

Lily Wells was her polar opposite and how her husband could cheat on the beautiful and sweet woman, Margo had no idea. But the woman accepted his illegitimate spawn, and for Margo, that meant endless weekends in their enormous house.

Like it or not, the Wells family was *her* family.

After the frail woman had passed away, her weekend visits grew far and between, until Logan started pitching fits about it. Despite Grandfather Wells hating her guts, Margo's visits resumed and her relationship with her brother had blossomed.

She loved Logan more than anything else in the world. He understood her, accepted all her quirks, even her weird insights, without question.

Both Wells heirs were gifted. There was no mistaking that. Their shared genetics were responsible, she supposed, but what did that matter?

He chose science as his career, and she chose the government. Breaking into the Supreme Court's mainframe to get access to their court documents was not something she'd encourage others to try, but it had gotten her noticed by certain important people.

Sure, she was better when it came to litigation, but Margo was also something of a skilled hacker. She could get through any firewall or security system she encountered. Only one gave her trouble, but even *Draco Fortis* was no match for her techy skills.

Soon Margo's unusual talents were put to use, and she'd been recruited by a special black ops department that dealt with an entire world that was unknown to society. Classified was a word she'd become very familiar with these last few years working for the DPCA.

She checked the lock on the janitorial closet where she'd gone to open the envelope one last time before tearing it carefully along the fold. She bit back a gasp. The last thing Margo ever expected to see was a picture of her brother in the company of those, those *animals*!

"Oh no," she murmured, frowning hard.

Margo had first learned of the existence of Shifters only a few months ago. People who could morph into animals and were just as wild and dangerous. As far as she knew, which was what the DPCA told her, was that Shifters included Werewolves and some subspecies of bear.

It was believed a genetic mutation was the reason for such creatures. Margo suspected otherwise, but never voiced it aloud. She was not a fan of being ridiculed for her beliefs. The one time she spoke out, her boss had quickly shut her down.

"Fairytales don't exist, Wells, only monsters," Mother often said.

But nothing could have prepared her for the feelings running through her as she looked at the grainy images of her brother in the company of a pink haired woman. The same woman who, in the next image, turned into a sleek black cat.

Holy cow! Shifters could be cats? That one photograph changed everything. Beneath the pictures was a typed letter with instructions. Mother wanted more info on the cat.

Margo's orders were to collect intel from Logan, but he was her family, and despite what she told her bosses, his safety came first. That meant getting him the fuck out of there.

"Where you off to? Margo? Margo!"

Her temporary NSA team leader, Declan Baudelaire, stopped her on her way down the hall. She looked down pointedly at the soon to be dismembered hand gripping her elbow. Margo did not like to be manhandled.

In fact, touching of any kind was only permitted by invitation only. And desire his having made that suggestion a time or two, she'd firmly refused to get involved with anyone from work. Her mama always told her not to shit where she ate. Besides, office romances were never as kinky or gratifying as they sounded.

To think she'd quit practicing law only two years into her practice and had given up her judgeship all for this. No way she was going to stand there and be questioned by her boss. Not when she was worth twice what he was in the field.

She knew it too. Margo never had a problem with knowing, accepting, and very boldly stating her worth. Had done so with her first job with the FBI. Then again, with the NSA. And now, with the covert DCPA.

She'd had quite the career already, considering she was just in her thirties. But there was one thing Margo did not do, and that was explain herself. Not ever.

"I'm taking a leave of absence, Declan. Two weeks."

"But we're in the middle of—"

"Two weeks," she snapped.

She was already in the parking lot beneath the main building and on her way to rescue her brother. What in the hell had the fool gotten himself into now?

She tied back her curls, the damn things had a mind of their own. Huffing out a sharp breath, Margo threw her car into gear. There was only one thing she loved in the world *almost* as much as her brother.

And that was her *still hot from the factory* Camaro SS convertible in cream blue with performance seats and 455 horsepower engine. The damn thing purred when she turned the engine.

Prrrrr.

But Margo did not take time to appreciate the fine as fuck machine. She flipped switches and waited for the GPS to direct her. The console had been completely redone with her own customized hardware, including some state of the art, not available anywhere, tracking software.

Lucky for her, Logan had no idea she'd micro-chipped his ass when they'd gone out for his birthday a year ago. He never could go toe to toe with her when it came to booze.

Like a fucking puppy, she'd stuck him with the needle, inserting the tiny chip into his ass that she'd hoped she would never have to use. Should have seen this coming, she thought with a shake of her head.

They both led busy lives, and it was true she hadn't seen him in a while. Guilt had started to eat away at her, but she was just as career focused as he. Another Wells family trait.

Monthly check ins via email did not make up for real sister and brother bonding time they used to share. Even with Grandfather Wells disapproving glare in the background. Margo had always loved her visits with her brother.

He'd been so pale and thin as a kid. She loved holding his hand and looking at the contrast between her gold brown skin and his fair complexion. No one would ever guess they were related. Not unless they looked at their eyes.

Margo had the Wells hazel green eyes, flecked with gold. With her darker skin tone, they practically popped out of her head. She used to hate the way her eyes drew stares, and eventually, questions when she was in her youth. She'd grown accustomed to it, made internal adjustments so it wouldn't bug her.

Being brilliant meant having a thicker skin than most, and as far as Margo was concerned, her mixed heritage was her own damn business. No one else's. She was not interested in debating race, religion, or anything of the like.

Those were human problems, and Margo was in search of something more. Something *unrevealed* to the populace. Something that explained why the hairs on the back of her neck stood straight up when something was about to happen. Or the knack she had for guessing the right number to play at the roulette table. Or when to get off the highway before traffic backed up.

Margo was searching for proof that magic existed, but all that would have to wait. First, she had to save her brother.

"Don't worry, twin, I'm on my way," she muttered.

THREE

Present...

Egros sat down in the living room of the Keep. It had been a very eventful day. Elena had claimed her mate and announced it to all, reunited with her father, who turned out to be one of the Assembly, that was like the Council but for Guardians only, and he'd realized he was completely wrong about her choice for a partner. Logan was her fated one, her conpar, and that was something no one could cast asunder.

Afterwards, Holley had gone into labor, and the Guardians welcomed their first offspring in a hundred years or more. Kingston was a father, and they should all be rejoicing. Storm and Furio had opened champagne, nonalcoholic for their mates, now both expectant mothers, and they'd passed out cigars. It was quite the event.

Only, Egros did not feel like celebrating. To be honest, he felt a little bit like an ass.

Okay.

More like a complete and total ass.

He looked at the faces of those around him and his heart squeezed inside his chest. They were almost all paired up. Each of his fellow Guardians had seemed to find their mates, all but Byram, the Vampire, in the last year or so. Yes, he was grateful to the gods for giving him a second chance to remain one of them, but he could not help but feel apart from them all.

Witches did not have fated mates. Not to his vast knowledge, anyway. He'd thought Elena might be amenable to being with him, but even then, it was only a half-assed gesture meant to help the Panther Shifter in her time of need. Of course, everyone thought him in love. He wasn't. Just lonely and perhaps a bit jealous.

How very human of me, he thought with a sneer.

To think he'd almost ruined his life and all because of ignorance and stupidity. And yes, envy too, even if it wasn't the kind everyone thought. It didn't matter. All that mattered was that they'd somehow forgiven him.

All of them. Unbelievable. And yet, he was so very grateful.

Elena sat on her mate's lap looking happier than he'd ever seen the female Panther Shifter. Logan Wells, her *conpar*, that was the Guardians word for beloved fated mate, was a brilliant scientist.

He was also a human, or *normal,* as supernaturals tended to call them. Somehow, he fit in with the motley crew of Shifters, a Witch, and a Vampire. They were all members of the Guardians of Chaos, having vowed to keep magic free for all beings.

It wasn't just organizations like the Loyalists who plagued them, but it was the humans too. Truth be told, the past decade had been full of so many technological advancements that keeping magic secret was becoming quite the task. For a male Witch, there was no duty more sacred.

Magic was the single most important secret in the entire universe. A fact that Egros had been taught years ago behind the stone walls of St. Barnabas' School, when he'd still been a member of the Coven Pyke.

He shivered at the thought of his youth and that horrible place. It wasn't the teachers or even the bullies of his school days that made him freeze in place. No, only one man could cause such an intense reaction.

Bartholomew Pyke.

The man had been missing since that fateful day Egros had gone to live with the Guardians. He'd even been declared dead in a court of law. Of course, Egros had never believed his father had run off and wound up dead. Not Bartholomew Pyke. The old bastard was simply too mean to die. Regardless, he'd left the Coven, and lived the life he was meant to be here in the Keep with his fellow Guardians and friends. For the first time in his life, Egros had friends. He hoped he still had them, at any rate.

Recent actions left him riddled with guilt and for a moment, he wondered if he would be banished from the only real home he'd ever known. Guess even a gifted Witch had to wrestle with the green-eyed monster once in a while.

It was not simply jealousy, though that was what they had all assumed. Egros cared for Elena, but he was not in love with her. Not really. She was beautiful, yes. And yes, it was true he'd offered to see her through her heat. But in retrospect, it was because she was his friend.

He simply couldn't bear to think of her in pain. The fact she'd chosen a normal over him had caused him to lash out because of the danger she was putting them all in.

She didn't seem to understand that humans were the single most destructive force in the universe. They were the complete opposite of everything Egros believed in.

Guardians protected magic. The cornerstone of their beliefs was the idea that *from chaos comes creation*, but humans did not abide chaos. They were rigid with structure and schedules. Intolerant of anyone who was different, but they had no qualms about paving nature, leveling jungles needed for something as vital as clean air to breathe, polluting oceans until they were unlivable, chopping down forests, fracking for oil, and those were just their environmental monstrosities.

In his experience, humans were also responsible for curbing creativity, punishing those who dared to be different with derision and hate.

Order. Order! ORDER!

Always calling for order, but the daft bastards did not seem to realize that order was confining. It was restrictive and led to intolerance.

The only thing that came from intolerance was destruction, and that was the root of all evil. Not money or sex or even religion. Not politics either.

Nope. It was humanity's ever increasing appetite for destruction that was pure malice at its worst.

Egros' magic pulsed and buzzed along his skin, and he closed his eyes. He should be feeling joyous. At the very least, contentment. But no. He was anxious.

Their leader, Kingston and his mate, Holley, one of the most powerful Witches he'd ever met, had welcomed their young into the world this very evening. The birth of a half-Witch Dragonling was rare and momentous. It was neither the time nor place to get into one of his moods.

He closed his eyes and counted to three. That tactic still worked after all these years, believe it or not. When he finally reopened them, the purple sparks that had begun to dance along his fingertips were gone.

Good.

The idea his powers were becoming unbalanced was something every Witch, male or female, feared. He still wore the pendant with his magical inheritance locked away. There was no way he could trust himself with the added powers of his mother's family when he could not control what he already had.

Best to keep it locked away, he thought with a frown.

The pendant warmed against his chest and Egros exhaled unsteadily. He could feel the magic there calling to him, and he answered with the only words he could.

Not yet.

It was the additional *maybe not ever* that he kept to himself. Elena's giggle had his head turning in the direction of the so in love couple. The Panther Shifter was currently basking in the glow of her *conpar's* affection, and Egros was happy for her.

Truly, he was. She lifted her hand, admiring the pink sapphire ring her mate had given to her, which Egros had magicked to grow and recede as needed when she shifted from Cat to woman.

It was a rare and precious stone, but that was irrelevant. Logan was fabulously wealthy. Not that it mattered. Elena had to be one of the most down to earth women Egros had ever met.

He nodded at her whispered thanks, a bit embarrassed that Logan had given him credit for the spell at all.

Bloody hell.

The gods knew he didn't deserve it. But he replied with a nod, gracious as ever. Egros was just glad his fellow Guardian and her mate were speaking to him at all. Amazingly enough, he had been forgiven by the people he'd hurt the most.

The evening air was chilly in springtime, even as they readied to meet summer. He could hear crickets waking, waiting to rub their wings together, sounding their own mating call. The trees stretched and groaned, their buds tightening with the drop in temperature.

Egros listened to it all, blocking out the noise of those gathered round in the warmth of the Keep. It was the time for birth and renewal, for growth. The whole world seemed waiting to blossom, and Egros knew his job was simply to watch it happen.

Like with his Guardians finding their mates. Like Elena and Logan, a couple who were truly meant to be together. He saw that now, clear as day, and he wished them well.

Shame filled him, and he frowned. He still couldn't believe what he'd almost done. Coming between a supernatural and his or her mate was the worst kind of trespass. For Guardians, a *conpar* was more than a mate.

A conpar was the Guardian's most sacred fated mate. One who was beloved and cherished above all. Anything and everything else were second to that one being perfectly suited for that one lucky Guardian.

Only those most blessed and deserving found their conpar. When that occurred, new stores of magic and powers beyond imagination opened up for the Guardian. The better to protect his or her mate, of course.

Usually, it meant extra strength and endurance, but there were other boons as well. For Storm, it meant blue swirls of magic that allowed him to blink from one location to the next with a mere thought. For Kingston, control over fire and flame was now part of his magical repertoire. Furio's Stallion had powers much like the mythological Pegasus ever since he'd mated his beloved Jessenia.

The *Italian Stallion*, as his fellow Guardians called him in jest, could actually fly with the help of magical wings made of green fire. And Elena had actually become the *Panther Incensed* of legend with pink flames dancing on her skin and coming from her ears.

All these added powers served to make the Shifters in question stronger, faster, and better at their job, which was ultimately to protect magic. In doing so, they were protecting the universe for their *conpars*, making it a better, safer, and more magical place.

A place of pure creation.

Loneliness started to weave its way into his mind. As usual whenever he got into one of his more pensive moods. That hated longing he could not help but feel for someone to call his own tried to overshadow the wonder and happiness he'd felt for his friends.

The pendant around his neck buzzed and

hummed, and Egros felt his magic pulsing inside of him. He had to work at keeping his cool, and it was an energy sucking task. More so than a heavyweight champion going twenty-three rounds inside the ring with his equal.

By the time he was finished tightening the screws on the metaphorical box where he put his magic whenever he felt dangerously close to losing control, Egros was sweating.

"You alright?" Elena asked, suddenly.

"Yes," he replied, uttering the lie easily.

He could not tell her the truth. Had to hide the truth from them all. Egros Pyke was just as lonely and unwanted as he'd been as a child. The Witch was unworthy of their company.

No, he would never share their fate. He would never find his soul mate, his conpar. It simply was not meant to be.

Witches were not the same as Shifters. They did not operate on instinct alone. Shifters were dual natured beings and their animalistic sides used senses Witches simply did not have. He'd often wished he could sniff out his own mate as easily as a Shifter did. Yes, it was sometimes nothing more than a literal sniff. Imagine having the ability to scent things like lies, arousal, and a mate? Amazing creatures, Shifters.

Yes, they used magic, but it was on a different level. Both sides of their natures were always converging and working together. Witches were more like normals in the sense they were not sharing an existence. Magic was inherited or gained, but it was something that needed tending and care. Magic untethered or unlearned was unpredictable and untrustworthy.

Of course, a Witch's relationship with magic was also profoundly different than a Shifter's or Vampire's. Not that Byram shared much info on that. As a male Witch, and the last of his line, Egros had the magic he was born with, or that which transferred to him at birth. He also had access to the stores of magic willed to him by his mother.

His father's magic had not transferred to him at the time of that man's disappearance. Whatever had happened to Bartholomew Pyke, he'd taken his magic with him. And for that, Egros could only thank the hateful man who'd sired him.

He was just fine with what he had, unlike many power-mad Witches. Yes, other creatures wanted power too, but Witches should know better.

"What has you so lost in thought?" Logan asked, disturbing his reverie.

"Oh, nothing," he replied, grateful to the normal.

"Egros is usually a deep thinker. No worries

though, love, if you see him struggling just tell him a joke," Elena teased.

It was well known amongst the group that Egros did not get many punchlines. He was far too literal. Looking around at the group of them, he was proud to be part of this group of Guardians who had found not only one, but four of their conpars.

Down the hall, he could hear their Alpha cooing to his new son. Greyson Mount Baldric was the first of the new generation that Egros predicted would be ruling the halls of the Keep sometime very soon.

He did not mind the tiny addition. Even with all the wailing that was bound to keep him up late at night lest the Keep install some extra soundproofing within the walls.

It was all good, though. Children created their own brand of chaos, and to Egros nothing could be more perfect. Kingston was lucky to have found his true fated mate in Holley.

The Dragon had been mated before, or so they had all thought. But the female Dragon had not been his conpar, and the difference was incredible. Holley completed him in a way that could inspire poets. Just imagining it made his mind boggle.

Kingston loved Holley so much he broke curses

and battled warlocks for the chance to be with her. And now, the once stoic Dragon smiled and laughed easier than in all the years Egros had known him.

If only I had that chance, Egros thought sadly.

Four

He needed to get out of there, to break up the monotony of the scenes playing out before him, else he would go mad. How could he act happy all the time when he was utterly alone?

Ugh.

Egros managed to disgust even himself with those selfish thoughts.

"I'm going to go get a drink. Want something?" Egros asked Elena and Logan.

"No, thanks," they replied together.

The couple was all wrapped up in one another, as they should be, and he was tired of feeling like a third wheel. He was getting ready to stand when Furio shouted at him.

"Yo, Egros! You think you can help me set up the artificial lights in the greenhouse for Jessenia?" the Stallion Shifter asked from across the room.

The male Witch was jarred from his many thoughts. A good thing, of course. But before Egros could answer, something flashed outside the window. He narrowed his eyes, raising his hand for Furio to wait a moment when the ready to anger Shifter snorted impatiently.

Then something hit the glass window, causing an explosion that had glass flying everywhere and Egros on his feet. Using magic, he raised an invisible shield that repelled the dangerous shards. Snarling, he was ready to blast the intruder to smithereens until he saw *her*.

"Get the fuck off my brother!" snarled the petite, full human female.

Glossy curls crowned her head, and her golden brown skin glowed in the lamplight from the sconces on the wall. She'd jumped in through the now broken window and seemed unafraid of the lethal group who faced her with claws and fangs unsheathed.

Amazing.

It wasn't the fact she wielded two guns in her small hands, or that she had one aimed directly at his balls that stilled him. It was her eyes. Golden hazel and glowing with anger, and maybe something more. Human or not, she'd found them, and that was a problem. The Guardians were secretive even amongst their own. A human should not have found them.

"Margo, what the hell are you doing?" Logan yelled at the female.

Anger roused, Egros turned on the male, but then understanding dawned. The normal had said *brother*. Logan was her brother.

Bloody hell.

Egros' gaze flitted between them, somehow, yes, they were related. Everyone was yelling and talking over one another, but the moment it was decided she was alone and wouldn't be killing anyone, most of the others left.

Only Elena, Logan, and Egros remained with the stranger. Well, stranger to him.

"You don't understand," Margo said, her untrusting gaze flitting between Elena and himself. "They've got you brainwashed, or under a spell, or just something!"

"That is ridiculous. I told you we are mates," Elena growled, and Egros knew the Panther was holding on by a thread.

"How do you even know about Shifters?" Elena snarled.

"The United States government knows about a lot of things. I happen to work for an agency that has been tracking Shifters for some time."

"What? Don't tell me you're with one of those military crews that hires Shifters to take out rival governments."

"What? Um, no," Margo replied, cocking her head to the side in a way that was way too endearing.

"Logan, I don't know what you are thinking, but your pink haired girlfriend is not human."

"Firstly," Egros cut in. "She is not his girlfriend. Elena is Logan's mate. Their bond is unbreakable. Secondly, Shifters do not cast spells. That would be impossible. Of everything you are bound to see and hear in this place, I assure you there is nothing untoward happening between your brother and Elena."

"Untoward? Really? And just who the fuck are you, Mr. Darcy?" she asked, her wickedly beautiful eyes narrowing at him.

For the first time in his life, Egros was about to tell a normal the truth about himself. He was not particularly worried, and that alone should have been a red flag. But his mouth was opening before he could over-think it.

I can always magic her later.

"My name is Egros Pyke, and I am a Witch."

FIVE

"*I am a Witch.*"

The sound of his voice revealing that one phrase was on constant replay inside her mind. First, he was a dude. Not that she was sexist, but she sort of thought Witches were chicks with pointy hats or sparkly wands. Egros Pyke had neither.

After a few days in the mansion they all called the Keep, the man did not seem inclined to develop those things she'd always deemed witchy, either. He refused to reveal any proof that he could perform magic, assuming he had any.

In fact, the damned man deflected every inquiry she made about his supposed declaration that he was a Witch and any powers he might have right back at her.

He was clever. Infuriating, but clever. And no, she was not disappointed. *Much.*

Four days had passed since Margo Wells had busted through the window of this old mansion that everyone who lived there called the Keep. The window had been seamlessly repaired, and no one seemed to hold it against her.

But still. Four days, and Margo had not managed a meeting with the leader of the cultish group of weirdos that had kidnapped her brother. She'd been interviewed over and over again by the man in front of her. For some reason, he could not get it through his thick skull that she was there to rescue her brother Logan.

He wanted to know about some group called the Loyalists. She'd come across the name infrequently, but it wasn't her department. Still, he seemed pretty convinced they had somehow brainwashed her to do their dirty work.

Whatever.

She was there for Logan, whether or not he believed her. He stared at her for a moment, jotted something down in his infernal notebook, then stared some more.

Well, if he thought she was going to whimper or beg, he had another think coming. She was Margo Wells, DPCA Agent, marine, and lawyer.

So, she calmly stared back at the man, *er*, Witch. He didn't seem nervous or afraid, despite the fact she knew exactly what they were.

"She knows what we are, man," the one named Furio growled at Egros.

"Some normals do at some level. At any rate," Egros replied, easily.

They were seated in the dining room, and Margo was getting impatient. Hell. She had been impatient since day one. The events following her busting in on them replayed through her eidetic mind.

"Who named you Egros?"

"My father."

"Hmm." She'd pursed her lips.

"Must be a real dick to name his kid that."

"Indeed, he was." Egros had replied.

The man looked like he was fighting his grin. The large clock against the wall ticked away the minutes, but neither of them broke eye contact. It was a test of some sort, she was sure. But whether of strength or wills, she did not know. Besides, Margo did not want to look away.

He was fascinating. There was something about him that drew him. Her blood raced inside of her, and her heartbeat seemed deafening even to her ears.

Her head started to spin, and visions came flooding

in. It was difficult to sort them. That had never happened to her before. Almost as if they were conscious and aware on their own, wanting to show her all the possibilities.

Curious.

"Um, okay," Elena, her brother's psycho girlfriend had butted in, and Egros seemed startled to notice the female Shifter standing there.

"You got this, Egros?" she asked.

"Yes," he replied with a certainty Margo was not sure he actually felt.

"I think we can manage."

"Okay. Um, I don't want to bother him, but I'm going to go let Kingston know what's going on," Elena replied.

"Certainly," he agreed.

The female was all snarls and growls, but Margo was used to that. Shifters were something she'd seen before, though never a Dragon or Stallion. Witches, though, she was mighty curious about them.

"Is he going to see me today?" she asked before the male Witch could fall off into one of his many long silences.

———

Egros looked down. He knew she was right, but he wasn't exactly in a position to make demands. The Alpha should be here, interviewing her.

Their visitor was not exactly welcome. But neither was she threatening them at the moment, which was a pretty nice change. Still, Margo Wells seemed to know much more about Shifters and supernaturals than any normal should.

Far too much.

Protecting the supernatural world and keeping it hidden fell under the Guardians' purview. He needed to investigate just what she knew and how she found them. It wasn't like the Keep was on a bloody map.

Elena remained standing there. She watched the byplay between her new sister-in-law and Egros, eyebrows raised. He had the distinct feeling she was laughing at him.

"Uh, so you need any help before I go?" Elena asked.

"Of course not," Egros replied. "Ms. Wells and I were just chatting."

He kept her gaze, eyes never wandering from the woman in question. She fascinated him. No doubt about it. And yet her very presence created a huge problem for the Guardians. A problem that had Elena and the others worried.

"Chatting, are we?" Margo said, leaning forward with her elbows on the table.

He must have done something right somewhere, because only the gods themselves could have given him the will to not glance down at the abundance of cleavage on display. Was she teasing him on purpose? He had to wonder.

"There's more to it, Eg," she crooned. "Don't you agree? More than just chatter between us."

Oh yeah.

The female was definitely playing with him. So Egros did look down, and after two very long seconds, flicked his gaze back to her glittering hazel eyes.

"I would think that an accurate assessment, Ms. Wells."

Margo gritted her teeth. He could practically hear the steam coming from her ears. She was pretty when she was angry, he noted with pleasure.

"Okayyy," Elena said, eyes bouncing back and forth between them like she was watching a tennis match.

If she was going to try to use her extremely hot body and pretty face to get answers, Egros was not going to deny her the victory of him being distracted.

She was gorgeous, and he liked looking at her. Liked the way Margo's eyes tilted slightly at the corners, her curved eyelashes outlining them in thick black fringes. Her brows were naturally thin and arched.

Very pretty, he mused, shocking himself with that description. Egros was always the consummate professional. His sex life was low on the list of priorities. Like eating. When he was working, he could go for days without food. As it was, he'd been without a woman for months now.

"Did you just call me an *egg*?" His head whipped back to her face, confident he'd misheard the inept descriptor. Still, it wouldn't hurt to be sure, he figured.

"No, I called you *Eg* with one g."

"Right." Egros cleared his throat. "I don't know if that is any better—"

"Listen up Eg, whatever it is we are doing here, I don't think we can put it in the same category as two old biddies sipping tea on a Tuesday afternoon, do you?"

"Um—"

"Look, I know there is something up with you guys. I have seen the claws on some of you, after all. And the agency I work for has come across chatter about the Guardians. That's you, right?"

"What else do you know?"

"Not much. The *DPCA* is what we like to call an intelligence gathering agency. We've been watching and collecting information on Shifters, Wolves, and Bears, because that was all we were aware of. Till now."

Shocked speechless, he merely waited for whatever she was gonna say next.

"So when I saw, we have more things going on between us, I mean, we have more things going on between us. Do you agree?"

"Indeed, Ms. Wells."

"Glad we understand each other," Margo said, and stood.

"Now look, I drove six hours to get here, and I have been waiting four days to talk to your leader or whatever the hell you call him."

"I apologize for the delay, it cannot be helped."

"Yeah, I figured you'd say that. But I am damn tired of waiting in this room."

"Ms. Wells, I'd like to talk more about the DP—"

"Department for Paranormal Creatures and Activity, Eg. We've been aware of you for some time. But I admit, proving the existence of paranormal creatures beyond Wolves and Bears, like Witches for example, is definitely going to be good for my career."

"You can't do that!"

"See, and that's why of all these guys sitting here

with their women, you are alone. Strong women don't like when men tell them what to do, Eg."

"What? I don't see what that has to do with anything. This is very serious, and we need to talk about it," Egros grumbled.

"Don't get uptight, Eg. You're a good looking guy. You just need to lighten up," she replied, and winked.

"Now, I am through here until I speak to the big guy," she said, and turned away from Egros.

"Hey, Logan?" Margo shouted at her brother.

"Yeah, Gogo?"

"What's there to do around here?" Margo asked.

"Well, you wanna check out my lab? I can show you what I am working on, then we can..."

The woman was an enigma. She stood up, dismissing Egros without so much as a backwards glance. And dammit, he wasn't done with his interviews. He needed to have something to present to his Alpha, but the confounded woman would not sit still long enough.

She'd been vague in her answers, withheld more than her share of info, and seemed to not notice when he'd tried a simple compulsion charm. His magic was definitely wonky. Especially when it came to her!

"Blasted," Egros muttered, shuffling his notes in a pile.

"What has you cursing?" Byram asked, walking out of the shadows in that way the Vampire had about him.

Egros was used to it by now, so he was not startled. But he could see why people, even supes, thought the bloodsuckers creepy.

"Margo Wells is infuriating."

"I see, why not just bespell her then and be gone with the normal?"

"You don't think I tried? She is a human, Byram, you of all people should understand their frail natures. If I mess up a spell, it could damage her permanently."

A thought that had his power raging through his blood. Egros shook his head. It was no good. He would have to make a potion. Yes. That should work. Anything else was simply too dangerous, and he was not about to risk the woman.

"I said," Byram repeated. "Why not use something stronger?"

"Because," Egros said, and refused to explain.

Yes, he was being childish, but what could he say? The thought of harm coming to the curly haired vixen was simply too much for him to take. No, that would not do.

Not at all.

Six

Egros sat at his desk in the room he'd always thought of as his potions' room. The Keep had always seemed able to oblige the inhabitants with whatever they needed, but who knew a conpar's needs would surpass a Guardian's?

He snarled and pushed the blasted science geek lab stuff out of his way. Okay, fine. He was being a brat, and he knew it.

Ever since Logan had moved his equipment into what was once Egros' space, and for a damn good reason too, he'd been feeling out of sorts. Was he even needed anymore? The human scientist had found a much better solution for stemming female Shifters' heat cycles than he or any other Witch ever had luck with.

Maybe the Guardians would be better off with him as their alchemist? Fuck. Now he was being ridiculous.

Logan was a genius, yes, but Egros was a Witch. The room was now set up so they could more easily work together, and really, it was fine. So what if it was like a Hogwarts meets tech geek science lab?

Whatever.

As long as he could work, he was fine. Besides, Egros enjoyed working with Logan. He'd been disappearing into his many projects for years when the outside world got too tough.

Focus was his friend.

Egros grimaced as he added the wrong ingredient to the batch of healing ointment he was making.

Damn it.

What was going on? He knew better than to add dried fire ants to his salve. That would cause more pain to whatever injury he was tempting to heal. Elementary stuff, and he knew better. For the first time since ever, at least, since he could recall, Egros' mind kept wandering away from the task at hand.

Where was his head?

As if he didn't know, he thought with a distinct growl. He shook his head, hearing his mother's sweet voice echo in his brain from long ago.

"Witches do not growl, my son."

But he did, at least when he was a child and he used to play at being a Wolf or Tiger. Now, he supposed he did it out of habit. The byproduct of living with Shifters for so long, he supposed.

The reason he could not focus was, of course, the woman. One tiny human female had him making mistakes he would not have done in Witch school. Margo Wells should have been of no consequence to Egros Pyke, Witch and Guardian of Chaos.

He'd always been able to push all distractions out of his head when he was working. And yet, his brain was simply not cooperating. How was he supposed to commune with his powers with all these confounded images playing over and over again in his brain?

Only a handful of days and interactions with the vivacious normal, and Egros was reduced to this! Frustration runneth his cup over or whatever the fuck the saying was. He closed his eyes, willing himself to get back to work, but it was no good.

Her image remained firmly imprinted inside his brain. She was so different from anyone he'd ever known. Her glossy curls were at least ten different hues of brown, from the deepest mahogany to the brightest gold. They surrounded her head like some tawny halo, perfectly complementing her golden brown skin.

Did he mention how smooth and clear that skin

seemed? Her face, obviously carved by angels, Egros had to stop himself from reaching out to touch her one time too many. He'd never been the type of man to just assume he had rights over a woman's person, and yet he was having a difficult time keeping his hands to himself.

She was just so, so, — everything. She was so everything. Curvy and petite, with a wry wit and a ready laugh when something struck her as amusing. She'd answered their questions without telling them a thing more than she wanted to. Her secrets confounded him, her scent intoxicated him, and her hazel eyes hypnotized him.

The fact Margo Wells was completely comfortable amongst a group of Guardians amazed Egros. She was not scared or hostile. She was calm, cool, collected, and utterly attractive. And he was completely fucked.

Egros was responsible for causing serious discomfort to her only brother. A trespass she would surely never forgive. And could he blame her?

Not really, no.

But regardless of his feelings, he could own up to the truth. As far as he saw it the truth was this. Margo Wells was perfection.

Or as Fergie would say, she was *bowchickawowow smokin' hot*. Egros grinned, thinking of Storm's rather blunt mate. The redhead had a penchant for high end shoes and could out cuss a sailor. But she'd grown on him, and Egros was glad for her company and insights.

Fergie would definitely approve of the tough as nails female as a prospective mate, but what the hell was he thinking? She would never consider the likes of him suitable. The thought pained him, but he steered his brain to what the other Guardians might be thinking.

Elena was a little less trusting of the full human, but since Margo was related to Elena's mate, she was willing to offer her protection. Egros assumed Elena would eventually warm towards the female. She was, after all, practically related to her.

Holley, still recovering from childbirth, would want to meet Margo forthwith. The Witch was always excited when newcomers came to the Keep, but after being bound within its walls for nearly three hundred years, Egros could not blame her.

Then there was Jessenia, the kitchen Witch, mated to Furio. Her talents had superseded all expectations, including Egros'. She was tougher than they'd thought as well, rushing in to rescue her mate when the Loyalists had captured him. Still, Egros could not imagine the kind Witch being anything other than welcoming to Logan's sister. If nothing else, Margo's fondness for Jess' shortbread cookies was bound to win her over.

What the hell was he doing sitting there thinking about all this? Why should Egros care how the others found Margo or if they'd welcomed her? It was not his business.

With a dissatisfied grumble, he looked down at his ruined potion. Having messed up again, he grimaced and tossed the ruined ingredients into the special wastebin designed specifically for magical refuse.

It was one of many inventions he'd patented with the Council of Covens and sold to other Witches in the specialty shops available only to supernaturals. Egros was a firm believer in sharing his gifts, but he was also practical.

Money was a necessary evil, even in the supernatural world. Of course, as the heir to the Pyke fortune, he had inherited plenty. But Egros would never touch his father's money.

The minute he'd come of age to inherit, he'd given as much of it as he could to the orphanage that had seen his fellow Guardian, Furio, through his rough childhood. He funded hospitals and clinics for paranormal creatures, and studies that could help their kind thrive in secret. Putting the Pyke fortune to good use was his way of making up for his father's horrible past.

All these years later, Egros had amassed a fortune ten times what his father had left with nothing other than his talent and wit. Money did not really matter to him. He had all he needed right there.

Besides, as a Guardian, he lived in the Keep. The *manetuwak* or spirits therein had always provided whatever it was he wanted or needed. Sometimes doing so before he'd asked for it. Something he greatly appreciated.

His rooms were furnished to his preference, as was his clothing, and the workrooms he used for potions and other casting. But even the Keep could do nothing to stop his mind from wandering back to *her*.

The air seemed thick with frustration. *His*. But could anyone blame him? The woman was a total enigma. Her answers had been vague when questioned about why and how she'd come to the Keep. She'd smiled and zipped her lip, refusing to tell them anything more detailed until their leader, Kingston, was available. Of course, that did not stop the questions from filling his head.

Why was she there? Was it simply to get her brother? How had she found them?

All good questions that needed answers but

contemplating those would not answer the question most on Egros' mind.

How would her lips feel pressed to mine?

Fuck. This was bad. He had no business thinking anything like that about Margo Wells. Normals were not allowed in the Keep, unless mated to one of the Guardians within. And far as he knew, Witches did not have fated mates.

Even if the thought pained him, it was only the truth. Margo was not his, and regardless of his attraction to her, she would have to go. Worry had him frowning as he thought of the extensive mind wiping process the female would have to endure.

After his failures at using simple charms on her, he knew this was the only other option, and yet, he hesitated. The human mind was a fragile thing, and one wrong move could turn a perfectly capable person into a vegetable.

Unacceptable.

His power thrummed and sizzled at the thought of any threat to the female. His chest reverberated with what sounded more and more distinctly like an animalistic growl.

He was being an idiot. How many times had he wished he was Wolf like Storm, or a Dragon like Kingston? Especially when he'd been younger. But he was a Witch, not a Shifter. And that wasn't too shabby a thing to be if he did say so himself.

There's more to it, Eg. Don't you agree?

Her words played back in his head. Once more, his chest rumbled, and his magic pulsed. Egros stilled. Physically, he was frozen in place, but his mind was moving at a hundred miles per hour.

Since when did his magic have opinions or feelings? Never. Not about any one person or thing. Certainly never about a woman.

He grabbed his computer. The thing was magically enhanced with spells as well as Draco Fortis security software for paranormal searches on *Ghoulgle*, the magical net for supernaturals. Nostradamus, an underground Ghoul, and his super fly girlfriend, Emily, had invented the search engine as the end all for information for magical beings.

Graves Enterprises was another solid structure in supernatural software development. They were the best in the business, far as he knew. Owned by one of the Macconwood Wolf Pack's Wolf Guard, Egros frowned and started thinking. Who would know more about this kind of thing than one of their mates?

Without hesitating, he sent an email off to Sherry Morgan-McAllister. The woman was the single most powerful Witch alive in the world today. The

Morrigan walked the Earth once more, and if anyone would have the answers, it was her.

Of course, whether she would share them was another question entirely. Still, he had to try.

Grrr.

SEVEN

Margo took a bite from the still warm cinnamon bun that sat in a massive tray on the long table in the dining room. This place, *the Keep*, was incredible. The lights seemed to glow at the thought, and she bit back a grin. Incredible and apparently not above preening.

The last few days had been like a strange vacation of sorts. She'd eaten well, slept better, and spent some much needed brother and sister time with Logan. She'd also met and got to know his mate, Elena, a bit better.

After months of watching Shifters covertly for her job, being able to interact with them was quite thrilling. And boring. They were just like regular people, except they looked better, ate more, and had ridiculous amounts of energy.

Sighing, she was glad Logan had come to get her from her borrowed room to have breakfast. The food in this place was insanely good, and all due to Jessenia, one of the Shifter's mates.

So yeah, it was pleasant so far. Especially the glimpses she'd gotten of Egros. He'd confessed to being a Witch, and Margo's pulse had raced.

Still, she hadn't exactly seen him perform magic. Her hunt for proof that magic did in fact exist was so close to fruition, she could taste it. But if being evasive was a skill, he had that shit down cold.

"Let's talk about you being a Witch," she'd said *during one of their question and answer sessions.*

"I'd rather discuss you," he'd replied, *a cute grin on his face.*

"Can you do a trick for me? A magic trick?"

"I'm not a circus magician, Ms. Wells. I do not do tricks."

She'd obviously insulted him, but the look on his face was so worth it. His sometimes dark eyes had grown even darker, and she'd had to bite back her grin. He was entirely too tense. With the new legalization of certain recreational herbs, Margo wondered if he wouldn't perhaps benefit from a little herbal therapy. Not that she ever indulged. As a law enforcement agent, she was not allowed to partake. College her would be so pissed.

"So, how is it going?" Logan asked.

"Well, your guy here has questioned me time and again and I still haven't met the boss," she replied.

"yeah, sorry about that," Logan frowned. "Apparently, it's customary for his kind to stay in his caver, *er*, bedroom protecting his mate and newborn," Logan explained badly.

"I see, and will this caveman ever come out of the Dark Ages to speak to me, you think?"

Logan spit his coffee onto the table and glared at his sister. She handed him a napkin, smirking as she did. Margo never tired of frustrating him.

"Not funny, Gogo," Logan said, still coughing.

"You need to lighten up," she replied. "Tell me, which one of you replaced the window? It is seamless," she noted.

Her eyes had wandered to the window where she'd busted through a few nights ago. She stared, amazed that there was no evidence of her entrance at all. Even if they were handy, she doubted anything other than magic could have cleared that up without even a drop of spackle or glue residue. Sure, they could simply be talented at construction and home repairs, but she doubted it.

Yeah. Right.

If her work with the DPCA had taught her anything, it was that things were never what they seemed. The secret government agency had been aware of the existence of Werewolves and Shifters for some time, though they were somewhat limited in their knowledge.

Notoriously private, paranormal beings sometimes worked with the human government on the dl. Margo would have killed to be in on those assignments.

Alas, she was relegated to the legal department after an incident in the field that had left too many dead and more wounded. Due to an NDA, she was not permitted to talk about that now. To this day, she found peace in knowing her actions during that skirmish had saved tens of thousands.

And her family thought she was some bleeding heart lawyer who traveled the world to help those less fortunate. Ha! Even her brother had believed that lie until now.

"What?" Logan asked, helping himself to more coffee.

"How long have you known?" she asked without any buildup.

All these years, they'd never directly lied to each other. Omissions, certainly. Both their jobs had called for that sort of thing. Logan had worked for companies involving top secret pharmaceutical formulas he was not privileged to discuss. And she worked for the government, enough said. So, yeah, without preamble, she asked him flat out the one question that had been on her mind the last few days. How long had he known about the paranormal world? She waited, shaking her head when his brow creased.

"Don't tell me any stories, Logan. How long have you known?" Margo asked again. She believed in getting straight to the point.

"That you're scary without coffee? Most of our lives, Gogo," he replied, using the nickname she hated.

"Most of our lives," he reiterated, and offered her a refill of what turned out to be truly excellent coffee.

She mock glared at him, but didn't bother replying. Instead, Margo took a healthy swig of the piping hot stuff.

Mmm. Now that was good coffee.

Eyes closed as she indulged in a second swallow, Margo felt the hairs on the back of her neck rise as someone else entered the room. It was *him*. The man she'd dubbed Eg. The only male Witch she had ever heard of.

Somehow, she just felt it whenever he entered a room. It was unnerving and exciting at the same time. Not that Margo would ever admit she liked it when she felt his broody eyes on her almost as surely as she'd imagined his hands. Another thing she wasn't rushing to tell anyone.

Okay, fine. Since the second after she'd crashed through the enormous picture window and her eyes found the tall, dark haired man standing protectively in front of her brother, her curiosity had been piqued.

She'd spied Logan and Elena, whom she'd admittedly referred to as the *cult skank* before she'd officially met her and had taken no notice of the others. Just their heat signatures. Certain she'd had enough of the specialty Shifter strength rounds in her guns. Margo had busted into the Keep determined to save her brother.

Only, Logan didn't want to be saved. He was quite happy. More so than she had ever seen him. It was not that difficult a concept, but Margo had to admit she'd been surprised to see her bro so in love. In love and claimed by a Panther Shifter who'd defend him to the death. And that was the only reason Margo didn't push the issue.

The Guardians, or whatever these people called themselves, seemed to her like a group of mercenary soldiers fighting the good fight, but not exactly getting paid. Their mission was unclear, but she was damn sure her boss would want to know. That had been her first mistake. Trying to send a text off to Mother in front of him, Egros Pyke, the self-identified male Witch, had led to the confiscation of the phone and other equipment.

They allowed her to keep her foldable knife, so she'd feel safe. Apparently, they weren't worried about that particular skill set. More fool them.

Elena walked in, and before she greeted anyone else, she bent to kiss Logan lovingly on the lips. Something whispered between them had Logan's cheeks turning a dusky shade of red, while Elena's eyes sparkled in a matching hue.

Who knew her fathead brother could be so happy? Margo swallowed back a sob of joy that threatened to burst from her lips. She was thrilled for him, at the same time her heart broke a little.

They'd always done everything together. Their first time riding bikes without training wheels was with one another. They'd taken their first SATs together. Hell, they'd even gotten stitches for the first time with each other. Ironically, that was on the same day they'd learned to ride their bikes.

Oh Logan, I am so happy for you, she thought, and meant it.

If only she could stop the ache inside her chest from spreading.

EIGHT

argo watched the exchange unashamedly. Their love was obvious, sweet, and tender. Still in that ever hopeful, blooming springtime stage. Much like the weather outside.

New Jersey was notorious for inconstant weather in the months of April, May, and June. But every day was a promise of something warm and wonderful, and she saw the same promise in her brother's eyes when he looked at his mate.

Great. She was happy for him. No, really, she was. Even if his happiness seemed to highlight Margo's own perpetually single state. Once that thought had entered her brain, Margo could only see one solution. He was tall, thin, with a swimmer's build and a look of careful consideration on his handsome face every time she'd seen him.

Egros Pyke was what her Auntie Beth had always referred to as a tall drink of water on a hot summer's day. She'd never known what the old woman had been talking about, till now.

Dayum.

Now, where had that thought come from? Sure, it had been a hot minute since Margo had indulged in a little *somethin' somethin'*, but since when did she find skinny, tall, goth looking dudes hot?

Since now.

She hated it when she argued with herself. But *inner frisky her* did have a point. The man seemed to exude a mysterious sexiness that she was dying to explore.

Okay, so on further perusal, Margo admitted he wasn't rocking a full on goth vibe. He did wear a lot of black, though. And that inky dark hair of his fell all the way to his chin in front, like some 90s alt-rock star. Still, Eg seemed unintentionally indifferent to his appearance.

People worked so hard to look cool, but Egros Pyke did it without even trying. He looked like one of the front men she'd hung posters of all over her college dorm room. That was the stuff she and Logan used to listen to back when they were in their teens.

Fine. Big bad secret agent that she was, Margo still had a weakness for brooding bad boys. And dayum, but this guy looked just like that actor who played Loki in the latest Hollywood production of super-heroism.

Margo was a sucker for good old fashioned comic book universe action flicks. Especially the ones that featured smexy bad guys with dark good looks and all that intensity.

Ooh. Gave her shivers.

Snap out of it, she scolded herself.

Margo was too dang old for this. She was a grown woman, and she could damn well control her carnal appetites. Squirming in her seat a little, she purposely ignored Eg's entrance. Now was not the time to drool over any man, *or* Witch, for that matter.

"Morning, Egros," Logan said, bringing the man directly over to where brother and sister had been chatting.

Fucking great. Thank you very much, she thought angrily at her genius idiot brother.

"Good morning, Logan, Ms. Wells," Egros returned, inclining his head slightly.

"Please, join us," Logan said, engaging the man in a

conversation about formulas that went way over Margo's head.

Good, that would give her a second to breathe and collect herself. Their conversation sounded like background noise, and that was fine to Margo. Smart as she was, she had no patience for science. Give her something to investigate, a case to argue, and she was all over that like bees on honey.

But that wasn't the issue. It was the scent of mint and fresh rosemary that seemed to be coming from him, driving her nuts. She wanted to get closer, bury her nose in the crook of his neck and just breathe him in.

"Excuse us, Ms. Wells," Egros murmured, startling her with his deep voice. "Um, we can talk shop a bit later, Logan. I don't think your sister is all that interested."

"My sister? Oh, sorry, Gogo, forgot you were there." Logan grinned and stuffed another bite of cinnamon bun in his big, dumb mouth.

He did not just call her that. Ugh! *Inner frisky Margo* turned into *inner seething Margo* on a second's notice. She was ready to scratch her brother's eyes out for the slip.

Dumb fathead.

She hadn't called Logan, and his abnormally large

skull, that since they were little. Even thinking it now made her giggle a bit at the naughty thought. Auntie Beth would not like that one bit. She'd been more mom to Margo than her actual mother, and had taught her kindness was, in fact, a virtue.

One she was in short supply of at the moment. Especially where her big-mouthed brother was concerned.

"Gogo?" Egros inquired.

Great. Margo glared at her bro. The idiot did not even realize he was making her uncomfortable, did he? That was the thing about being a fathead. Logan was usually pretty oblivious about stuff that was common sense for others.

"An unfortunate nickname from when I was a kid," she reluctantly explained.

"Really?"

"Yeah," Logan added, unhelpfully. "She was always so impatient. No matter where we were off to, it was always *'Go, Logan go!'* So I shortened it to Gogo whenever we were hanging out."

"I see. So you didn't grow up in the same household?"

"Duh," she snarled. "Don't you have something to do? More inane questions to ask me?"

"Gogo!" Logan admonished, but she was so done with him.

"Ah, still impatient?" Egros asked, and dammit, the man smirked. Not unkindly, but still.

"Only when I'm being *handled*."

"Well then, we'll have to make sure not to let that happen."

"You're damn straight," she replied, and bit into her pastry with relish.

Chatter around the table was friendly, but Margo sensed everyone was waiting. She noticed the seat at the head of the table was still empty. How long did a man have to spend alone with his newborn and wife, for fuck's sake? Didn't he know she was there?

The DPCA would kill for the information she was secretly stockpiling inside her photographic memory. Shifters, Witches, *magic*. All of it was real. Not just what the government agency had told her, but so much more.

If she could just somehow bring back proof of this place and its inhabitants. Maybe even arrange for a meeting between Mother and the one called Kingston Baldric. Then she would finally be vindicated.

Tired of being laughed at behind her back for her belief that there was more out there than some Wolves and Bears. But Margo was right. There was. She just had to figure out how she was going to prove it to her boss.

"So," she said, deciding to cut the shit. "How many of you are Shifters? What kind of animal do you turn into? And how many of you here are Witches? And are *you* really a *Witch*? Wouldn't you be like a Warlock or a Wizard?" she asked, pointing at Egros.

"Uh—"

"Well—"

"You see—"

"Margo!" hissed Logan.

"What?"

"That isn't polite, and you know it." Logan frowned.

"That's not polite? These folks can turn into beasts that can rip our faces off before we can blink, and you think I am being impolite by asking them to explain what they are?"

"Margo," Logan growled.

"I want answers, Logan. It's been days and all we've done is eat. The food was delicious, but I'm not gonna forget my questions because of a couple dozen cookies. And you know me, brother. I won't stop pushing until I get what I want."

"Can't you just stop being an agent for one minute," he grumbled, tossing his hands in the air.

"Excuse me," Egros said. "If I may interrupt?"

"Go ahead," she said, narrowing her eyes at the man.

"I apologize, Ms. Wells. You must have many questions. As do we. You haven't answered our inquiries, and yet you demand we answer yours—"

"I did not demand. Not yet," she replied, and crossed her arms over her chest.

She hated when people pointed out the flaws in her logic. Besides, there were things she simply couldn't answer. These people didn't have the clearance necessary to hear it.

"Pardon me, then, for that misrepresentation. But you must understand we have the right to protect our secrets—"

"Why? Why do you have that right? I have a right to know who and what you are. For all I know, you are keeping my brother hostage!"

"I think we both know, that is not true."

"Look," Logan butted in. "We should wait for Kingston—"

"Shut up," Margo growled at her brother.

"Yeah, Logan, perhaps you should be quiet," Eg added.

"Don't tell my brother what to do or I'll—" she snapped at the wickedly handsome Witch.

"Or you'll what?"

Egros was now standing toe to toe with Margo. She was so mad, she was growling. His eyes were flashing like purple lightning at her. She felt the hair on the back of her neck stand up. It felt like little shivers of electricity were dancing all over her, tickling her skin. They were both breathing heavily, and Margo swore she could taste his rosemary mint scent.

It was delicious. Egros blinked, his eyes zeroing in on her mouth, and Margo swayed a little on her feet. The noise surrounding them fell away, and all she could do was stare at his lips. Need and arousal warred within her, but before she could do anything stupid, like throw herself at him, a very large someone cleared his throat from right next to them.

NINE

Egros was two seconds away from plastering his face to hers in front of all and sundry.

Thank the gods for Kingston. His arrival was just in time. At best, the tiny female would have planted the knife she kept in her back pocket somewhere between his third and fourth rib as he had no doubt she could with unerring accuracy. At worst, she'd kiss him back.

That end would only serve to destroy Egros' life as he knew it. Somehow, he'd subconsciously accepted that as fact. Kissing Margo Wells would change everything.

But was that a risk he was willing to take?

His magic swirled and gathered deep inside of him. Rising up from that place in the pit of his stomach, all the way to his chest. It beat there, pulsing in time with his heart. For a brief moment, her eyes glittered, and he wondered if she would be the one to break this spell. Perhaps she'd take the decision right out of his hands.

Excitement and anticipation buzzed along his skin, his magic racing along with it. Egros had never felt so alive, so enthralled by a female. Never like this, never before, and he'd stake his life on never after, as well.

"Well! Looks like I've arrived in time," the Diamond Dragon announced.

He walked around them, further into the room, with the air of an Alpha Dragon Shifter. Kingston had every reason to be supremely confident, not only in his position as their leader, but in his life.

Of course, Egros knew of the man's inner demons and struggles, and he could not be happier for Kingston than he was now. A closer look at his friend and Alpha revealed Kingston most likely had not slept a lot the past few days. And yet, he seemed infinitely content with his lot in life.

Unlike this currently sweating and agitated Witch. The lucky bastard.

Egros thought unkindly. He cleared his throat and pushed away his annoyance. With a slight bow of his head in the Dragon's direction, Egros stepped back from the tempting female.

Of course, Kingston Baldric, ever the Alpha, took in the situation with keen eyes. He tilted his head slightly, and Egros knew he was asking him a question. One he did not dare consider. So, the Witch ignored it, keeping his eyes frontward.

"So," the Dragon said, sitting down at the head of the table. "You are our Logan's sister."

"Yes, Logan is *my* brother," Margo replied, seeming to correct the Alpha's use of the possessive *our*.

"I see," Kingston growled, one eyebrow raised.

Shit. Not many people dared hold the man's stare, but the little vixen was doing just that. Egros' magic stirred. Not at all happy with the way the Dragon was openly glaring at the female.

Though, to be honest, Egros was quite shocked, and for some strange reason, proud that she could hold the enormous man's stare so long. Finally, and to his relief, Margo averted her gaze with an angry puff of breath.

That made Egros grin. She was gutsy for a human. He'd give her that. But she was also prudent. A life-saving virtue if ever there was one.

"How did you find us?" Kingston asked.

The Dragon did not believe in dilly dallying and chose to speak directly. Egros waited for her reply, curious as to her response. In all their interactions, it was the one she'd most vehemently refused to answer. Margo exhaled heavily. He already knew she had no desire to confess her methods.

Now, seeing that expression on her lovely face made Egros even more curious. He turned, taking a closer look. They'd both reseated themselves at Kingston's insistence, and he found the damn chair constraining as he waited. She tapped the table with her short, polished fingernails, and her hazel eyes flitted to her brother.

Was that Guilt? But why?

"Fine," she grunted. "I micro-chipped Logan."

"You did what?!" her brother shouted in outrage.

He'd stood up so swiftly, the chair he had been sitting on crashed to the stone floor. Margo's only moved back as she also stood, going toe to toe with her taller brother.

"Don't take that tone with me, *fathead*," she retorted.

It was amazing how much they looked alike. Skin and hair colors so vastly different, and yet their hazel eyes blazed with passion as they took identical stances against the other.

"I might have always been on the run as a kid, but

you were the one always getting into trouble. I did it so I could protect you—"

"Protect me from what? I am a grown man—"

"Who was abducted by Shifters! Dangerous man eating Shifters!"

"Um, we don't eat humans," Storm said.

"Actually, I'm a vegetarian," Furio added unhelpfully.

"Shut up!" Logan and Margo screamed at the same time.

"Hold on, everyone, please just a minute now," Egros stood up, getting between Elena and Margo, who were staring each other down again.

"*Ohmygawd!* You guys! What the hell? I was napping," an angry, and very pregnant, Fergie came walking into the room in her custom Ferragamo slippers.

How she got the design house to create them for her, he did not know, or care, for that matter. Egros had other things to worry about. Besides, Storm probably procured them, and the Wolf certainly had his methods.

"Butt out, Egros," snapped Logan.

"Stop telling everyone what to do, Logan," Margo snapped.

Was she defending him now? Egros wondered. And

was it perverse he felt happiness at the very idea the beautiful Margo had stood up for him to her own brother?

Fuck. Yes. It totally was. Pathetic, Egros. Very pathetic.

He rubbed a hand over his face as everyone resumed their shouting and talking over the other. It was a goddamned disaster, and Egros' magic was starting to zap at him anxiously.

"Quiet!" Kingston roared. "Now, we are all going to sit down here and discuss this rationally."

"Fine, but first someone needs to dig that microchip out of my ass!" Logan bellowed.

That particular announcement was followed by a unanimous round of *not its* from the entire group. Egros included.

Much as he still felt he had a lot to make it up to both Elena and Logan, he was not digging in that guy's ass cheeks for a damn thing.

Nope. No fucking thank you.

"Um, yeah. Okay, so Logan? We can figure that part out later. Now, I have a mate and newborn Dragonling to get back to—"

"Dragonling? OMG! You really turn into a Dragon?" Margo gasped, and Kingston closed his eyes.

The Alpha more than likely did not mean to reveal

anything about himself. But the cat was pretty much out of the bag, and there were only two ways this could go. One, they enlightened their fellow Guardian's sister-in-law as to the actual facts about the world. Or two, they erased her memory.

Both he and his magic were in favor of the former. Suddenly, he felt the most absurd need to protect the little vixen, to keep her from harm at all costs. As if she needed him to, he thought disgusted with himself.

"Egros," Kingston said, his eyes white with his beast. "Take Margo to your office."

Fuck.

He knew what those words meant, and everything inside of him raged against it. Still, Egros could not disobey a direct order.

Much as he wanted to. Shit. He was going to have to erase everything that had happened in the past few days, the Keep, the supernatural world she'd recently uncovered, not to mention *himself*, from Margo's memory.

What fresh fucking hell was this day turning into?

"Egros?"

"Yes," he replied to the Dragon.

"Come find me when you are done."

He nodded, too angry for words.

Margo was arguing with her brother, and Elena

was trying to get his attention. The Panther Shifter had picked up on what their Alpha had ordered Egros to do. It was up to her to break the news to her mate.

Not an easy job, for sure. But Egros' was worse. He'd formed some sort of attachment to the woman, despite they'd only spoken less than a dozen times.

Remember your vows and focus, he told himself. But that didn't make him feel any better.

"Come with me, Ms. Wells."

Then he turned and walked away. She was curious and would follow him to his workroom. Once there, he'd perform a forgetting ritual. With any luck, that would suffice.

But when had Egros ever been lucky?

TEN

The Witch walked around her in a slow, yet perfect circle. It felt decadent and naughty, calling him that. She didn't know why. It was simply who he was.

A Witch.

But she could almost imagine his power reaching out across the void, calling to her in a seductive song. Foolish nonsense, but Margo always had an active imagination.

Whatever magic was, she was too new to it to have any understanding of its capabilities. But damn, she was giddy with the high of being right.

All the naysayers and those who'd looked at her like she was crazy could suck it! Ha! Magic was real, or at least, it seemed that way. She'd never been so happy, but she still needed proof. And with a little maneuvering, this guy was going to give it to her.

She looked around the room and frowned. No windows, no doors except the one they'd come in from. It was dark and depressing. Boring too with shelf after shelf of books, and all sorts of geeky equipment that could only belong to Logan.

Her brother was an odd one. Brilliant, but odd. Anyway, this place was not at all what she'd imagined a Witch's lair to look like.

She snorted at the word *lair* as it popped into her head. Eg turned and raised an eyebrow inquiringly. But Margo ignored the question and looked, really looked, at him.

Shaking her head, she took in his stiff shoulders, and constant frown. His hair fell across his forehead as he shrugged, then went back to gathering notes and vials. Margo wasn't precisely sure what was about to happen, but that pesky inner sight of hers was on full alert.

Something was going down. Something she wasn't too sure she was going to like. Eg's agitation was getting to her. Before she could stop herself, or question her own actions, Margo placed her hand on top of his.

"Okay. Stop banging things and look at me," she commanded.

"What? Um, why?"

"Just do it," she said, and waited for him to comply.

His fingers wrapped around hers, and she was stunned to discover it felt good, holding hands in the dark crowded room.

"What's going on, Eg?" she asked, using the nickname she hadn't bothered to ask permission for.

"What did the Dragon tell you to do?" she added.

Margo was far from stupid. Her foresight was a curse sometimes, but in her line of work, she'd learned more often than not, it was its own reward. She braced herself, waiting for the moment he would come clean.

Finally, she gazed into Egros' shamrock green eyes. Green, huh? She mused. She could have sworn they'd been blue, or violet, maybe even brown before. Whatever the color, his eyes sure were pretty. They glittered in the darkness, bright with resolve to tell the truth as they stared into hers. Or maybe she imagined that.

No. Not imagined.

That extra sense she sometimes loved, sometimes hated, told her he meant to be truthful. The pull she felt growing so powerful between them, he felt it too.

She was certain of it. Well, in that moment she was, anyway.

In all honesty, this place, the people in it, all of it combined, was like some crazy fantasy. Something she'd imagined or saw on TV. A make-believe playground for grown-ups that she'd read in a book, maybe.

But what author would bother making up such a place? And in New Jersey too. Ha! That was laughable. The Garden State wasn't known for hidden mansions in forest paradises, and that was exactly what she'd thought of this place when she spied it several nights ago. Among the pines and beeches, black walnuts, and more in the Jersey pine barrens sat the Keep like a stone fortress amidst all the burgeoning green.

Of course, at the time, she hadn't thought much beyond finding her brother. Fathead he may be, he was hers, and she would always have his back. Now that she had found him, and knew he was safe and sound, Margo realized she hadn't planned the 'what next' part of this failed smash and grab job.

Egros knew, though. He knew, and he was about to tell her. That fact made her heart warm just a little bit more towards the too handsome Witch. From green to gold, his eyes changed, and she blinked to make sure she wasn't just seeing things.

What the what now?

"Margo," he said her name, and her attention flashed back to him. "Kingston told me to bring you here so that I might wipe your memory of this place and all you have learned since your arrival."

"What? Sonovabitch! That's not fair," she sputtered, angry beyond the capability of coherent speech.

"I didn't even learn anything besides the fact there were more than Bears and Wolves out there! I already knew about paranormals! The US government has a branch dedicated to studying you!"

"What?" he asked, confusion evident on his handsome face. "Explain, Margo. Please."

It was then she noticed he'd been using her first name. Their hands still entwined, she looked down at them, then pulled away. What was she doing? She shouldn't be attracted to him. Not here and not now.

"Look," she replied, closing her eyes and gathering her thoughts.

"The DPCA knows about Shifters. We aren't part of the military or the FBI or CIA, for that matter. We are something else. A top secret branch of government that has been aware of people, paranormals, who turn into Wolves and Bears for years now. Some have been tapped by other secret branches of the military and have done work for them, but not us. We've simply watched and gathered information," she began, barely making sense to herself, let alone the confused Witch sitting there.

"So, you're telling me you are in cahoots with a secret government agency that knows something, but not everything about the paranormal world?"

"Yes," she nodded. "We don't interfere, we simply collect information. And Egros, you can help me. I mean, you're a Witch. That means magic is real. And let me tell you something, I have been looking for a way to prove that for years. You can't take this away from me—"

"Who me? No. I told you, Kingston says you need to have your memory wiped. I am sorry, Margo, but—"

"Why does he get to decide?"

"He is our Alpha. You don't understand—"

"Then help me, Eg. Make me understand," she pleaded.

"Not for my job, but for me. I've, I've been seeing things my whole life. Images, snapshots, sometimes whole scenes playing out like video clips in my head. My Auntie Beth thought I was crazy, had me locked up for a few months when I was a kid. Not even Logan knows," she whispered, wiping her face with her fingers.

She hated crying. Crying didn't fix anything. Only hard work and determination had ever helped Margo when the going got rough. That, and patience. Patience was another of those dang virtues she'd always strived for. Auntie Beth, God rest her soul, had given her a strong moral compass, like many good Christian women had. Her own mother had been absentee, which was likely for the best.

But without any other adults to take full custody of her, she'd learned to hide that truth about herself. And, God, how it hurt to have to do that! Without any prodding, Margo confessed to Egros about her sight, and the years she'd spent hiding it.

"Incredible," he whispered.

"Me? Nah. Crazy, maybe. I mean, it's not like I turn into a Wolf, or a Panther, like Elena."

"Me either," he said, offering her a tissue and a smile. "Actually, Shifters don't *turn into* Bears and Wolves, *they are* Bears and Wolves. And Dragons, Stallions, Panthers, and more, Margo, so much more than that."

"What more? Tell me, Eg. Teach me, please. I will be a good student. I swear it."

Margo watched his eyes darken now to almost black, and she wanted to grin, knowing she had him. Men were so easy to figure out. She just had to smile and show some enthusiasm, and they followed her around like puppies. She tried not to let her disappointment show and was stunned by the fact she wanted him to be different.

Why should that even matter?

"Come on, Eg," she said, trying to shake off that bit of weirdness. "The world deserves to know the truth about all of you, your friends, and magic. If magic exists, it's only fair—"

"Stop right there," he said, shaking his head and she knew then that she lost him.

Even more compelling was why she should feel so relieved knowing she'd lost her only lead?

Margo had no time to contemplate her strange reactions to this man. No, not when he was talking again, and *surprise surprise*, she actually wanted to listen.

"The world is not fair. Never has been. And humans are among the most cruel, judgmental, and greedy beings out there."

"Hey!"

"Can you honestly say humans would react well to the news their neighbors are actually dual natured creatures? Beings who can shift to different forms, *sometimes multiple different forms*, from animals to mythological creatures, and more than that. Would the average Joe or Marcus or Steve like hearing that their wives and daughters and sons live next door to thousand pound Bears or two ton dragons who can breathe fire? Shifters have the increased strength, speed, stealth, and deadly traits their wild cousins have only with the addition of cognitive reason. And I already said there are more than your regular zoological creatures from A to Zed. So, what then, eh, Margo?"

"I don't know what you want me to say."

"I want you to think, and be honest with yourself, then answer my question. Would the average human like knowing that supernaturals exist?"

Fuck. When he put it like that... ugh. Margo gritted her teeth. Anger and impotence cursed through her. Egros was right. She knew he was right. But after so many years of trying to understand her own precognitive abilities and working to prove magic actually existed. Beyond that which she'd recently found out at the DPCA, Margo wanted to show the world that magic was real. Was she just supposed to let all that go now?

Frustrated tears pricked her eyes, but she wouldn't give him the satisfaction of crying. She stared him down, willing her anger to simmer down. But it was no good. Margo was torn between wanting to scream and wanting to kiss him.

Damn the man for being so stinking good looking. The sympathy she saw filling his gaze, as if he regretted his harsh words, just wasn't fair. After all, he wasn't rude or wrong even. He was simply being honest with her. Margo respected honest.

"So, do all paranormal beings hate humans or just you?" she asked, trying to regain her composure.

"I hold no hatred in my heart for you or any human, Margo. This is not personal."

"It is to me," she replied, glaring.

"I was given a direct order by the leader of our group. I could not disobey him, even if I wanted to."

She huffed out a breath and walked to the farthest wall. It was made of some kind of stone and looked ancient and unbreakable. But she never was one to take things for what they seemed. Margo lifted a heavy iron pot and hit the thing, once, twice, allowing her rage to flow through her.

Egros just stood there, watching with concern heavy on his face. When she was utterly spent, she felt his arms come around her. He took the heavy iron pot and replaced it on the shelf. The damage she'd done to the wall began to smooth away and repair in front of her eyes. Margo stopped, stunned.

"How did you do that?"

"It's not me," he replied, gently. "The Keep is

inhabited with *manetuwak*, magical spirits. They protect these walls, repair them, when need be, and see to our needs."

"Wow. That is pretty amazing," she mumbled.

"It is. Look, Margo," he began.

"Fine," she replied, cutting him off.

Margo turned and faced him. She wasn't afraid of the male Witch, but she was hurt by his words. Not so much the words themselves, but the truth behind them. It was irrational, and unreasonable, but she couldn't help it.

"Margo—"

"You're right, okay? Just leave it at that."

She stormed over to a chair and sat down heavily.

"Well? What are you waiting for?" she asked.

"What do you mean?"

"Let's get this over with."

Breathing unsteadily, she waited for him to make the next move.

Eleven

His green eyes darkened to amber, as if his own sadness affected the color. She blinked, sure she was seeing things, but no. From shamrock green, to black, to amber. Only a shimmer of that emerald color remained in the now honey-colored depths.

"Here," he said, stalking over to where she sat.

He picked up a tumbler of clear liquid, could have been water for all she knew, but it wasn't. Somehow, Margo knew that glass contained something that would take away her memories, clear her mind of this place, finding her brother, and *him*. The thought saddened her.

"Drink this," Eg said, getting a second vial ready.

Margo tossed it back, grimacing at the sharp, bitter

taste as it slid down her throat. The next one he handed her was sweet and floral, like hyacinths on a warm spring day. The one after that was terrible, it tasted like water after a handful of dirty pennies had been left to soak for a month. She wiped her tongue on the tissue he handed her, not embarrassed in the least.

"Ugh, how many of these do I have to take?"

"That is all. Now, I need you to look into my eyes, Margo, and follow the direction."

Always a good pupil, she sat there silently and gazed into his then sky blue eyes. That was strange, wasn't it? His eyes didn't just get darker or lighter the way some did when a person was angry, or happy, or horny. They didn't change from blue green to green blue like her friend Doris' did depending on what color top she wore.

His eyes were a revolving door of colors. Each one vibrant and expressive. And hot. Did she mention hot? Margot squirmed in her seat as liquid pooled between her legs. The thought of Egros Pyke and his multicolored eyes left her feeling both needy and lusty.

Knock it off, she told herself, listening to the sultry timbre of his voice. Eg held her gaze, asked her to relax, to trust him. Oddly enough, she did.

His blue eyes widened as he continued to speak, sparks of purple swimming in their depths. She was certain he was not even speaking English anymore. But that didn't matter because Margo was no longer listening to his words.

No, now she was floating down the river of her own consciousness. The water was warm and comforting, and the pull of the tide gentle and pleasing.

Egros was really quite handsome, wasn't he? She smiled and took in the sharp cheekbones and straight nose. A nose that had never been broken. He looked young, but by his own admission, he was twice her age if not more. Something about paranormals aging slowly.

Yes, he sure looked tempting sitting in front of her, face a study in concern. He looked even better sprawled across the king-sized bed, naked beneath silk sheets, in the vision she was seeing as she continued to float on.

That long, lean body of his was like a swimmer's, with tight muscles and hidden strength. In her vision, Eg was wrapped around her, his pale skin the perfect foil to her golden brown. Those powerful legs and arms wound tightly around her gasping form. His long-fingered hands stroking, touching, caressing her everywhere while he whispered and grinned, and kissed her lips.

Dayum. Was that real? She wanted it to be.

Next, she saw them walking side by side through some woods. Could have been the forest that surrounded the Keep. Butterflies and dragonflies flitted around them, dancing in the breeze.

Egros was leaning down, saying something to her, and Margo, well, she was laughing gaily and carefree as she had never been before. The river in her mind grew wider, and scenes flitted by faster. Mostly of Egros and her, happy, then scared. Some men in dark suits were trying to take him away.

Mother appeared, and there was violence next, but she couldn't see what. Her heart squeezed in her chest, and panic filled her. She couldn't lose him. He meant too much to her.

Darkness came, and shadows seemed to overwhelm the scene. She couldn't reach him. Men in suits, Mother, and some faceless monster pointing with one gnarled hand. She felt his greed and lust, not for her but for Egros and something he had. This monster wanted to rip it from his body, his heart, his very soul.

She could not see him clearly, only felt his malice. And it was evil. Pure, unadulterated hate radiated from the monster like toxic sewage from a chemical plant. She could not let him get his decrepit fingers on Eg. Not while she was still breathing.

No. NO!

"No!" she yelled aloud.

"Margo? Margo? Come back to me, here. Are you okay?"

"NO! Wh-What?"

She blinked her eyes. She was panting, and sweat was dripping down her face. She was still there, trapped somewhere between shadow and fear. But slowly, she came back to herself, and her focus was on him.

Egros was crouching in front of her, both hands on her face. She couldn't recall details of what she had seen, but her pulse was still racing. Her heart was pounding. Confusion filled her, but it was quickly replaced by relief.

She shoved away the doubt and social constraints that would have prohibited such a thing, and the next thing she knew, Margo vaulted into his arms.

"Thank God," she whispered, holding him tight to her chest.

"Easy, I got you," he whispered.

His arms came around her like steel bands, holding her tight to his lean, muscular body. In that moment, the only thing she wanted to feel was the profound joy that had swelled inside her like the tide the second she saw Eg and registered he was alive and well. Not in the clutches of some faceless madman, but living, breathing, and with her.

Thank fuck, he was with her.

Margo was not used to feeling such strong emotions. As a marine, a lawyer, and a DPCA agent, she'd learned to compartmentalize her feelings. How else could she live and see the things she'd seen? But this wasn't the same. This was emotion so raw and powerful, it knocked her off her feet.

"Are you okay? Margo?" Egros repeated himself.

"Not really," she said, leaning back.

"But I am going to be," she said and slammed her mouth to his.

For a second, she thought he was pushing her away, but Egros was only standing up. His hard lips firmly sealed to hers. Those long arms she was starting to really believe she loved, like loved *loved*, tightened around her in an unbreakable embrace as he held her close. *So very close.*

Egros nuzzled her face with his, prodding her gently until she tilted her head the way he wanted her to. Then he growled against her mouth, and it was all kinds of sexy. Margo leaned into him, breathing him in as his tongue pressed inside her mouth.

She sighed, opening for him, allowing him to explore her mouth. Nothing had ever felt so right. Her hands reached up and wound around his neck. He was so tall, she had to stand on tiptoe, but she did not care. The deliciousness of it all was way too sweet for silly worries like that. She hadn't had enough deliciousness in her life, and Margo sure as fuck was not about to squander it away with worries.

It had been a long time since she'd been kissed stupid by a man, *er*, Witch, or anyone really. And Margo really liked to kiss. She wished she'd had a mint, or maybe practiced more or something in her youth. Anything to keep him there, kissing her.

Embarrassing? Maybe. She just didn't want Egros to ever stop. Of course, that was when he leaned back, eyes blazing red and chest heaving from being breathless.

"What? Is it bad?" she asked, concerned.

"What? No, hell no," he replied.

"Good," she returned, leaning up to kiss him again. But the damned man leaned back farther, and he was just too tall for her.

"It's just, um, are you sure about this?"

"What?"

"This here. You, me, kissing, touching, *um*, maybe, *er*—"

"Are you trying to ask me if I am sure about sex?"

"Yes. That. Very much that," he ground out, and pink stained his cheeks.

Fuck, he was adorable. Was she sure about sex? Yes. Margo was surprised to discover she was, in fact, very, *very* sure.

"Margo," he whimpered when her tongue snaked out to tangle with his. "I don't want to take advantage—"

As if any man could ever take advantage of her. The Witch had a few things to learn about Margo Wells, but she could teach him later. *Much later.*

Like when they were sweaty and spent and starving from exertion, when the high of being alive and being with him eased. Though Margo was pretty sure he would always evoke such feelings.

It was crazy. It was fast. And proof or no proof, she was pretty fucking sure it was magic.

Yes, her heart and brain both screamed aloud. Being with Egros was pure magic. And she reveled in it.

"Egros?" she said, breathing him in.

"What?" His voice was deep and gravelly with need, sending spirals of desire shooting through her already amped up body.

"Shut up and kiss me."

He'd never been one for public displays of affection, not that is office was public but still. Egros was more a bedroom, lights off, locked door, kinda Witch.

Passion had never overridden his senses before. Certainly not like this. Then this saucy little vixen spoke, and he was helpless to do anything but obey.

"Shut up and kiss me."

How could Egros refuse a command like that? Especially when it came from the one woman in the world he wanted more than any other. Hands down.

His cock ached, heart squeezed, and magic pulsed all in time with his desire for her. Hell, he would've given her anything she wanted, anything at all for a single kiss.

He tried to control himself, told himself this was Logan's sister and he best not act too rash. Then she asked him for more in that husky voice of hers, and all reason went out the window.

Egros was hers to do with as she pleased. If she wanted kissing, then fuck yes, he would kiss her. Damn fucking straight, he would.

Egros would have kissed her for hours and been content. Only the feisty little vixen had other plans. Margo already had her hands down his pants, and whatever brain cells he had left jumped ship.

Egros hissed out a breath as her fingers closed around his cock. Fuck, that felt amazing. She squeezed and moaned while doing so, as if she enjoyed touching as much as he liked being touched.

Fucking hell.

He went cross-eyed at the sharp sting of pleasure from her caresses, the vixen using her nails against his skin, adding a bite to the sweet sensations and making his blood hotter than Hell itself. Having been to the Underworld, he could vouch for the temperature.

Of course, Egros' dick had been rigid since the moment he'd laid eyes on her. In truth, he'd been walking around fighting a semi boner for the last four days. But there was no fighting it now.

Not when she was wrapped around him like a

python, and her delicious mouth was sealed to his. Margo pushed against him, and ass that he was, he let her go.

Well, of course he should let her go! Fuck's sake.

He wasn't an animal. He wasn't even a Shifter. Egros was a Witch. They didn't have fated mates and animal urges, but right then the Fates themselves sure as fuck could've fooled him.

His magic was pressing against him, demanding he take the woman and bind her to him. In fact, he almost thought he heard the word *mine* ringing clearly in his ears.

What the actual fuck?

Egros shook it off, allowing her to step back. He'd been raised a gentleman, and gentlemen stopped when a woman said stop. It might feel like it was going to kill him, but nothing an ice cold shower and some mind-numbing work couldn't cure.

Don't be so sure of that, his inner asshole snarked.

He closed his eyes, telling himself to shut the fuck up. The little bit of brain power he had left was currently busy reminding him to breathe, so he was a little deaf when she'd opened her lips to speak once more.

"I'm sorry, what did you say?" he asked.

Margo grinned, and that smile damn near knocked

him to his knees. How was it legal for one woman to be so damn beautiful? And sexy to boot! And how could she be so calm when he was fighting the urge to bend her over the chair and take her hard and fast—

Fuck.

He really needed to stop thinking like that or he was going to embarrass himself.

Truth was, there wasn't enough cold water in the reservoir that piped into the Keep's many bathrooms to staunch his need.

Double fuck.

He was going to need an ocean to put out the fires of lust burning inside. Maybe two. Desire raged like a blazing inferno, and he couldn't recall ever feeling quite like that.

"Tell me you have a condom," Margo repeated.

He stared. Wait. What? She licked his lips, kissing him and rubbing her sexy little body against his. The female was so soft and warm, her brown skin ravishing in the golden hued lamplight.

What the fuck? He was a terrible poet, and worse, he knew it. But she was perfect and worthy of more sweet words than a Witch like him was capable of.

Perfect. Mine, he thought.

"Eg? Condom? Where?" Margo asked again, biting on his lower lip.

The sting of pain sent zips of pleasure right to his aching cock, and Egros growled and pulled her tight against him. Kissing her neck, he bit the flesh there, loving the moan that escaped her lips. He was still unclear what brought this on, but he was not going to question it. He couldn't.

"Condom. Now. Now. NOW!" she said, slapping at his arms.

"Top drawer," Egros growled.

Ever since Elena had mated Logan, the couple had been responsible for piles of condoms all over the damned place. Annoying at first, but he was grateful now.

He sucked on her tongue and tugged on her lower lip with his teeth. So sexy, so hot, she wiggled and writhed, making him mindless with every ministration. But no, that wasn't true. His mind was right there, every step of the way.

What was he doing making out with Logan's sister? Reason tried to push its way in between the passion exploding between them, but his magic pushed back, zapping him right in the ass so that he moaned once more into her mouth.

She kissed him harder. Her hands winding through his hair, and all his objections faded away under her sensual assault. Egros was putty in her hands. Well, not really.

He was more like rod of steel in her hands, but he wasn't about to repeat that aloud. Made him sound like a 70s porn star.

Fuck.

She smelled so good, like sunshine and daffodils. Good and clean and sweet. He wanted to treasure her, to keep this kiss sacred in his mind forever. Without him really conscious of it, his magic rushed forward, taking a snapshot of that kiss, and sealing the memory of it in 4D for him to keep always in the palace inside his mind.

"Mmm," she moaned, as if she too had felt and approved of the gesture.

She kissed him deeper, her breasts pressed against him so tightly he felt the unsteady beating of her heart against his skin. And that was when Egros Pyke said goodbye to his own heart.

Willingly he let it go, sending it to her as only a Witch could, in a sacred spell whispered only in his mind. He would love his sweet Margo until the end of time with every inch of his being.

She had the most incredible mouth. Plump lips soft as pillows, sweeter than cherries, and did he mention demanding? Gods, he loved the way she got rough and demanding with him. Not afraid to show him what she wanted at all.

Margo placed two hands on his chest and pushed. She shoved him backwards, till he landed softly on the small sofa in his office. Before he had a chance to ask her again if this was what she wanted, to second guess what they were doing, she was back. And good lord, the woman got down on her knees in front of him.

Egros swallowed, eyes wide as he looked into her lust filled eyes. He knew this had nothing to do with the potions and spells he'd tried to erase her memories. Something had happened to her, something magical.

He felt something inside her he couldn't quite explain. She seemed hellbent on hiding it, but whatever it was, Egros had sensed magic. And it was coming from her.

His attempts at wiping her memories had not worked. But something had occurred. Whatever this attraction between them, he needed to know she was acting with free will. Then, as if she had read his mind, she spoke.

"I am very in control of myself, Egros Pyke. Something happened back there, but before we talk about it, I need you inside me. I need to be close to you. To feel you. I'll beg later if you want me too, but right now, I need you to take these off," she growled and tugged at his pants almost as rough as a Shifter would have.

"I don't need you to beg, love. I just need to know it is me you want."

"You, only you," she whispered, caressing his face.

He didn't think twice again. Egros snapped his fingers and his clothes disappeared. Hers too.

"Oh fuck, that is so hot," she whispered.

One soft hand reached down and stroked his dick, the other gripped his knee to keep her steady. Then the little minx leaned forward and licked him from balls to tip, closing those sexy fucking lips of hers over the head of his cock.

Egros moaned aloud, back arching as she sucked him deep into her throat. His pulse raced, heartbeat roaring in his ears. Her scent surrounded him, filled him, and his magic pulsed and sizzled in response. Fuck, if she didn't stop, he was going to come.

"Stop. Won't come without you," he growled, and she sat back, grinning like the Cheshire cat.

Margo rolled the condom down until it covered his cock, then she straddled his thighs. He leaned forward, sucking one taut nipple into his mouth. She tasted even better than she looked. Her gorgeous curves and all that golden brown skin, so smooth and hot, like warm silk, he thought as he slid his fingers along her firm thighs.

Egros could not get enough of her. She was fire and light, elegance, and grit, and he was completely in thrall of her. Margo lifted herself high, positioning him at her entrance.

Her eyes sparkled all gold and green as she lowered herself ever so slowly. Egros held his breath, watching every nuance of emotion flicker across her gorgeous face as she took him deep inside her tight pussy.

"Oh!" they groaned in unison.

This was beyond his scope of expertise. He was a Witch, not a gigolo. But damn him if he could not admit this was the most incredible, the hottest, the best damn sex of his whole life. If he ever said differently, Egros would be a fucking liar. And he was not that. Other things, maybe, but never that.

"You done?"

"Huh?" he asked, unsure of what she meant.

"You done thinking?"

"Uh, yeah."

"Good. Cause when you fuck me, I need you to be here with me. Only me," she commanded.

"Yes, of course. I am here with you, Margo. Only you," he growled, sucking on her neck.

"As long as we understand each other," she said, then rocked her hips.

Egros growled, knowing full well the minx had the upper hand. He nuzzled her skin until he found her plump nipple again. Pulling it into his mouth, he sucked hard, and was gratified when her pussy squeezed him tighter.

A pull and tug on the other nipple, and Margo was moaning aloud. Egros grinned, pressing her breasts together with his hands, he flicked his tongue from one bud to the other, back, and forth, harder faster, and she rewarded him for his efforts by fucking him harder and faster. He took the right nipple between his teeth and tugged, causing her pussy to tighten around him.

Egros growled with the bud inside his mouth, then he tugged again. Margo was whimpering as she rode his cock, faster and harder. Every time his teeth tightened on her bud, the little minx's pussy spasmed.

One more tug had her coming hard and hot all over him, her sheath squeezed him with every ripple and jerk of her orgasm, body tightened like a whipcord until she slumped against him, breathing heavy.

That was when Egros turned her, so she was facing the armrest of the sofa. He pressed down on her back gently, and she went, lowering her face and arms so she was gripping the fabric between her nails. Margo was breathing more easily, but not for long. Not if he had anything to say about it.

By the time he was finished, he wanted her gasping for air and calling his name. Fuck, yes. He ran his hands down her back, cupping her ass cheeks and spreading them. He circled her back entrance with his thumb, loving her gasping moans as she pushed her perfect peach of an ass back into him.

Fuck, what a sight!

He took his cock in his hand and rubbed it against her pussy, still using his thumb to play with her ass. Margo whimpered and moaned, wiggling to try and get him to push deeper. He gave her an inch, then another, pulling back when she got greedy, only to give her more when she stayed still. Finally, she growled at him, and fuck if that wasn't sexy as all hell.

"Dammit, Eg," she said.

"Tell me what you want. You just have to tell me," he whispered, his voice so low he barely understood himself.

"I want you inside me. Fucking me. Not-oooh— oh fuck, yes!"

Egros didn't wait for her to finish. He plunged deep inside, ramming into her hard and swiftly. She had him so riled up, he couldn't think, he could only feel.

So, he did. Egros felt. Her. All of her.

Fucking her relentlessly, he felt his magic roaring through him. The power he'd kept locked away pulsing in the pendant at his throat. Fuck, he needed to keep control, but then Margo was moving her sweet ass against him, and he couldn't concentrate on anything but her.

Her back bowed as she begged him to work her harder. How could he do anything but? Egros let go of the leash he had on his emotions, then he really started to plow into her. His hands held her hips so tightly he was bound to leave bruises, but fuck, it felt so good. And from the sounds she was making and the response he was getting from her body, she loved it.

"Yes, yes. Oh god, Eg!" she yelled her nickname for him, and surprise surprise, the moniker was already growing on Egros.

Their lovemaking was fast and furious, and fuck it all, amazing. Egros wanted the female to be his, longed to mark her somehow, someway. But Witches didn't do that. Did they? Fuck if he knew.

Egros didn't know much of anything right then. He didn't want to know. Only wanted more of Margo. Fuck, he wanted all of her. And so he took, and took, and in taking, taking, *taking*, he gave, gave, *gave* everything he had.

Egros offered her everything. All of himself. His hopes, dreams, wishes, and more. Everything that made him Egros Pyke, Guardian of Chaos and Witch. He poured it all into the sweet, sexy little vixen who bucked and bowed beneath his ministrations.

And when they came, they came together. It was long, and poignant, and glorious. Egros felt a wave of pure, white hot pleasure rush through him as he clutched at her hips and breasts with his hands. The rush was both sweet and surreal. It went on and on and on.

When they were both sweaty and spent, nothing more than a tangle of loose limbs draped across the couch like lifeless bolts of fabric, he admitted the cold hard truth even if only to himself.

Egros Pyke was in love.

THIRTEEN

Margo woke up alone and deliciously sated. She stretched and stood, trying to make sense of what had occurred.

She'd agreed to let the Witch brainwash her, or whatever. But the potions he gave her didn't work on her messed up brain. Instead, she'd found herself floating along a river of absolute consciousness. That was where her memories were stored and visions of future events yet to pass swam.

The future was never certain. She'd read enough fantasy books to accept that. But something had happened there. Something real and beautiful, and if she wasn't careful, she would lose herself too it.

Her clothes were in a neat pile at the foot of the sofa. They appeared cleaned and folded. By magic, she guessed with a rueful grin. The Witch never did admit to anything, but he sure as fuck made their clothes disappear like lightning when she'd come onto him with lascivious intent.

She dressed quickly, since there was no shower in the potions room or whatever the heck they called it. Her stomach rumbled, and a snack sounded very good right about then.

Margo had no sooner walked into the room than every Shifter in the immediate area turned their glowing eyes on her. She froze, feeling like a piece of meat at a carnivore convention, fingers itching for her gun. But that wasn't the end of it. Oh no, Elena, Furio, Fergie, and Storm all tilted their heads towards her, and *sniffed*.

Freaky shit.

"What's going on?" Logan asked, taking a bite of the perfect red apple in his hand.

"Uh, nothing. Got anymore of those?" she asked.

"Basket," he said, munching on his piece of fruit while jotting notes.

Elena was elbowing him in the rib, and her fathead brother still didn't look up. Margo rolled her eyes and grabbed an apple, then scrounged around the cabinets for some peanut butter.

"My goodness, stop elbowing the poor man when he's working. You know he can't hear you, right?"

"Logan," Elena hissed, but he just nodded and tilted his head to kiss her.

The Panther accepted the peck he gave her but growled something about idiot men. Not that Margo could blame her. Logan did turn into an inattentive idiot when he was on the verge of solving a problem.

"Elena, you got a question to ask me or something?"

She decided to put the woman out of her misery. And clearly, the others too, since they all moved forward, surrounding the kitchen island where she sat down with her snack.

"So, Margo, why do you smell like my man Egros?" Furio asked, right before his mate stomped on his foot.

"Really?"

"Ow, Jess! What'd I say?"

Jessenia mumbled something, giggling, when the big guy wrapped his arms around her. He nuzzled her neck and said something that caused the shorter woman to blush prettily.

All of the Shifters seemed to constantly touch their significant others. A hand on the arm, a kiss on the cheek, fingers toying with their hair. But none of it was aggressive or proprietary. It all seemed gentle and loving to Margo, and she was an excellent judge of these things.

"Um, Margo," Jessenia began, to Margo's utter amusement.

"Yes," she replied, slicing her apple into perfect slices before smearing the right amount of peanut butter on each one.

"We were wondering, though it is really none of our business, but um, why do you, um," the woman hedged.

Her cheeks were turning a delightful shade of pink, so Margo thought it prudent to draw this painful process out as long as humanly, *or inhumanly*, possible. Discomfort, other people's, not her own, was one of Margo's favorite things.

"Look," Furio butted in, clearly the impatient one of the gang. "We just wanna know why you smell like Egros."

"Is that what you want to know?" Margo asked.

"Yeah."

"I see," she replied, taking her time to bite and chew. "Any particular reason you all want to know this?"

"Egros is one of us," Storm inserted himself into the conversation. "We care about him, so if you are using him- OW!"

"Geez! You guys have all the subtlety of a couple of army tanks in a church!" Fergie growled.

"Really, get out, all of you, or I swear you are not eating tonight," Jessenia said.

The men all grumbled, except for *fathead*. Margo's genius brother was still plucking away in his notebook. Clueless. Yes, the man was totally clueless, but he was her brother and she loved him.

"Okay," a very pregnant Fergie said, rounding on her.

"Two questions. First one, are you going to finish that?" she asked, pointing at Margo's half eaten plate.

"I was planning on it, but I am a good sharer," Margo said, offering the now drooling female a bite of peanut butter smeared apple.

"Thank you," she replied, munching on the treat and moaning happily.

"Second question, is Egros any good in bed?"

Margo's mouth twitched. The man himself was standing in the doorway, eyebrows raised at Fergie's impertinent questions. He stood silently, waiting for her reply with one eyebrow arched perfectly over curiously gold eyes.

She was going to have to ask him about his revolving change of eye color, among other things. Her chest seemed to warm with his nearness, and she was surprised to find she felt aroused as well. What was she doing in the kitchen with these females instead of in bed with her man?

Her man. Where the heck had that come from? She was not sure, but she liked it. There was definitely an affinity for that kind of possessive terminology in the most basic part of her brain.

"To answer your questions, Fergie, first, you can have the rest of my apple. And second, I don't know, we never made it to the bed."

Then Margo stood and moved across the room. An uncontrollable need to kiss him burned inside her, overwhelming reason and decorum. She grabbed him by the collar of his black shirt and pulled him down for a kiss.

The sounds of gasps, whispers, someone clucking their tongue, and a whistle reached her ears, but Margo didn't care. Let them watch. All she wanted was to kiss the man, the Witch, standing in front of her. The incredibly sexy Witch who was kissing her back like he was starving for her.

"What the hell are you doing to my sister?"

Ugh. The fathead was still there. Before she could tell him to back off, Logan had stormed over and tried to pull them apart.

And that was when Margo learned Magic was real.

Because the second her brother had laid his hand on her, her sexy, hot as fuck Witch boyfriend, zapped Margo's twin with a bolt of magic so powerful, he went flying across the room in a cloud of purple smoke.

"Holy shit!"

"Logan! Are you okay?"

"What the fuck, Egros!"

"Hey, that wasn't me!"

The cacophony of voices rose to a deafening roar until, well, someone actually roared. That someone being a grumpy ass Dragon holding a squalling, red faced newborn in his massive arms.

"Does someone want to explain what the f-word is going on here?"

"Um—"

"Well, the thing is-"

"You see..."

"Quiet!" Margo yelled, turning to face the angry Dragon.

"I think I just zapped my brother."

Everyone went silent at Margo's declaration, which was good because she wasn't finished. Her pulse was racing like mad, and she felt dizzy. Somehow, some way, she'd sent her brother hurtling across the room like a shot without laying a single finger on him.

"You?" Elena asked, bending over Logan's prone form.

"Is he okay?" Margo returned.

"I mean, he's unconscious, but yeah, he's not bleeding or broken," Elena said, though she could tell the female was pissed.

"Good," Margo said, turning to face Egros who was frowning and looking at her curiously.

"Are you alright?"

"No. Um, put your arms around me," she said.

Thankfully, Egros did just that. His swimmer's build was deceptively lean, but she knew he was more powerful than other guys who boasted gym built muscles.

His strength was to the marrow, and it was just one of the many things she liked about the Witch. Unsurprisingly, she liked a whole lot about Egros Pyke. What she knew, anyway. And she planned on learning more.

"Margo?"

"Excuse me, everyone," she said, and passed out for the first time since she'd drunk way too much Black Sambuca at a party when she was in law school.

She never drank the hard stuff anymore. All because of that one fateful night. Being underaged hadn't stopped her, but puking her guts out for days on end afterwards sure had.

Didn't matter now. Whatever Margo had done to Logan, it had used up a lot of her strength. Having Egros catch her before she fell to the floor seemed like the best way to go in her humble opinion. He looked down at her, cradled in his arms, eyes purple with worry before hers closed.

She'd wanted to tell him it was okay, but the truth was Margo wasn't sure if it was okay. Sleep was pulling her under, and she couldn't fight it. Not now. So, she gave in.

With any luck, she'd dream of Egros. The gorgeous Witch was already filling her dreams, she thought. Before her mind went blissfully blank, two words flashed across her sleepy brain. She wasn't sure what to make of them, but Margo would worry about that when she woke.

Egros.

Mine.

Fourteen

"I told you to take her memories of this place, Egros. What the hell happened?"

Kingston's grumble was lower than normal in deference to the now sleeping child in his arms. Holley was getting some much needed rest, and the Alpha Dragon was on daddy duty.

Egros sort of knew how he felt, seeing as how he'd been unable to let go of Margo ever since she'd asked him to hold her. More like told him, really.

"Can't you put her down yet?" Logan said unhappily from his chair.

Elena was holding an ice pack on his head where it had collided with the bottom corner cabinet. Egros felt bad about it. Well, not really. He would have, if the man hadn't been griping at him for the past hour and a half.

Egros gritted his teeth against the snarl that rose in his throat at the man's question. Witches did not snarl, for fuck's sake.

"No. For the eleventh time," he said in his most reasonable voice. "I cannot put her down. There is something going on here that we need to examine more closely—"

"Why don't you start by telling the story about how you magicked my sister into fucking you, you bastard? Tell us that one, so I can rip your goddamn head off!" Logan retorted.

"I think you are forgetting who you're talking to," Egros answered, his magic building inside him at the man's insolence.

It rose and rose until he felt it surround him, covering him and Margo in gold and amber circles of magic. It was odd. He'd never manifested magic this way, but then again, he wasn't certain it was even his.

"Everyone calm down," Kingston commanded, and the weight of his Alpha voice was felt by all in the room.

"Fine, but he needs to know Margo is an adult. She makes her own choices. And she chose to be with me, Logan, whether you like it or not."

"I don't like it."

"And I am really not interested in your opinion."

"That is still no reason to use magic against him, Egros," Kingston said, and Egros could tell he was disappointed.

Now for the hard part, he thought.

"Yes, Kingston, about that. You see, it wasn't me who zapped him."

"What do you mean?"

"Yeah, right," Logan muttered.

"He wouldn't lie. Not ever, and certainly not about this," Elena said, surprising even Egros by taking his side.

He glanced down and saw Margo looking up at him, her eyes dreamy with sleep and glowing faintly of purple and gold. She blinked and the glow was gone, replaced by her usual hazel green color.

"He means, it was me," she said, reaching up to touch his face with her warm hand.

Egros turned his head slightly to kiss her palm, loving the way her eyes flashed at the gesture.

"Are you alright?"

"Are you always going to ask me that?"

"Yes."

"I thought so," she said, smiling and using his arms to balance herself as she sat up slowly.

"Ms. Wells, how do you feel?" Kingston asked.

"Fine, but Eg's right. I zapped *fathead* when he tried to pull us apart. I don't know how I did it. But it was definitely me."

"Then he did something to her when he fu—"

Several growls sounded, but none as loud as Margo's own distinct cluck of displeasure.

"Logan Wells, you may be my brother, but I fuck who I want to fuck. And I do not ask you for permission, are we clear? Or maybe you need another zap," she said.

"No. Sorry. I was just worried, Gogo."

"Fine but keep a civil tongue in your mouth please and thank you before I get Auntie Beth after your sorry ass."

Egros knew she was bluffing, but damn, if he didn't enjoy it. Margo slid off his lap and sat next to him, but she kept her hand tightly clasped in his. A gesture he liked way too much to be healthy.

"Eg is just telling you what he knows, and it isn't any more than I do. He did as you asked. Gave me vials to drink, but it didn't work like he expected."

"She's right. If Margo were any other normal, she'd be back in her own life right now and we wouldn't even be a memory to her," Egros explained.

"What are you saying? My sister is a Shifter?"

"No, not a Shifter," Egros said. "I believe your sister is a Witch."

After an hour of Margo going over the events as she'd experienced them, with Egros chiming in with his own perceptions, they left Kingston alone to do some digging. It was after dinner, and Egros' stomach was growling. It stood to reason she was hungry as well.

"Want to get some dinner?" he asked impulsively.

"Yes," she replied easily.

"Italian or Chinese?"

"How about Indian?"

"Wonderful. I know a place that does an extraordinary biryani."

"Great, just let me use the restroom and I will be right with you."

"I'll be waiting," he said.

Smiling as he watched her walk down the hall to the room she'd been using, Egros ran a hand over his head. Fuck, this was moving fast, but he couldn't help it. Everything was easy when he was with Margo.

Nothing else seemed to matter when he was with her. Not his clothes, or his name, or his magic. She just put him at ease if there was such a thing.

He liked her. Loved her even, though fuck knew it was too soon for that. He wanted her, that much he knew. Everything felt right when she was with him, and his magic went wild whenever she was near.

Yes, it was rash to ask her to go out, but he really wanted her to go with him.

———

Someone knocked on Margo's door just as she exited the bathroom. She really needed to wash her face after that crazy power nap.

Her phone hadn't gone off in days, but she dropped it in her pocket, anyway. Force of habit, she figured.

"Who is it?" she asked, but that was all she got out before a slew of women filled her room.

Fergie, the pregnant redhead, was munching on a bag of chips. She was followed by Jessenia, also pregnant but not eating, Elena, and a tawny skinned woman with long, straight hair holding a baby.

"Hi, I'm Holley," she said softly. "So Egros really asked you out to dinner?"

"How do you all know that?" Margo asked.

"Shifters. We got good ears," Elena winked.

"Okayyy," Margo replied. "So, I am going to dinner with the man. What do you want?"

"Um, well, we just wanted to help," Holley returned, but Margo just stared blankly.

"Fine, you need it plain and simple, right? Well, the thing is, we all love Egros, but he is a stick in the mud. But he seems to like you, and we want to make sure he has a good time."

"Are you trying to get me to have sex with him? You know we did that already—"

"OMG! TMI!" Elena growled, covering her ears, and closing her eyes like a six year old forced to eat lima beans.

"Look, you just can't go dressed like that," Jessenia explained, rubbing her tummy.

"Okay, I am pretty sure if we just think about it a door should pop up here," Holley said touching the wall.

Margo was about to tell her she was nuts when suddenly, a large wooden door appeared where nothing, but wall had been moments earlier.

"Yup, here it is. Welcome to *The Ladies' Room*," she said, grinning.

Inside, Margo was stunned to see rack after rack of beautiful gowns and designer clothes. It was as if these women had their own personal department store right inside the Keep. Even better were the shoes and boots, all things she'd liked in fashion magazines over the years. Most were beyond even her budget, and amazingly enough, they were in her size.

"What is this place?"

"The Keep is filled with many spirits, and they like us to be happy," Holley explained, cooing at the now awake baby in her arms.

"He is beautiful," Margo said.

"Thank you. He will be strong like his father, but smart like me," she replied, eyes twinkling.

Margo smiled and, with Holley's permission, touched the baby's perfect little head. He was truly beautiful and seeing him secure in his mother's loving arms sent pangs of longing through the badass lawyer turned government agent.

Odd. Very odd.

"Okay, so with your hair and eye color, I am seeing greens and golds. Oooh! How about this?"

Fergie waddled over to a rack of clothes overflowing with exactly the kind of designer clothes Margo had always admired but shied away from. Flowy wide-leg pants that rode low on her hips and crop tops were not exactly the right fit for her job.

The DPCA did not have a policy on it per se, but she'd always gone with fitted slacks and button-down shirts. Simple, plain, professional. Plus, she could carry a weapon under her many blazers without it showing. Not that she used her gun very often.

"That is beautiful," she said, ruffling the fabric between her fingertips.

"And perfect for dinner. Come on, take that off," Fergie replied, snapping her fingers impatiently.

"Fergie! Margo, ignore the pregnant psycho. You can use the divider to get changed and only if you want to," Jessenia emphasized.

Margo took the bundle and snorted at the women's antics. They must be really good friends, she thought, and a part of her longed for that kind of camaraderie. She'd never made friends easy. The curse of being the only child of an extramarital affair. Logan was her friend, but he was her brother so he kind of had no choice.

She dressed without even realizing it, pondering her sudden melancholy. She was being silly, Margo decided, stepping out from behind the divider. Holley was standing between Jessenia and Fergie, who were involved in some sort of pregnant lady slap fight, and Elena was looking through a rack of tall skinny jeans that only she could wear out of the four of them.

It all seemed so friendly. Comfortable, warm, and crazy. Like a family, she guessed. Everyone stopped whatever they were doing when she cleared her throat, and Fergie was the first to speak. Margo was really starting to like the nutty redhead.

"Damn, Egros is gonna shit when he sees you!"

"Um, I know I am still learning the vernacular, but is that what we want him to do?" Holley asked.

"She means, he's going to love it," Jessenia interpreted.

"Oh, I see."

But the confusion on Holley's face was evident even as she nodded. Margo grinned, and Jessenia rolled her eyes at Fergie. Baby Greyson cooed, and Holley's attention was diverted, but Margo couldn't fault her. The baby was just perfect.

"You look really good," Elena said, and the woman looked pensively. "Egros is a good man. Despite what happened."

"Logan told me about it," Margo confessed.

She'd known since day one about his trying to stop her brother and the Panther Shifter from getting together. She'd been mildly interested, but after recent events, Margo had to admit, she was downright curious.

"We never, um, you know," Elena said, pink eyes going wide with what Margo assumed was embarrassment.

"I know that too," Margo said, and somehow, she simply did.

"He was just trying to help. And our kind, you know, *supernaturals*, don't trust easily. Anyway, I didn't want you to get the wrong impression. I've partnered with Egros in the field and couldn't ask for anyone better to watch my back. He's proven his loyalty time and again."

"Thanks, Elena," Margo said. "I appreciate it."

"I just, well, don't hurt him, Margo. That's all, I guess."

Elena rubbed the back of her neck, clearly uncomfortable with the discussion, but Margo stepped forward and took her hand.

"I get it, Elena. And I could say the same thing to you about my brother. Logan is all I have in the world."

"I couldn't hurt him if I tried," she replied easily, and the love she had for him shone in her bright pink eyes.

Amazing, Margo thought. The power she felt in Elena's grip, and the love shining in her eyes, told her the woman was complicated and powerful, and even better, she truly loved Margo's brother. That was good.

Something was changing inside of her. Margo felt as if something deep within her had been asleep her entire life, only awakening now in these walls and with these people.

Elena seemed confused by their conversation, but Margo got the message. Even if the woman did not understand, she did.

These people loved Egros. He was their family. And as she turned to the mirror and saw herself, curly hair down around her shoulders, pale sage crop top and wide linen pants with slits up the sides revealing her legs with every step she took in the leather sandals on her feet, she was stunned.

For the first time in memory, Margo looked relaxed and happy. Her brown skin was practically glowing, her smile radiant, and her hazel eyes were more green than gold at the moment.

"Dayum, I look good," she announced, and the other women stopped their chatter.

"You'll do," Holley said, nodding.

"Hell, with any luck Egros will be *doing you* before dessert!" Fergie replied crudely.

Margo just laughed and covered her mouth with her hand, stemming the snort that threatened to escape. These ladies! They were hilarious. And she couldn't have asked for a better group of women to be around.

"Margo?" Egros' voice drifted in through the walls, and she turned with bright eyes to see the door gone.

"Where is he?" she asked the women.

"Oh, the guys aren't allowed in here. This is our space. Just walk up to the wall and the door will appear," Holley explained.

"Magic," Margo whispered.

And it was.

FIFTEEN

E gros started to wonder what the heck was going on after twenty minutes had passed agonizingly slow, and still no Margo.

He walked into her room, anxious when he saw it empty. Using his other senses, he quickly found a magical residue in the air. It was familiar, good. The *manetuwak*, he realized. The spirits of the Keep not only worked hard to keep the Guardians and their mates safe from outside forces, but they also used their powers to see to it that most every need was met.

Which included *The Ladies' Room*, a place for the females of the household to gather, chitchat, and try on Fergie's ridiculously large collection of designer shoes. Egros wondered how his Margo would fare with those four women. He wasn't worried.

His vixen could hold her own with anyone. Hell, he'd never seen a more competent woman in all his life. He waited another ten minutes, but patience was not his strong suit. Without any other recourse, he simply called her name.

Then she appeared. Like magic. Well, she used a door, actually. But *that* had appeared like magic.

"Holy fuck," he murmured.

Having only ever seen her in black slacks and button-down shirts, the change was surprising. Hell, he could hardly keep his tongue in his mouth. She smiled at him, as if she knew exactly what he was thinking. Soft linen, so thin it was sheer in places in sages and golds hung from her rounded hips in flowing waves.

With long slits up the sides of each pant revealing her gorgeous curvy legs with each step, and a crop top in the same material leaving her midriff bare, she was a vision. Like a goddess from Ancient Egypt, or maybe one of the Greek Pantheon.

Margo's smile was mysterious and intoxication, Mona Lisa, but better. The woman was gliding towards him, nothing as mundane as walking for his sweet vixen.

For fuck's sake.

His cock was fighting a losing battle with his pants.

The blasted thing threatening to bust a hole through the fabric, he was so hard. Egros' heart was pounding as she neared him, the woman was so damn beautiful she stole his breath. Margo stopped just short of touching him, and he thought he'd die from lack of contact.

"Ready?" she asked in a husky little whisper that had him closing his eyes and gritting his teeth.

Fuck yes, he was ready, for anything, everything. For her. Only her.

Mine, his magic growled.

"You said Indian food, right?" she asked, bringing him abruptly back to the present.

"Yes, if you like."

"Sure," she replied, shrugging.

She raised her eyebrows, and he damn near tripped over himself leading the way. Egros stopped short, then turned and took her hand.

"Please, after you," he said, remembering himself.

"You don't have to treat me like a prom date, Eg."

She laughed, and he loved the sound. He was acting silly, but he couldn't help it. He wanted this date to be perfect, and he hadn't been on many. Come to think of it, he hadn't been on any.

Sex, of course, but that had been an equal exchange based on need. Egros had never had a real relationship with a woman, except for the women at the Keep, and those were all purely platonic.

"Is the restaurant far?" she asked, stepping beside him.

"Far? Well, I suppose."

"How long till we get there?"

"Oh, we will be there in a few minutes."

"How if it's far?" she asked, cocking her head to the side, and sending a mass of curls tumbling to her shoulder.

Fuck, she was beautiful. So much so that he didn't really understand her question. He just took her hands, placing them on his chest. Then he moved his to her waist.

"Hold on," he whispered near her temple.

Egros closed his eyes, casting a simple transportation spell that he'd used a million times or more. A magical wind rose around them, and Margo gasped in delight. She shuddered against him, but he held her safe and secure. He would never allow harm to befall her. Not ever.

The fact she trusted him meant the world to Egros. He vowed then and there to endeavor to keep her trust for as long as he lived. She might not know it, but he wanted more than a date and a night with the beautiful woman. Much more.

"The best place for biryani," he said, once the wind had died down.

"Oh, my god!" Margo gasped, clasping a hand to her chest as she looked around at the busy Kolkata street.

The air was warm and full of spices since they were in a market district with restaurants and shops aplenty. Evening was falling and tourists and locals milled about, some exploring, others going on with their daily business.

"We're in India?" she whispered, and Egros smiled.

How could he help it? He nodded and took her hand, so they didn't get separated in the crowd.

"How did you do that?"

"A spell," he replied, easily.

"Magic. You used magic? I thought you weren't going to show me any of that," she replied.

Her eyes were bright with excitement, and he felt ten feet tall, knowing she was impressed. A small hint of worry and doubt snuck inside his brain as they entered a local establishment and found a cozy table for two.

It was a fact that Margo had been looking for proof of magic her entire life. Now that he'd shown her some, what if that was all she wanted? What if she planned to reveal him to her superiors at the DPCA?

All the doubts of his youth came creeping in while perusing the menus, and Egros' spirits fell. What if he had read this wrong? What if she was just looking for another round of what had transpired earlier between them before outing him and his fellow Guardians to some normal government agency?

His cock was willing, but his heart almost beat right out of his chest. Pain at even the thought of her doing such a thing filled him. Fuck, how was he supposed to find the truth?

No, his magic seemed to shout at him. Looking at Margo as she navigated the menu, asking him questions while sipping the steaming tea a waiter had brought for them, he knew she was enjoying herself.

"I can't make up my mind. Can we just get one of everything?" she laughed.

"If you like," he replied easily.

"I know! You pick. I trust you," she said.

And those words washed away every doubt that threatened to crumble his happiness. Egros lifted their still joined hands and pressed his lips to her palm, love for her filling him.

She was amazing. An honest, good, and fierce woman, beautiful as she was brave, and he was proud to be with her.

"Everyone is staring," she whispered, her hazel eyes glowing with emotion.

"Americans always get looks when visiting foreign places," he explained.

Though Egros was used to that kind of thing, he had a feeling they were staring because she was just so gorgeous. He'd been to this part of India before, and it should have been old hat, but not now. Not with her. With her everything was new.

They ate and laughed, shared stories about their lives and antics. He loved her enthusiasm, her joy. She was as real a person as he'd ever known. He was in love for the first time in his life, and the real truth, was Egros was terrified. He was a powerful Witch, but he had no idea how to not fuck this up.

"Furio really did that? I mean, he totally looks like this Jersey wise guy type, but really? He picked up the guy and threw him in the river?"

"Well, he wasn't really a guy. He was a marine Shifter, and he was being a total ass."

"I see. And that makes it better?"

"No, not really, I guess," Egros replied, laughing with her.

"Ice cream for dessert?"

"I love ice cream."

"Good, come with me."

Egros paid the bill, and they walked hand in hand to the alley where they'd arrived. He didn't see the men tailing him until it was almost too late. But somehow, Margo had. Her hand tightened in his, and before the first spell hit them, she'd turned around and raised her hand.

Purple and gold light emanating from her palm, and Egros was so stunned he could not move. Wait, that wasn't why he was suddenly frozen. Something was pulling on him, on his magic, and his knees buckled.

"Egros! What do I do?" she yelled over the loud din of magic blasting through the air.

But he could not answer. His voice was stuck in his throat. It was like his strength was being siphoned and he could only watch in horror as a tall, black cloaked stranger faced off against them. The others were still trying to zap them with weaker spells, but Margo's deflection spell was holding.

"Give me what's mine, boy!" snarled a familiar voice, and Egros' eyes went wide.

"Eg, who is that revolting piece of shit?" Margo asked, her eyes glowing gold as the man Egros had not seen since he was thirteen years old pulled off his hood.

Time had not been kind to Bartholomew Pyke. His face was wrinkled and ravaged with pockmarks and scars that had not been there when Egros had last seen him. He looked wild and manic, like a junky who'd gone too long without a fix and would do anything trying to score.

"Need you to let go," he finally managed.

Margo, quick as she was, looked down and dropped his hand. She pulled a small caliber gun from a thigh holster he hadn't even known she was wearing and aimed it at the two goons now siding with his father.

They were Witches but had obviously been messing with Dark magic. The deep scars and missing appendages, fingers, noses, and more, he could only imagine, told Egros they'd been practicing blood rituals to commune with Demons. A sort of power bartering system that rarely worked out for the Witch involved.

"The magic! It is mine!" Bartholomew raged, but Egros did not waste time on him.

He wrapped an arm around Margo's waist and transported them out of there. Once they were safe and back in his room at the Keep, he ran his hands over her, checking for injury.

"Are you hurt? Were you hit?"

"I'm okay. Hey, Eg, I'm okay," she said, taking his face in her hands. "Tell me what's going on. Who was that man? Were they Witches? I felt magic, but it seemed wrong," she said, brow furrowing in confusion.

Egros sat down heavily on the bed. He ran his hands over his head and face. How to explain the sordid details of his childhood? Hell, his very existence.

"That man was Bartholomew Pyke," he confessed. "He's my father."

Sixteen

" *He's my father.* "

That was probably the last thing Margo would have expected Egros to say after their run in with some magic spewing thugs. She sat down beside him and waited. Her years as a lawyer, and an agent, had taught her silence was the best tool to use when someone wanted to confess something. And Egros clearly had something to say.

"My mother was a young, innocent Witch from a powerful line. When she'd met my father, she'd been visiting relatives in the area. He was the head of the Pyke Coven and looking for a way to replenish the magical stores he, and those in his family before him, had squandered."

"Magical stores?"

"Yes," he said, and she could feel his anger, though it was not directed at her.

"You see, Margo, magic is finite. There is only so much of it in the universe. It can be passed down from generation to generation or willed to another. If you are a less scrupulous Witch, it can be bartered, bought, and sold.," he explained hurriedly.

"I see."

"No, you don't. Not yet. But I will continue to explain, because you need to understand that with magic there must be balance. If used inappropriately, there is always a cost. It is not the stuff of fairytales and animated movies. You can't just squander it without consequence."

Egros heaved a sigh, and she felt his worry and grief as if it were her own. Not knowing what else to do, she moved closer, allowing her leg and hips to touch his. Confident she was on the right track when he didn't shy away, she stayed there, waiting.

"My father killed my mother. I have no real proof, but he did. He wanted her magic, but she'd already willed it to me. Her family had ancient powers, huge stores of magic that would be dangerous in the wrong hands," he said, voice so low it was barely above a whisper.

"Then she did well, leaving it to you," Margo said, her belief ringing true with her words.

"I don't know," he replied sadly. "I've never even unlocked it. You see here, this stone pendant is the key to my inheritance."

He lifted the necklace he always seemed to wear, and she studied it. The stone seemed to simply float inside a silver circle, hanging there by magic, she mused. Why she hadn't noticed that before, she could not say? It was beautiful, hauntingly so. Sadness filled her at the thought he'd never tried to unlock his mother's gift to him. That he'd never felt worthy of it.

"I thought my father was dead, you see. So, I figured I had time before I tried to unlock it, to see what was there. Besides, my mother told me the time to reveal the power within would choose me."

"Wow. You were never curious?"

"Sure, I was, but Margo, the thing about magic is it's seductive. Like any kind of power. Did you notice the missing fingers and scars on my father and his men?"

"Yes."

She'd been taken aback by the horrendous appearance of the three men with long black cloaks who'd followed them into the alley. Margo had been on the best date of her life, and she figured they were going to try to mug them. Imagine her surprise when it turned out to be some sort of attempted magical robbery instead.

"Dark magic requires sacrifice. It is the most forbidden craft, and yet, it is used by those desperate enough to try and barter with Demons for power."

"Demons exist too?"

"Oh yes, my sweet innocent. There is much in this world and the next that you don't know. And you are better off not knowing. I'm sorry. I will try to find some stronger spell so you can forget—"

"What? What are you saying?"

"This was a mistake. All of it. You shouldn't be here—"

Margo flinched and moved away from him. He might as well have slapped her! It sure as fuck would have hurt less. Her heart squeezed so hard she couldn't breathe. How was it possible for him to walk away? To even think it!

"I'm not made of glass, Eg. And we already proved I can't be brainwashed or whatever the fuck you call it," she snapped.

Her chest heaved with the effort it took to breathe, and Margo stood up, pacing back and forth in his room. The jerk! She was angry at him for even suggesting she was too weak to stand beside him.

"Am I magic?"

"What?" he asked, truly stunned.

"Am. I. Magic."

"Uh, well, you have used magic. I can't be sure, not exactly. But tonight I felt as if you were pulling it from me."

"So, what am I?"

"Margo, I don't have the answers you are looking for—"

His eyes were a sad, deep blue as he looked up at her, but she would not be swayed from her line of questioning. She was on to something here, even if he was in denial.

"I can't be just human. I have had visions of the future, glimpses, my entire life. When I first saw you after I busted through that window, I felt like I knew you, Eg. And when we kissed, it was like coming home."

"Margo," he growled, and the sexy sound sent a wave of arousal washing over her.

"I know you are upset, and that is understandable. If I was facing the man, I believed killed my mother, I'd be pissed as hell too. But don't push me away to try to protect me, Eg. I am stronger than I look."

"Fuck. I know you're strong," he growled, and stalked her to the farthest wall.

"Do you know that? What else?" she asked, desperate to know.

This Witch had her so wrapped up in feeling, she didn't know whether she was coming or going. Wetness coated her sex, her pussy throbbing with need as he neared her. She'd never been turned on so fast in her life. Everything was different with Egros. It was better, hotter, more honest, and even fun.

Life was not perfect, and neither was she, but it was magical. He was magical, and she wanted to be with him. She couldn't imagine being without him. So yeah, when he'd even suggested she leave, she'd gotten angry.

Margo never got angry with anyone except Logan. And that was because her fathead brother worried the shit out of her. If she lost him, she'd be all alone. In fact, Margo had never had anyone to call her own. Except maybe now she did.

Was Egros hers?

She swallowed audibly.

Holy shit.

Another swallow, followed by some deep breathing.

I love him.

The realization stunned Margo. She might have

thought it earlier, but now it wasn't just an idea. It was fact. She didn't just love to fuck him. She loved *loved* him.

"Do you think I am weak, Eg? Is that why you're pushing me away?"

She watched emotions play across Egros' face. His eyes shifted from blue to teal to gold to that deep purple she loved so much. They stayed that hue when he'd made his decision, anticipation made her tremble.

"Weak? Fuck, no. You are not weak. You're strong, and gorgeous, and fucking mine. You hear me, Margo? You. Are. Mine. Mate. Conpar, Mine," he growled.

He smelled so good. Rosemary, mint and sex, pure unadulterated sex. Need rose like the tide, and she couldn't help herself. Margo grabbed him by the collar and tugged him down to meet her hungry lips.

She was so done with talking. Pure satisfaction had stroked her, like hands, when he made his declaration. It was primal and possessive, and she fucking loved every syllable. She wanted to be his. Need to be. Just as she needed him to be hers.

"Mine," he growled between kisses, and she felt something pulsing between them.

White hot and delicious, it danced across her skin, and his, engulfing them both in purple flames. Magic, she thought with wonder as he stripped off their clothes with a wave of his hand.

Egros' hot, hard body held hers against the wall. He lifted her with minimal effort, and she wrapped her legs around his waist, moaning as he entered her swiftly and without error. Margo was so wet, soaked for him, allowing his long, thick girth to stretch and fill her in smooth stroke after stroke.

His tongue plunged into her mouth in time with his cock, and she could only hold on and enjoy the ride. Fuck, it was so good. He was so good. Fucking her against the wall, hard and fast, his magic covering them and touching them everywhere.

The sounds of their flesh slapping together filled the room with their grunts and pants a close second. Margo's pussy clamped around him, holding tight as the first wave of ecstasy swept through her. Egros growled, his kisses traveling from her mouth to her throat. He licked her neck, teeth grazing her skin while his cock pounded into her aching cleft.

Fuck, so good. So close.

The magic surrounding them burned brighter, hotter, going from purple to gold to white as she started to come. The pendant around his neck started to smoke, and as he pumped once, twice, three last times, spilling his seed into her, the thing broke.

"Margo!" he roared her name, cock still pulsing as he came, and came, and she came right along with him.

Her orgasm crested, and Margo's mouth opened in a soundless scream. Never had she felt such intense pleasure. So good, it bordered on pain. Then it was pain. Actually, owie fucking pain.

"Fuck, oh fuck, oh fuck!" she screamed, and Egros released her slowly, lowering her to her feet.

"What's wrong?"

"Eg?" she gasped in question as the broken pieces of the pendant lifted off the floor. "Are you doing that?"

"No! I'm not. Margo?" he yelled.

But it was too late. The stone was whipping around her until the silver circle rose, level with Margo's heart. Then both stopped, joining once more, stone inside the circle, and both struck, slamming into her chest and sending white and gold lights into the atmosphere, practically blinding them both.

The force of that thrust propelled her back into the stone wall, but Egros was faster. He'd moved like lightning, fast as any Werewolf she'd ever tracked, to cushion her body before she could make impact.

She'd have told him she appreciated his gesture, but it was wasted since her chest was burning hotter than if she'd been shot. Margo grunted against the pain, and just when she thought she couldn't stand it, it was over.

Whatever force had been holding her upright, it ended with that final punch of pain that had so suddenly stopped. Margo slumped down. She was conscious, but not physically. She would've hit the ground had Egros not caught her.

"Margo? Are you okay?"

"Eg?" she asked, staring at him in wonder.

Fear and worry tainted the air with an acidic smell that made her nose twitch, but it was Eg's strange appearance that had her wide eyed.

"What is it, love?"

She sat up slowly, hands touching his face. His now very hairy face. He covered her hands with his, stopping when he felt the beard now coating his cheeks.

"Let's get you up," he mumbled, standing and lifting her easily.

"What happened?" she asked when he dropped her gently on the bed.

Egros did not answer as he sat beside her and summoned a mirror in front of them. She was always awed when he used magic, but it was getting easier for them both, she mused.

Margo was rubbing the spot on her chest that still burned a little when he scooted behind her. His face was back to normal, no more hair. But as for Margo, well, she was not one hundred percent herself.

"What the heck is that?" she gasped, looking at the mirror, then down at her chest.

"I think that is my mother's pendant, love."

"But it is in my chest!"

"Yes. Now, don't freak out. I am sure there is a good reason—"

"Egros, did you do this?"

"No, I swear it. Tell me, when you saw me before, when I was worried for you, was it just a beard that suddenly grew?"

Margo turned her head to look at him. She liked his big warm body around her. Loved what they had just done to one another, even though it ended rather strangely. But how was he so calm?

"What? Your beard? Who cares about a beard? Wait a sec," she said, closing her eyes to bring back the memory of only minutes before.

When she'd been concentrating on her own pain, Egros had somehow changed. Her best guess was that his fear had spiked some sort of magical adrenaline rush, except his reaction was bizarre, to say the least.

During her years with the DPCA, Margo had watched and gathered intelligence on various Wolf Packs and Bear Clans, and the one thing those Shifters had in common was they were fiercely protective of their families. Their husbands and wives in particular, though they used the term *mates*.

When Egros thought she was hurt, he'd responded the same. He'd started growling, and once that happened, his body began to morph. Purple and gold flames engulfed him, transforming him from the Eg she knew and loved to something else. Something bigger, badder, hairier. He was like some sort of bipedal Wolfman.

"Here, I have an idea," she said and lifted her hands to his head. She couldn't articulate what she'd seen, but maybe she could show him.

Once she started concentrating, it was like a whole new world opened to Margo. A world within his mind. She gasped at the pleasure, knowing she was sharing information, sending it directly into his head.

And it wasn't just visions she sent him, but her feelings, and something else, too. Something wild and pulsating, powerful and slightly willful, she discovered when she tried to coax it aside.

Magic. It was magic. And it was theirs, she felt the truth of that and Egros' ready acceptance instantaneously. Emotion filled her heart, and Margo felt tears slide down her cheeks.

"I can feel you inside my head, love. The magic, it's so great, so much of it, and it belongs to us both. Can you feel that?" Egros spoke in whispered wonder.

"Is it hurting you?" she asked.

"Not at all. It is amazing, love. You are amazing!"

"So, what does it mean? What happened to you? And to me," she said letting go and turning back to stare at the stone and silver circle now embedded in her skin.

It no longer hurt, and she frowned as she touched it. Strange that it was not raised, either. It felt like her skin, like it was a sort of magical tattoo.

"My mother told me love was the key to her magic, but I assumed she meant her love. I was wrong," Egros said. "She meant you, and my love for you. I think we are soulmates, Margo Wells. And I know I love you more than anything else in the world."

She closed her eyes at his words. Was it true? She'd never had much affection in her life, but she wanted it. Here and now. Margo wanted Egros' love and affection. And she wanted to give him hers in return.

She turned around and straddled his legs, felt his hard cock slide between her slick folds. She wanted him so badly, but first she had something she needed to say.

"I love you too," she told him, lifting up to take him in.

Eyes on each other, they made love with nothing between them. No lies or pretense, no secrets, or hidden expectations.

Only love. And this, Margo thought, this was the real magic.

"I love you, my *conpar*," Egros growled, the new animalistic side of him coming out to play as their passions rose.

"I love you too," she replied, moaning in earnest as he lifted his hips to meet her downward thrusts.

Faster and harder, Margo rode him, loving the way his new powers had him growing fur and fangs with his increased desire. The rumbling growl in his chest as he suckled her breast had moisture dripping down her thighs, and when her orgasm hovered out of reach, her sexy Witch licked the surrounding skin of new tattoo and that was all she needed to start coming.

And so on it went, all through the night, Margo and Egros loved on each other, insatiable for one another. They shared their bodies, minds, hearts, souls, and magic with one another, filling the void that had kept them so lonely for so long.

"It was worth it," he murmured before drifting into sleep.

"What was?" she whispered.

"A lifetime alone to finally find you. I love you, Margo," he said, and she sighed, snuggling closer.

"Love you too."

SEVENTEEN

"You did what?"

"I, um, *magic bonded* with your sister," Egros told Logan the next day over breakfast.

"What the fuck does that mean?" he snapped.

Egros scratched his head, he was far too happy to let Logan's annoyance bother him. He'd hoped to catch everyone at breakfast, and he was lucky enough to do just that.

Holley was off nursing Greyson, but everyone else was there. It was confession time.

"I sent a question to the Morrigan a few days ago when I started noticing things about Margo and myself," he began, eyes flashing to where his conpar was sitting, looking at him sweetly.

She was cunning, his mate, and he was so damn in

love, she was all he could see. Dangerous for some, but for him, like with other Guardians, it meant being the best version of himself. One who could better protect her and magic at all costs.

"You sent a request to Sherry Morgan-McAllister without consulting me?" Kingston asked.

"Forgive me, Kingston, but this was a Witch matter and there was no other recourse."

"I see," the Dragon replied and gestured for him to continue.

"I had always operated under the assumption that Witches do not have mates, and that something was wrong with me because of my, well, oddities even as a child. Turns out I was wrong and right."

"How do you mean?" Jessenia asked.

"I've always felt hollow, alone," he said, turning when Margo joined him.

"Me too. I love you fathead, but you know I never had many friends or family who loved me back. Just you and Auntie."

"Oh, Gogo, why didn't you say anything?"

"Cause, I had books and school and my jobs to keep me busy. I didn't need you worrying about me," Margo said.

"Now that I have found Margo, and she's found me, things are different. I felt a pull to her the second I saw her, and now I know why. You see, way back in my mother's lineage, the Morrigan has discovered an ancient line of Druids, *shape shifting* Druids."

"Is that like even a thing?" Fergie asked.

"Yep," Margo replied, grinning.

"It is," Egros added. "I have a fated mate. May I introduce you all to Margo Wells, my conpar."

His mate giggled and leaned into him, and Egros readily wrapped his arms around her, nuzzling her neck with his nose and lips. Daffodils and sunshine, mixed with a hint of his own rosemary mint scent.

Perfection.

The table erupted with questions and congratulations, but he only had eyes for his sweet, feisty, and *so fucking beautiful it hurt* Margo.

"What about her job? I mean, doesn't she like want to out us and everything?" Furio asked.

"Actually, I think it is time Kingston and I have a chat about the DPCA. I think we can work together, maybe share information, and sort of stay out of each other's way. After all, you guys could use someone on the inside to help with covering things up, can't you?"

Egros knew she'd piqued Kingston's interest when the Dragon raised one eyebrow. He grinned and let go of her hand when she moved to sit down next to the Alpha.

"Margo is special, you know," Logan said from beside him.

"I know."

"Good. So, then I don't have to tell you that if you hurt her, I will develop an elixir to strip the skin off your ass while you sleep, right?"

"Um, no, Logan, you do not have to tell me anything like that."

"Logan," Elena said, rolling her eyes. "He's just kidding. Sort of. Okay fine, not really," she growled when her mate just stared at her.

"But, like I already told him, if she's your mate, you would never hurt her."

"Of course, I won't I love her, Elena."

"Good."

"Um, who are those guys?" Fergie asked, pointing her oatmeal laden spoon towards the large window.

"Fucking hell," Egros growled when he recognized the same two Witches who had attacked him and Margo in the alley the day before.

Another second and his father entered the clearing in front of the Keep. The bloody bastard!

"I've come for what's mine," Bartholomew Pyke sneered. "Are you still the sniveling brat I left behind? Too afraid to face me," shouted the old man.

Long ago, Egros would have been scared. But not today. Not when he had so much to protect.

"Who the fuck is that guy? And what happened to his ear?" Storm said, moving in front of his pregnant mate.

"That is my father. And I will deal with him."

"Not alone, you won't," Margo said from beside him.

Egros looked down. He hadn't even seen her move, but there she was, eyes blazing. Every instinct inside him was screaming at him to order her to stay put, but he could not do that. Margo was a warrior in her own right. She wouldn't appreciate him stifling her. He just had to make sure nothing happened to her, or else he'd burn the whole fucking world down.

"We can't have that, can we?" she asked, looking into his eyes as if she'd read his mind.

Holy fuck. She had. Egros' eyebrows disappeared into his hairline, but she just grinned and nodded.

"I love you too. Now, let's go kick your dad's ass."

"Sounds like a plan," Kingston said, joining them.

"I can't ask you to do that. This is my fight—"

"When is this cump gonna learn, we're family, Eg. Hey, I like that nickname. I think it's gonna stick."

Storm clapped a hand on Egros' back and for a

moment, he felt like the kid he used to be when the big black Wolf used to come and watch over him.

"Fine," Egros said, overwhelmed with feeling. The fact the Guardians still accepted him after his past mistakes. That they would risk themselves for him was almost too much to bear.

"We're a family, Egros," Elena agreed.

"Um, the missing ear tells me he's made a blood sacrifice to some Demon. That means he is ripe with evil power. His minions, too. Be careful out here," Egros warned.

"You too," Margo replied, cocking her pistol and taking his hand.

Love thundered inside of him, and he'd never felt quite so strong. He looked at where his father was waiting, still shouting obscenities, and readied himself mentally to face the biggest monster of them all.

His father.

Margo noticed two things when she stepped into the courtyard beside her man, the other Guardians of Chaos flanking them. Jessenia, Fergie, Holley, and baby Greyson remained indoors, the spirits of the Keep would be protecting them as they watched worriedly at their mates and friends going off into battle.

First, Bartholomew Pyke was one ugly bastard, and Egros must have taken after his mother in the looks department. Thank fuck.

The second thing, he had more than two men with him. As they stood, half a dozen other Witches stepped out of the woods, hands ablaze with magic.

"I see you've grown more powerful. Good, more for me," Bartholomew spat.

"And you've grown simple, old man, if you think you will get even a drop of what is mine," Egros returned.

"How can a weakling like you ever hope to use your bitch mother's magic? It is mine, boy."

"Never weak, and never yours, father. Mother's magic is ours now. Go now, and live," Egros said, holding Margo's hand.

"You've given it to your whore? Ha! I will rip it from her screaming body after I've killed you," Bartholomew said.

Egros growled and Margo seconded that emotion. The man who sired the love of her life was a foul, disgusting parody of a man. When she looked at him, Margo saw only darkness and evil. A creature totally void of all humanity.

That was the real difference, the link she'd been missing when studying the world of the paranormal. Magic was not just theirs. It belonged to everyone. The supernatural and the human. That was what the Guardians protected, and the realization made her love Eg even more.

Speaking of her man, Egros continued to growl as his father made threats against her. Her chest warmed and pulsed, and she felt power flow freely between them., covering the two of them with purple and gold flames.

Damn.

Her man was sexy when he was angry. His body began to bulk up slightly, and his power pulsed, mixing with hers. The Morrigan was looking into her heritage, but it did not matter what she found. Margo now accepted her visions as part of the magic that was always hers. Combined now with Egros' powers and that of his mothers, she was learning more about magic than she ever dreamed of.

Even better, she was learning what it meant to love and be loved. Really loved. And this pitiful excuse for a father was not taking that away from her. No way. No how.

The sounds of fighting grew, but she could not take her eyes off the scene unfolding before her.

Margo watched as Bartholomew raised his hands and inky black tendrils of what she assumed was dark magic began to shoot out at Egros. Her mate growled as he deflected all but one, the tiny dark spiral escaped his spell and zapped a single curl right off Margo's head.

"Hell no," she growled. "Don't you know not to mess with a woman's hair?"

Egros threw his head back and roared, his form swiftly changing from Witch to the bipedal Druid Shapeshifter of his ancestors. They'd talked about what it meant to be a conpar, and she knew that Guardians were gifted with a special boon to their powers when they found and claimed their mates.

Last night, Egros had claimed her with his words, his body, and his magic. Margo, being a tough as nails modern woman, claimed him right back. She watched in awe as his body changed, increasing in size, strength, musculature, and hair, she couldn't forget that. His nails elongated into claws and fangs protruded from his mouth. Swirls of gold and purple magic surrounded him, and the same flames danced protectively along her skin.

Like a magic suit of armor, she thought. *Like a me sized shield.*

"What is this?" Bartholomew Pyke asked, fear

tainting his voice as he looked at the beast that was his son.

"*This* is something you can't handle," Margo replied. "*This* is *mine*. And you really pissed him off."

Then it was her turn to stare as Egros charged his father. The Witches in his thrall came at her then, grabbing at her arms and legs while she sent magic shooting through her gun as she fired at them. Margo fell to the ground, more Witches came from the woods, hurling spells at her new friends.

They were weak, but many, and it took precious time to stop them. She tried to find Egros and saw him battling a large serpent made of black smoke that his father had conjured. The bastard was stronger than the rest, but she trusted Egros. Knew he would do anything and everything to make his way back to her.

The Guardians were holding their own, though Logan had been hit with a fireball that left him doubled over in pain. Elena's sleek Black Panther was tearing the throat out of the Witch who dared hurt her mate, and Margo nodded approvingly.

There were so many of them, she wasn't sure how to help. Then she closed her eyes as a vision came careening into her mind. It was fast and abrupt, but it showed her what to do. Margo turned to see a single puddle on the muddy and battle scarred lawn. She dropped to her knees and began to chant words that had somehow come into her brain.

A second later and the stagnant water began to swirl, deeper and wider it grew and grew, turning into what looked like a whirlpool that led straight to Hell's door. A sulfuric stench rose from the inky depths, and Margo stepped back.

"Toss them in here," she screamed above the wind, and Furio's Stallion turned, kicking one Witch right at the whirlpool.

Over and again, she worked with the Guardians to dispense of those Witches who had given their souls to evil Demons in exchange for drops of power. Every now and then, she could have sworn she saw a flash of fangs or glittering black eyes in the inky depths.

Beasts waiting for their feast, she mused and shivered.

She was no stranger to blood and gore. In fact, when it was her loved ones being threatened, she downright approved. As the battle died down, Margo found Egros with her eyes. He was standing over the prone body of his father. The man's remains turning to a black tar like substance before their very eyes.

His eyes met hers, the irises burning bright red. Her mate smiled then, love burning brightly in his gaze. Margo smiled back, sweaty and covered in mud and filth from the fight, but so in love and happy to find him unhurt that she wasn't paying attention.

That was when the Witch she'd thought she'd finished off grabbed her and pulled, tugging her down into the black pool that led straight to Hell.

To her death. To her end. Fuck.

"MARGOOOOOOOOOO!"

EPILOGUE

Egros ran towards where the bastard Witch had pulled his mate and despite the other Guardians screaming his name, he dove headfirst into the black pool. Straight to the pit. Straight to her.

"Margo!" he roared over the sounds of wailing and fire.

There were many levels in Hell, and not all of them were bad, to be honest. But this one was reserved for the damned. Souls, like his father's, who had bargained for more than they had to give.

He saw her then, being fought over by a pack of hellbeasts, unconscious and bruised. The Witch who'd dragged her there had already been gobbled up by the Demon he'd thought to ensnare. No others had come up yet, but they would. The smell of fresh meat too good to pass.

Fuck no, he snarled.

Egros' other form took over, the flames of his magic covering him and when he turned, he saw them surround her as well. One curious hellbeast got too close, and the magic zapped him, sending the creature howling. He raced to her side, snarling as others clawed and scratched at him, but he did not care for any injuries to his person. He only cared for her.

"Margo," he growled, his voice deep and gravelly as he scooped her into his arms.

Her clothes were bloody and torn, but he had her now. She was safe now. He turned his head, looking for the doorway out. The pool was starting to close, and he had to haul ass to get them there in time.

Time moved differently in Hell, so it wasn't surprising when he burst through to find snow on the ground and a plaque marking the spot where they'd gone under. Margo shivered, blinking up at him as he tried to catch his breath.

He was exhausted. Dirty. Starving. But so fucking happy to be back.

"Holy shit! It's them!" Storm shouted somewhere nearby.

The big Wolf tried to touch them, but Egros'

magic wasn't quite ready for that. Purple and gold flames covered him and his mate. He watched her breathe, heard her sigh, and when she opened her eyes and smiled at him, he kissed her.

That kiss was worth a trip to Hell and back any day.

"Egros!"

"Margo!"

The other Guardians and their mates came running out of the Keep. Everyone had changed, he thought absently. Fergie was holding what he could only assume was her and Storm's baby, and happiness filled him in thinking the Wolf had a family of his own. Greyson was toddling beside his mother, and Kingston's eyes glowed brightly with feeling as he looked at where Egros was kneeling with Margo in his arms.

Jessenia's stomach was hugely rounded, and she must be due any day now, he thought, while Furio stood beside her, eyes wide. Byram was there too. The Vampire the only one who reached out with a cautious hand.

"Glad you're back, old fellow. It took you long enough," he grinned, revealing his needlelike fangs.

"Sorry about that," Egros said, still a little breathless. "Hellbeasts were a bit of a problem."

"I see. Well, better get her inside then," the Vampire added.

Egros looked down to see snow was falling, and now landing on his mate. That wouldn't do. He stood and walked inside, nodding at his friends. He would explain it all later. Much later.

Egros used his magic to clean himself and Margo, she was still asleep, and he was too tired for an actual bath. Together, they lay down in bed and just slept.

On the third day of their prolonged slumber, Egros blinked to find Margo looking up at him, her hazel eyes wide and curious.

"What is it?" he asked, throat dry.

"You dove into Hell for me," she whispered

"Are you hurt? Shall I call Byram? He is the best healer we have—"

"Eg," she said, hands on either side of his face. "You. Jumped. Into. Hell. For. Me."

"I would do it again," he said, honestly.

"I know."

"I love you. My own. My mate. My conpar."

"I love you too, Egros Pyke. With everything I am, I love you," she said, and then she was kissing him, and everything else was forgotten.

His thirst and hunger, all of it flew out the window. Completely sated by his mate in his arms, where she belonged. Egros climbed up her body, determined to show her without words just how much he loved her.

He kissed every inch of her, sucked and licked, stamped himself on every inch of her glorious brown skin. Loving on Margo was better than anything. Her pleasure was his only goal, and filling her was the ultimate homecoming.

Hours later, they showered and dressed in loose, comfortable clothes. Then they went to the kitchen for some food. A feast waited on the table, and all their friends surrounded them.

"How did you know we would come out now?" Margo asked Holley, who was putting the finishing touches on a tomato salad with some heirloom varieties grown in her greenhouse.

"The *manetuwak* told me," she replied. "And since you are my sister Witch, I think it right I start teaching you what I know."

"I'm a Witch too?"

"Well, of course you are," Holley said, as if the question was ludicrous. "And he didn't need to bother the Morrigan with all that. She's here, by the way, over there."

Margo's eyes found his, and Egros smiled. It was what he'd always suspected, having confirmation was just icing. He turned to see a woman with mismatched eyes sitting down with Jessenia, her wild curly hair a myriad of colors as well.

"Come sit by me, Margo Wells. We have some things to discuss," Sherry Morgan said, calling his mate over.

Egros bowed at the female and nodded at Margo to go on. He knew his mate had so many questions about magic, and this was the perfect opportunity for her to learn. The Morrigan was the most powerful Witch alive, and he had nothing but respect for the female.

"Well Egros," Kingston approached him, and Egros averted his gaze in deference to the man's dominance, and out of respect.

"Alpha," Egros said, still looking down. Kingston waited a bit for the Witch to meet his gaze.

"I am so very glad you're back, son," the big Dragon said, embracing Egros in a tight short hug.

Shocked, but grateful, Egros nodded. He was too choked up to speak.

"Sorry it took so long. Time moves differently there," he explained.

"I understand. And you and Margo, both can tell me and *Mother* after dinner," he said, nodding at a large, conspicuous man sitting at the table.

Egros recognized the name from when he was still

interviewing Margo upon her arrival at the Keep. It seemed so very long ago. But that was a worry for another day.

Right then, he only wanted to eat and drink and simply be. The meal turned out to be fabulous, and as he laughed and made merry with Margo by his side, surrounded by friends and family, he came to one very real conclusion.

Life was precious, and it was good. Most of all, it was magic.

The Guardians of Chaos worked hard to keep magic free for all, but it was still a carefully guarded secret. The most important one in the entire universe. It was their job to protect magic and the chaos that breeds creation.

So, yes. Magic was a secret, but sometimes secrets were meant to be shared with one special person.

Margo was his special person. His mate. His conpar. She fulfilled him in ways he'd never thought he'd be lucky enough to experience. And that night, after they'd retired to their room and loved each other till they were breathless, he told her.

"Of course, I love you, I mean, who else would go all the way to Hell for me," she said, only half joking. "You risked your life for me, Eg. You shielded me from harm with your magic and your love. I don't know what I would do without you."

"You saved my life by loving me," he returned, meaning every word.

"And you will never have to find out what it's like to be without me, conpar."

"What are you saying?"

"I'm saying I want you to stay with me. Always. We are mated, but I know you were raised human, so. Marry me?"

"Marry you? Just like that," she asked, both eyebrows raised.

Nerves almost stopped his heart, then she smiled, and he knew his naughty little vixen was teasing him. Fuck, he loved this woman. From head to toe and everywhere in between.

"Yes, of course, I will marry you! I've been dreaming of you for years, Eg. You're my one. My only one."

"Thank the gods," he murmured, holding her naked body tight to his.

Margo raised her eyes to meet his and took his face in her soft hands.

"I love you, Eg. Always have."

"I love you too, so much more than I could ever have imagined."

And then he showed her.

Again, and again, and again.

T he end...

Did you enjoy this installment in the Guardians of Chaos series by C.D. Gorri?

Catch up with the rest of the Guardians today! Now available wide.

And don't forget to keep an eye out on more from this series and other Paranormal Romance & Urban Fantasy tales by subscribing to C.D. Gorri's Newsletter today.

Happy reading!

VAMPIRE SHIELD

GUARDIANS OF CHAOS

BLURB

He left her behind years ago. She's never forgotten.

The Loyalist Union of Logic and Order has a new leader, and they are threatening the balance of magic. Witches are being attacked, and Shifters kidnapped, their magic siphoned through ritualistic bloodletting. The dark and ancient Vampiric practice had not been utilized in an age, and that spells trouble for the supernatural world.

Byram Evers is the only Vampire known to have sided with the Guardians of Chaos. His Alpha sends him to investigate the mystery behind the magic bloodletting epidemic, and the trail leads Byram back to his former Clan.

Back to her.

Princess Kaelene of the Clan Withers has spent years obeying her father and bowing to the demands of Vampire law. Betrayed by love, she refuses all suitors, determined to live the remainder of her life alone. Then *he* comes back, and her world turns upside down.

Will Byram discover the truth behind the bloodletting and redeem himself to the only woman who ever mattered?

GUARDIANS OF CHAOS PLEDGE

I AM THE WATCHER IN THE STORM.

I am the sword who strikes true.

I am the iron shield.

I protect against those who seek to control the wild nature of magic.

I am the guardian of chaos.

To thrive, we must be free.

From chaos comes creation.

PROLOGUE

September 1898

Byram followed her scent through the labyrinth in the garden on the south side of her father's castle. King Aethelred of the esteemed Vampire Clan Withers would likely bleed him if he knew about their affair.

Byram was a low-ranking Vampire, and she was the king's only heir. The Princess Kaelene was everything beautiful and perfect in the world. She was too good for him, but that did not slow his pace.

Love was the only thing in this world worth anything to a man such as he—*well, love and blood.*

One was the means to sustaining life, and the other was the reason one should bother with it at all.

He was a fool for love. That was what his mother

had said when she'd looked at him with worried eyes. His mother had always been able to see into his soul, and tried to be encouraging, though cautious—kindhearted woman that she was.

Losing her earlier this year was the hardest thing he had ever experienced, making him hold on tight to the good that remained in his life. To the only woman left in the world who made sense to him, who made him feel anything at all. It was impossible. She was the princess, and he, he was nothing. He should not want her, but he did. More than he wanted air to breathe or blood to drink.

Kaelene.

Maybe it made him reckless, but he refused to dwell on that. He was working hard to improve his station. It was the only way he could have her, and Byram had to believe that someday he would be worthy of her, and King Aethelred might yet approve.

Byram's heart raced as the scent of honeysuckle reached his sensitive nostrils. Pulse quickening as he neared his prey, Byram found her crouched down behind a statue of the goddess. Her blonde hair cascaded down her back. The flaxen tresses so long they trailed across the ground like a bolt of silk, but he only had one mere moment to appreciate her beauty before her dancing gaze reached him.

"You found me," Kaelene whispered breathlessly as he pulled her up and crushed her to him.

She felt so good in his arms. Her curvy and petite frame was the perfect complement to his tall, lithe musculature. She felt perfect in his arms, always had.

"I will always find you, Pip," he murmured, dropping teasing kisses along her neck.

"Must you call me that? I'm not a child anymore, By," she whispered without heat.

The childhood nickname he'd given her came to his lips readily whenever they were together, but had she really hated it, he would have called her something else. Pip was short for pipsqueak, and she was tiny and petite. Also utterly annoying when he'd been ten and trying to impress his father, a guardsman to the king, and she a child of just four years, always trailing after him.

His annoyance had changed around the same time his voice did, and protective instincts followed as their friendship changed over the years. Pip was his best friend. She knew everything about him, and he her. Byram had never loved another, and likely never would.

"Missed you, Pip," he murmured, dropping his head to nuzzle her nose, her cheek, and her lovely bow-shaped mouth.

He could not help himself, Byram simply had to touch her. Whenever she was near, he had this overwhelming urgency to kiss her, lick her, claim her body the way he so desperately wanted to with his bite. Vampire claimings were nothing to be rushed into. Usually, it took centuries to secure the right to bite a mate. Made sense since they lived so long, and claiming was for life.

Having to spend eternity with one who did not know your heart was a nightmare he could not even imagine. But Pip was his. Always had been.

His fangs pulsed in time with his heart as he kissed, and kissed, and kissed her some more. It was always this way when he was with her. Byram was losing control of his predatory nature, and soon he would not be able to stop himself from feeding from her. Only a female's betrothed had the right to take blood from her.

It was different for the fairer sex of their kind. Females did not need to feed until they experienced their first breeding cycle, which usually coordinated with the meeting of their true mates. The males required blood as part of their regular diets right after they reached adulthood.

Contrary to popular fiction writers of the day, Vampires were not dead or undead. They were not what human myth thought at all. Sunlight did not burn him. Holy water had no adverse effects. Crosses either. They were born this way, not made, and even if they could be, the process of turning humans to Vampires was either forgotten or impossible.

It was a bold new world, and science was young, but Byram was excited by it. He had been studying medicine in his spare time, much to the disapproval of his Clan mates. Vampires had their own beliefs and mysticism, but he was never one to follow that which he could not see, hear, or touch with his own self. The Crimson Veil was the name of the god his kind worshipped, but Byram had never been much of a believer.

Only now, he prayed with everything he had to control his hunger around Kaelene. He could not bite her. Not yet. Once he did, it would all be over. The iron leash he held on to his control was the only thing saving them both from a fate worse than death.

The king would not be happy if Byram fed from his daughter. It would be an act of treason, far worse than falling in love with her already was.

"We don't have much time, Pip. They are sending me away to finish my training," he whispered, kissing her precious lips with aching tenderness.

Being parted was going to be hell. Oh yes, Byram

was a fool and a glad one at that. He had known the second he touched her with intent that it would either make or destroy him.

It was an addiction a Vampire in his position could not afford to keep. Alas, he was helpless against his desire to kiss her, touch her, bring smiles to her sweet face, and lusty moans from her lips.

"I want you," she moaned, head back as his mouth traveled down her throat and settling over the delicate pulse at her neck.

"Please make love to me," she begged, and fuck, he wanted to.

Weak, so weak. He was desperate to take her, to tear the clothes from the body of the only woman who had ever managed to break through the wall surrounding his heart. But not here. Not in the garden like some rutting beast.

"Claim me, Byram. To hell with father and the law. Claim me now and we can face the Council's wrath together," she whispered, moaning as he continued his sensual onslaught.

Temptress. Minx. My heart's only desire.

"Don't you think I want to?" he growled, cupping his hand around her neck. "They already know, Pip. The only reason we are still breathing is because you are too important for the Clan to make an example of. You are the princess, and I am no one—"

"Don't say that," she gasped, pulling back from him. The distance hurt, but no more than the pain he saw in her liquid blue eyes.

"The council does not know how we really feel about each other. It is the only reason I am still here and not in shackles somewhere. My captain is sending me away before they figure it out, Pip, but I will come back for you. I swear it," he vowed.

"And what do I do? How do I stop them and their plans for me? They're going to use me to forge alliances. Sell me like cattle," she hissed near panic, and he pulled her to him, squeezing her tightly. Fuck, he hated he was powerless to stop it from happening.

"You must try, Pip. Be strong. Wait for me."

"I am not strong like you," she sobbed, and his heart broke a little more.

"You are stronger than you think, Pip. Wait them out, and I *will* return. I will be worthy of you, I swear it—"

"You already are, Byram. I love you," she confessed with such misery his own eyes pooled with unshed tears.

"I was supposed to say it first," he murmured,

leaning back and cupping her precious face in his hands. His gaze never leaving her as he made his vow.

"I will come back, and when I do, I will be in a better position to put in my claim for you."

"Do you swear?"

"I swear I will come back for you, Pip. Wait for me to return. Promise?"

She turned her head slightly, kissing his palm, her warm tears wetting his skin, soaking into the cuffs of his shirt. Byram held his breath, waiting for her response.

"I will wait for you," she whispered, leaning up to kiss him fervently. "I promise."

ONE

resent Day

I will wait for you. I promise.

The ghostly voice from his past echoed through his mind, piercing the steel wall Byram had built around his heart. Fuck. It hurt to remember. He had spent a lot of time trying to forget, but now and then, she would creep back in.

Like a cold draft beneath a door he could not shut out, or that single ray of sunlight blinding him through the window shade when he was doing a buck thirty in his Vette.

She was the past, though, and there was no getting away from a person's past, try as he might. It was always there. She was always there.

I promise....

"Byram? You with us, bro?"

Byram turned and blinked slowly, coming back to the present. It was always difficult to return to the here and now after a bad night, and he'd had two more dreams this week, replaying the past. Not a new phenomenon.

Being a Vampire had drawbacks, and his crystal clear memory was one. Even if he wanted to, he could not forget her. Forcing himself to think about anything else was his usual routine, but sometimes there was no use. Sometimes the dreams crept back in. He'd experienced it a hundred times or more since the last time he'd actually seen Kaelene in the flesh. A low, rolling rumble built up in his throat and he closed his eyes, breathing harshly as he fought to control it.

Fuck.

He was losing control over his Vampiric nature. It was no secret, as he'd already talked to Kingston about the dangers of a Vampire suffering from the *famine*. That was their name for what happened when nothing could satisfy the beast within.

Usually, when a Vampire felt himself or herself slipping into the famine, there was only one thing he could do. Go Hunter or find the true death. It was the reason he'd sought Kingston and the Guardians in the first place.

After his initial discovery that Kaelene had betrayed him, Byram had feared the worst for himself. Vampires were notoriously difficult to kill, and even surrounded by Shifters as he'd been for the past century, none knew the actual strength he really held.

The Dragon was the only living creature who might be able to best him. Hard *might*. Eventually, they became friends, and Byram had started to believe in the work he did with the Guardians of Chaos.

Keeping magic free and maintaining the balance of the natural and supernatural world was a noble and worthy cause. Far more than wallowing in his own misery.

Stupid heart. Get over it already. Kaelene is not who we thought.

His chest rumbled, drawing the eyes of his compatriots, and he stifled the sound. The evening light filtered in through the windows of Kingston's office, and he felt the Alpha's eyes on him. Fifty or sixty years ago, the Dragon would have given him the battle he so obviously needed to sate his rage. But the beast was mated now, all the Guardians were. Byram was the only loner in the group.

Fuck. Steady now.

Loner. Alone. Always alone. Shit.

He had to do better than this. There were new

cases, new proof the Loyalists had recouped and were gaining their numbers. The freedom of magic, the supernatural chaos theory he and Egros had worked so hard to prove, was being attacked, and it was his sworn duty to protect it. No, he could not afford to wallow in his unfortunate past. He could not lose himself.

If Byram were to lose control, it would mean death for many, if not all. His future was not determined. Fuck the Fates. He'd trusted in those fickle bastards once before and look where it got him. No. He would not go Hunter or endure the famine.

Loyalty was the cornerstone of his vow, and he owed it to them all to stay true, loyal, and stalwart. Byram would not turn on his group of Guardians. Hell. It hurt him to think of hurting those he cared for.

Fuck.

"Byram?"

"I need a moment, Kingston. Apologies," he grunted, closing his eyes, and giving himself the time he needed to straighten his head out.

"Of course. Take your time," the Alpha grumbled.

Byram tuned out the others as they whispered amongst themselves. Mind racing, he focused on his breathing and allowed himself to indulge a few moments in his inner turmoil.

Was he really so far gone that turning Hunter, or begging death were his only options? Fury welled within him at what might have been, and he had to work to block out that single-minded rage.

Hunter Vamps were a plague to all. Those Vampires who had lost the will to live allowed madness and thirst to take over. They became creatures who barely resembled what they once were. Bat-like horrors bent on destruction. Byram would stake himself before he allowed that to happen. But luckily, he did not have to.

Facts were facts. Byram's thirst was growing, and no amount of bagged blood seemed able to quench it. More and more, Byram had been losing himself to memories he'd be better off forgetting.

Even now, he needed a moment to sort them before he spoke to his Alpha, Kingston Baldric of the Guardians of Chaos. The Dragon Shifter had agreed to end him if he showed any signs, though he did so with a heavy heart.

The memories plaguing him had been of the worst day of his life. The day he'd truly lost *her*. Kaelene was the one true love of his entire existence, but he'd been foolish in giving his heart to a princess who, in the end, had never really loved him.

Yes, she did.

He was in no mood to argue with himself, so he ignored that pesky little inner voice and replayed the facts in his head. Byram had returned to his former Clan a mere five years after being sent away, bristling with new ideas and experience. His old master had trained him in the art of war, and he'd studied science and medicine in his spare time.

He had money, knowledge, brawn, and risen in rank in the Clan army. Finally, he was worthy of putting in a claim for the love of his life, the Princess Kaelene. Only she'd broken her word.

He'd arrived home to the sounds of bells ringing in the old temple and scribes shouting word of the betrothal of the princess to the son of the king of a rival clan.

Byram had not bothered to stick around after that, He'd taken off, heartbroken and mad at the world. If only knowing she'd betrayed him when he had been loyal had been the worst of it, but there was more. The crown had seized his meager holdings, claiming unpaid taxes for his time away, and he was left with nothing. Nowhere to live or lay his head.

Kaelene was readying to marry another, Byram had been stripped of his land and rendered penniless, and worse, he felt the beginnings of bloodlust taint his vision. If he succumbed to it, he would be hunted and staked.

Maybe he should have allowed it, but then he would not be here today. He had to leave his Clan and his home, knowing he would never be fulfilled in his very long lifetime. Talk about a fate worse than death. Byram would be alone forever.

Fuck.

"I'm ready," he announced, cutting through the whispers of the Guardians, *his friends*, with his voice steadier than he felt.

"When is the last time you fed?" Kingston growled the question, interrupting his thoughts once more.

"Apologies, Alpha. I was just lost in my thoughts," he explained, ignoring the surprised expressions of his fellow Guardians.

Two

Byram had joined the Guardians of Chaos after wandering aimlessly for a decade or more following Kaelene's betrayal. This unique group of Supernaturals had been his salvation when all he wanted was to sink into despair.

The Guardians of Chaos had given him back his purpose in life. The least he could do was pay attention.

"I see. Take your time," Kingston replied, but it was clear enough he did not. Not really.

My own fault. Keeping secrets is a solitary game, old boy.

Fuck. He was talking to himself again. That was never a good sign. Perhaps he did need to feed. Vampires ate regular food for sustenance, but they needed to supplement that with a regular diet of blood was best to keep his strength and senses in top order.

"What was the question again?" he asked.

"The Assembly wants us to investigate a series of attacks happening up and down the east coast, At first, they sent Enforcers, which is why we are late to the party, but after this last incident, they called us in. So, Byram, what do you know about rituals involving Vampiric bloodletting and magic?" Kingston asked.

"Are you certain Vampires are the culprits?" Byram asked, mouth going dry at the thought.

Kingston's Dragon peeked through his eyes as the large man nodded and typed onto his keyboard. He wore a deep frown as he downloaded something onto his magically enhanced laptop. Holley, his mate, was standing beside him, her hand squeezing his shoulder as she looked at whatever had just popped up on the screen.

The female was a powerful Witch, and yet, the case they were about to take on seemed to spook her. The other Guardians in the room moved uncomfortably, all of them attuned to their Alpha's growing agitation.

Byram worked to silence the growl building in his throat. His instinct to protect the people here still surprised him, though it shouldn't. After Kaelene's betrayal, he never thought to find a purpose again, and yet he had.

Here. In the Keep. With these people.

They were his Clan now. His family. All of them were paired, having found their true and fated mates. Byram was happy for them—*well and truly*—grateful even for the new powers their matings had given them.

A small piece of him might be envious, but he squashed the thought readily enough. Byram might never have a mate, but he had them, and he would do anything to protect them.

A moment later and the large screen over his head blinked to life, showing a half dozen crime scene photos. Byram studied them silently, his expression grim. The victims had not been savaged or torn apart, as one might expect from a rampaging Vampire.

"The first murders took place outdoors before or after extreme weather, leaving no trace of anything other than exsanguination on the victims' bodies. However, the last three photos occurred indoors. These are all different crime scenes, but our guys picked up a pattern. Exsanguination, torches, some sort of ancient writing etched into the flooring around the bodies—like runes or hieroglyphs."

"Wow. Got pictures?" Fergie interrupted, and Kingston nodded.

"Yes, we do. Another group of Guardians has an Ancient languages expert who has been studying them. He has identified a few. The most prominent is an ancient sun rune, and he thinks it is symbolic of the rebirth of magic."

"Doesn't sound bad," Jessenia murmured.

"Oh, it is bad," Egros added. "It means whoever is performing the ritual, coupled with the bloodletting, is trying to enhance their own innate magic by siphoning it from others. Blood magic is Dark in nature. It is forbidden by most Witch covens."

"But blood is nature," Fergie argued, dragging a small grin from Byram.

The others considered blood to be off limits in magic, but for Vampires, well, it was everything. Blood was not evil or dark. It was the very source of life. Without it, nothing could survive. Not even magic. But he remained silent, willfully so, as the others discussed things.

"To the contrary, Fergie, there is absolutely nothing natural about blood magic. It is used to bring Demons onto our plane, and to hold power over others."

"Let's get back on track," Kingston grumbled. "Our job is to find the person or persons responsible for these crimes. Byram, I am looking at you because of the nature of these acts, and the evidence found in the runes by our expert. All suggest Vampiric activity. I am sorry if that is offensive—"

"Not at all, Kingston. I am a Vampire, and my relationship with blood is complicated."

"Shit, By, I didn't mean," Egros began, stuttering, but Byram merely raised his hand and shook his head.

He did not need apologies from the Witch. Vampires were notoriously secretive, and if the Guardians still held prejudices against him, well, he was partially responsible for keeping himself closed off.

"Anything else you can tell me about the crime scene?" he asked.

"Oh, I almost forgot, there was evidence of some sort of sticky residue on the bodies, around the mouths as if ingested before exsanguination. They took it to the human labs but could not identify it. The substance appears to be organic, but none of the investigators, not even the supes, could identify it."

"Does the substance have an odor?" Byram asked carefully.

Fuck.

This was not good. Even though he had been a Guardian for decades, Vampire Law forbade the sharing of secrets and rituals. Kingston had never ordered him to divulge anything he was not comfortable sharing, but suddenly, it felt as if the time for keeping silent was finished.

"Notes from some of the on scene Shifter investigators state the substance smelled distinctly like rotting flesh, but upon testing, there was no evidence of animal DNA anywhere."

"That's because it is not animal," Byram declared, mouth set in a grim line. "I can't be sure until I see and test it for myself, but I believe you are describing *Rafflesia* extract. An uncommon plant used in some ancient Vampiric rites. It has sedative qualities amongst supes."

"Rafflesia?" Holley interrupted curiously.

"Yes, otherwise known as the corpse flower," he explained.

"I know what that is!" Fergie, the she-Wolf, mated to Hudson, his fellow Guardian, interrupted.

The feisty redhead was one of Byram's favorite people, but he had no smiles for her as he flicked his attention to where she animatedly spoke to the lot of them.

"That's my girl," Hudson said, beaming beside her as he held her hand while she shared her news.

"It's like this giant flower that stinks like rotting meat when it blooms to attract beetles and bugs to pollinate it. It even gets hot, and they say it mimics a heart beating. It was on this *top ten most disgusting plants* countdown I watched the other day."

"Ew, that is gross," Jessenia, a Kitchen Witch mated to Furio, Stallion Shifter, replied, shaking her head.

"Gross, but all true," Byram said. "The extract was once revered by followers of the Crimson Veil, the Vampire God. There are less than a thousand of the blooms in the wild all around the world and considered endangered, but temples of the Crimson Veil have their own cultivators who grow and make the extract for ceremonies."

"Can you confirm this is the work of Vampires?" Kingston asked, brows furrowed.

"I have been away from that life a long time, Kingston," Byram replied. "But I recognize some of those symbols from blood bonding ceremonies from my old Clan. These over here, I do not recognize," he said, pointing to some of the ancient looking runes.

"Whatever they were trying to do with the Rafflesia extract and the victims, they failed. See the candles? If it was successful, they would have burned till nothing was left. Candles are symbolic in Vampire rituals, representing the dawn."

"So then, Vampires had something to do with this?"

"Yes," Byram admitted, his body trembling with rage.

The others around him gasped and whispered. He felt their tension as if it were his own. Dammit all to hell. It had taken years for him to earn the trust of his fellow Guardians, and even then, he could sense them holding back. It was not their fault. He was secretive, private, was forbidden to share certain truths of his species.

"I thought Vampires are forbidden to kill?" Egros, their resident male Witch, asked.

"They are," Byram answered. "Especially humans. Vampires have existed in secret, apart from other supes, specifically because of their strict rules. Whoever is responsible for this? They're breaking Vampire Law, and by doing so, they are putting a price on their heads," he growled.

"A price? Who would hunt Vamps?" Margo, former agent of the DPCA, Department of Paranormal Creatures and Activity, a primarily human organization for those secret government agents in the know and mate to Egros, asked.

"Other Vamps, of course," Byram replied. "If they know about it, the Vampire Council will have their own men hunting these rogues down."

"Men?" Fergie scoffed.

"My dear Fergie, Vampire society is notoriously patriarchal. Females are thought to be softer, frail, and are kept apart from anything that might be *uncomfortable*," he tried to explain.

Byram had to admit it was no easy thing in the face of such fearsome females as the mates of these Guardians of Chaos, not to mention Elena, who was a Panther Shifter and a Guardian herself. He'd never known women could be so empowered before leaving his Clan.

"So, wait a sec, you mean there are no women on this Vampire Council?" Margo asked, and he shook his head.

"What about female Clan leaders? Surely, they must object to being left out?"

"Um, there are no female Clan leaders. Vampire Clans have kings, no queens. Mates are referred to as consorts," he said through gritted teeth.

"What about the king's daughters?"

"They are given the term princess, but they have no power," he muttered, hurting at the mere mention of the word *princess*.

True, a princess had no control over her fate, but she could have waited. Should have waited. Fuck, he did not want to think about her now.

"So what you are telling us after decades of silence, is Vampires are assholes?" Furio remarked.

Byram wheezed a soft laugh. He supposed the Stallion Shifter was correct. They were assholes. And the truth was, he doubted things had changed even after a hundred years. Being practically immortal meant time moved differently for his kind.

"Indeed, Furio. I admit Vampires are a bit old-fashioned," he said, trying for diplomacy.

"Uh, old fashioned? I think you mispronounced misogynistic," Margo quipped.

"Or barbaric," Jessenia added.

"Or stupid," snarked Fergie.

Yeah. These women whom he respected were right. Vampire Law was archaic when it came to females. How had he forgotten that?

"You are all right. But that does not change whether the Vampire Council knows about this."

"No, it doesn't. And that is where you come in," Kingston agreed.

"You want me to reach out to the Council? I have no connections there—"

"We want you to reach out to your old Clan. Whispers of discontent have reached our ears, Byram. It's time," Kingston said.

Fuck. He was not ready. Would he ever be?

Byram's entire body vibrated with nerves. He ran a hand through his light brown hair, mussing it, and drawing amused stares from his Guardians. They had probably never seen him this way.

"About the victims, are they human?" Byram asked.

"No. Shifters."

Shit. This was bad. The only rituals he recalled involving Shifters and blood were dark, forbidden, and best forgotten. Kingston was right. He could not avoid his past any longer.

It was time to go home.

THREE

The sun was shining brightly in the clear skies, promising spring though winter was still clinging to the lush landscape of her father's mansion in upstate New York. Little had changed over the past hundred years, though modern conveniences had been added like electricity, plumbing, cable, and Wi-Fi.

And yet, there she was, wearing a dress that was out of style, with her hair pinned back like some nineteenth century doll. The house might have been upgraded, but the females in most all Vampire Clans were grossly old-fashioned, kept that way by the strict patriarchal society that ruled them.

Even princesses were afforded little to no leeway. What was Kaelene but a pawn in her father's manipulations, anyway? Still, she did not hate him. He was her sire, her protector, her benefactor, and she needed him. Without him, she would be chained to some hoity toity male who thought she was the grand prize in his ambitions.

It had been years since Father had attempted to force her into a betrothal. Blissful years when she'd been allowed to wallow in her past mistakes.

Stupid heart. Stupid youth. Whatever.

She'd given her trust and heart to someone a long time ago, and he'd abandoned her. Betrayed her trust a hundred years ago, and Kaelene was still gun shy. She listened to the sounds of footfalls and grinned.

Here comes trouble.

Her lady's companion of the past decade was rushing towards her, small feet pitter pattering on the tile.

"Marguerite, can you please get me some spearmint leaves for the citrus salad before you come in?" Kaelene called from the kitchen.

She smiled and hummed as she worked, loving the fact that though she still lived in her father's mansion, neither he nor the other males of the Clan Withers dared step foot inside Cook's domain.

The older female had been preparing meals for the royal family and guests since Kaelene's father, King

Aethelred, was a boy. A master chef and lethal with a knife, no male Vampire in the Clan was stupid enough to enter Cook's territory without permission.

The repercussions were such they might keep any trespasser glued to the toilet for days on end. A lesson some unfortunates had learned. Was it a wonder Kaelene sought refuge there? Away from all the testosterone and posturing. She could not deal with it. Not today.

"Here," Marguerite, her companion, said breathlessly as she returned from the small herb garden just outside the kitchen.

"Is it freezing?" Kaelene asked, taking the leaves, and rinsing them before turning back to her chopping block.

"Of course. It's February, Kae, cold as ice, but love is in the air," Marguerite replied, a dazzled look in her eyes.

"Okay, so what is going on? You're positively vibrating," Kaelene remarked, tossing the slices of navels, tangerines, grapefruit, and blood oranges in the bowl with lime juice, honey, and the newly chopped mint leaves. She did not know why she was making this salad. It had been years since she'd made it last, decades even.

It was his favorite. Byram Evers.

Kaelene stuttered in her stirring. She had not thought his name in such a long time, but for some reason it had been playing on the periphery of her mind all damn day. The man who'd caused her more heartache than she had ever known. The reason she had fallen from favor with her father and had sworn off all men.

"I was talking to Emil," Margie whispered conspiratorially, and everything suddenly made sense.

Emil had been making eyes at Margie for years now, but the male had only just recently asked her parents for permission to court her. Kaelene was happy for her companion and best friend. She deserved to find happiness, even if that meant Kaelene would be completely alone now.

Whispers had already been circulating throughout the Clan of the poor Rime Maiden, the virgin Princess who was as cold as ice, forsaking the touch of any male.

Well, screw the rumor mongers. Just because she refused to be a pawn in her father's games did not mean Kaelene had no feelings. She'd simply gotten very good at blocking them out. She had no choice.

Her heart had been stolen away decades ago, and the silly muscle refused to entertain thoughts of another.

"Wait for me," he'd said.

"I will. I promise."

That promise had cost her so much. Her happiness, her future, her freedom. Still, Kaelene did not regret a single moment she'd spent with him. Better to have loved and lost, she supposed. Her bruised heart beat slowly as she tried to pay attention to what Marguerite was saying.

"Murders? Margie, what are you talking about?"

"Emil told me. He said there's been talk of murders, and the Shifters suspect Vampires. They don't have proof yet, but the Council is spitting mad. The Shifters are sending a representative from the Guardians of Chaos. Magic is being attacked, and they think Vampires are involved some."

"So they are sending a Guardian? Wow," Kaelene replied, eyes wide.

Strangers were seldom invited to see the King of the Clan Withers. If the Council sent word of the incoming stranger, chances were he was not invited.

"Even better, Kae. He's here!"

"He who?"

"The Guardian!"

Curiosity spiked inside her as Kaelene covered the salad and popped it inside the fridge to chill. Cook was making a honeyed ham for dinner, and this would brighten the sweet and savory dish. Margie was practically bouncing up and down, waiting on Kaelene to finish washing and drying her hands.

She straightened her blouse and made sure her long skirt fell evenly to her boot covered feet. Her Clan followed the old ways, as most Vampire Clans did. Females were valued but had little rights. Her father insisted on skirts and dresses, and she obeyed him in this one small thing. It was her way of appeasing him after so greatly disappointing the male who'd sired her.

"Come on," Marguerite said, but they did not walk more than a few feet, arm in arm, when they heard the sounds of raised voices.

Kaelene glanced at her companion, then grabbed her skirts and hurried down the hall to the south parlor. Her father saw visitors there when he was trying to make an impression. It was beyond a doubt the fanciest, most imposing room in the mansion.

Located in upstate New York, the Clan Withers had significant financial holdings accrued over centuries of investing and what basically amounted to gambling. Wall Street was not so far, what with the internet and all, and many of the ruling families inside the Clan Withers had made wide decisions with their funds.

But whether banker, baker, or candlestick maker, everyone paid tribute to the King who in turn kept them safe by paying for their armies and elite warriors. War did not happen often between the nearly immortal creatures, but it happened. Money meant safety, security, and above all, comfort. Her father adored comfort. His, Of course. Not so much his only daughter.

But Kaelene had always been headstrong, and she'd given her sire no small amount of grief over the years. Fielding offers of matrimony while her heart held on to her silly childhood romance. There was a time when she thought the sun rose and set on Byram Evers, but that was so long ago. And why was he taking up space inside her brain now?

Kaelene could not help but replay their final parting and her whispered vow to wait for him. She had, damn him. Oh, how she had waited! Earnestly and loyally for more years than made sense.

For whatever reason, he'd failed her. He'd never returned and the tragedy of it all broke her heart all over again. Had she been unworthy? Did he ever really love her? Perhaps he'd just moved on—no, that was not why. Closing her eyes, she refused to give in to past hurts when she was about to enter her father's parlor unannounced.

He would ream her for this later, but that voice, the one speaking with such quiet grace and confidence, was mesmerizing. Familiar, and yet not. It drew her in until she held the doorknob in her hand. Kaelene gasped.

It couldn't be! Heart pounding, sweat beading her forehead, Kaelene hissed as he spoke again. She should flee from there. Run as far as her booted feet could carry her, but it was as if she were under some master magician's spell, she turned it and opened the door.

Shock and rage flooded her system, those, and something else, too. Something very akin to a feeling she'd thought long dead. Something that felt an awful lot like hope.

"Byram," she said involuntarily.

His dark eyes flashed emerald but returned to their normal hazel brown so fast she thought she might have imagined it. Was he in such mastery of Vampiric powers? She wondered, impressed with his skill.

Eyes were windows to the soul, even for Vampires, and black meant he was highly emotional, even if for just a moment. There was a time when his would have glittered with desire upon seeing her, but that was a lifetime ago. Byram was not hers any longer. Maybe he never was, and that thought depressed Kaelene.

"Princess," he murmured, and bowed formally.

"Daughter, what are you doing here?" her father hissed.

"Princess, is there something you need?" Morris, her father's advisor, asked from his right side.

He was an older Vampire, but youthful in appearance. His face was a cold, hard mask, and held so much anger, it was a wonder none reacted to it. He hated Kaelene, and the feeling was mutual. Morris was her sworn enemy. The vile male had tried to cow her repeatedly, to get her to agree to matches that would benefit their Clan, but Kaelene had refused all suitors.

Her heart had always belonged to one male. Even if he did not want her back.

"Princess?" Morris hissed, and the faint sound of growling reverberated in the room.

Shit. It was coming from Byram. His eyes were blazing red now as he moved himself between the aggressive advisor and Kaelene. That was not good.

She had no idea what the male was doing in her father's parlor, or if he had anything to do with the mysterious deaths Marguerite had told her about, but she was not about to put him in Morris' path. That man was dangerous. Besides, Kaelene had waited a hundred years for answers. Now Byram was here, and she could finally get them.

"Father," she said, ignoring Morris and Byram. "I have just come with a question from Cook about supper."

"Yes? What is it?"

"Oh," she said, blinking and smiling absently. "Sorry, Father, I'm afraid I forgot. Never mind, though, shall I ask Cook to make a place for our guest?" Kaelene asked, covering up her shock smoothly enough, she hoped.

"Yes. That will be fine."

"Good. Excuse me, gentlemen," she murmured, face carefully blank, giving each male a small bow before backing unhurriedly out of the room.

It was never a good idea to give one's back to a predator, and for the first time, Kaelene understood what that meant. Morris and Father were powerful, the latter ancient, and the former ambitious. She was used to the feeling of heaviness in the air surrounding them whenever she was in their presence.

It was not them who had her shivering beneath her layered clothing. It was him. Byram had changed. He stood, hands clasped behind his back, watching her with his head cocked slightly to the side and an impassive expression on his face.

When had he gotten so rugged? Gone was the smooth skin and carefully styled hair of his youth. In its place was a chiseled jaw bearing day old scruff—unheard of for Vamps. His tawny locks had grown down past his chin, and were tossed back carelessly, like some rockstar might do if he were wailing on stage. He was, in a word, sexy, and Kaelene felt little pieces of her stirring at only a glimpse of the man he became.

Damn her traitorous heart. She'd sworn to hate Byram Evers for the rest of her life after abandoning her the way he did. But even as she closed the door, glancing up to lock eyes with him one last time, Kaelene knew it was an impossible task.

As she closed the door and walked unrushed towards her suite of rooms, Kaelene's mind raced with memories. The times she'd lived for his smiles, the taste of his lips pressed against hers, and the feel of the hard planes of his body when they'd finally come together only days before he left.

Her blood rushed through her veins at the memories, flesh heated, and something inside of her called out in pain. It had been so long since she'd felt connected to anyone, but why did it have to be him? Hadn't his rejection taught her a lesson?

She could not do this again. Her life hung on the balance of her father's will. His whims determined her future. She'd learned that lesson the hard way. How many times had he tried to marry her off? Three in the past century?

Her first betrothal announcement had come mere years after Byram had left. She'd still been hopeful of his return, but she learned the hard way what her foolishness earned her. Lost in thought, she didn't hear the footfalls behind her until she was inside her bedroom and turned to see he had followed.

"What are you doing here?'

"Can't I say hello to an old friend?" Byram asked, looking haughty and aloof, and so fucking gorgeous, it was tearing her heart out.

"Friend? Is that what I was? Funny, I didn't think friends broke promises like you did—"

"Me? You are the one who could not wait a few measly years, *princess*," he hissed, and his eyes flashed angrily.

"What are you talking about?"

"You know what I am talking about, princess."

"Don't you call me that," she snarled, and he closed the space between them.

"What should I call you then? Princess Kaelene, you who are so above my station. Shall I call you friend? Lover? Betrayer?" he snarled.

"We were friends once," she answered, panting now as he inched closer.

Kaelene's pulse was racing as he closed his hands around her wrists and backed her into the wall behind him. She was enraged and turned on all at the same time.

Shame pinkened her cheeks because she knew he could tell. Smug bastard could scent her arousal, and she was helpless to stop her body from responding to his. It always had.

Byram's lip turned up into a knowing grin as he growled softly. That sound so sexy she had to close her lips tightly to keep from sighing. He lowered his face, millimeters from hers, and hissed softly, pressing his hips into her once before pushing off.

It felt so good having him pressed up against her. He was so big, so hot and heavy against her body. When was the last time she felt this kind of excitement?

Too long. Far too long. It had been decades since she felt so alive. Damn Byram for coming back now when she almost had her father convinced to let her be.

"Betrayer? Me?" she whispered, confused.

"Your husband must not be taking care of your needs, princess," Byram taunted cruelly.

Kaelene reared back as if he'd slapped her, pushing him off her. He went, thank goodness, or she would have never been able to move him. Yes, female Vampires were strong, but Byram had nearly doubled in size since last she'd seen him. All of it, pure muscle.

Sexy. Fierce. Wanna bite him.

"So, where is the lucky man? Don't I get to meet

him?" Byram asked, running rough hands through his hair.

He was losing his composure, and for a moment, she was glad. She wanted him just as ruffled and confused as she felt. Why should he get to stand there, looking so damn perfect and modern in his fitted slacks, silk shirt, and tailored jacket, when she was falling apart? Damn him for being so handsome still. More so now that he'd matured and filled out. He was not the boy she had given her heart to so many years ago. Byram was a man now, and more dangerous than ever.

"Well? Your husband, princess, where is he?"

"Who?" she asked, head spinning to keep up.

"what do you call him, then? Your mate, princess" Your lover? Baby? Cutie pie? Where?" he shouted.

"Husband? What are you talking about?"

"Do not play games, Kaelene. I was here when they announced your wedding," he growled angrily.

Kaelene's chest squeezed in pain. He'd returned? Byram had come back, and he'd seen her father's manipulations. She sucked in a breath, one hand pressed to her stomach, and turned to face him with her shoulders back and her head high.

"I am not married, Byram. I never was."

FOUR

"*I am not married, Byram. I never was.*"

Thunder roared in Byram's ears, and everything turned red under the fury that filled him at her words. Lies. Had to be. He'd seen the banners, heard the announcements, and counted the bells that day before he'd said his final goodbyes to the Clan Withers that day nearly a hundred years ago.

At the time, the Vampires held nearly all the property in the area and staying secret had been easier. Nowadays, keeping the reality of the supernatural world from being outed was a full-time job for supes.

As a Guardian of Chaos, Byram had another, more important job. To keep magic free and safe for all. The crimes he was investigating now had led him back here, to the last place on earth he wanted to be, and back to her.

A confrontation was inevitable, and a small part of him had been looking forward to it. He'd wanted to show her what he had become. The success story that was Byram Evers. From a low ranking Vampire in a Clan that mostly ignored him, to an esteemed Guardian of Chaos, he had come a long way.

The Clan had never felt like home, but the Keep sure as fuck did. At least, it had for a while before his hunger started growing unmanageable. Still, he had friends, a new Clan made up of Witches, Shifters, and a human scientist.

Byram was their healer, a doctor of sorts, having attended human medical school and studied under various supernatural shamans and healers. Byram had worked long and hard to become who he was, and yes, a small part of him wanted to taunt her with it.

All those years, plotting the day he'd be back and watch her rue the day she'd given up on him, on them, and it was finally here. But it was not how he'd imag-ined it at all.

The second he'd seen her, his heart had damn near stopped inside his chest. She was beautiful as ever, more mature, womanly even. Her skin glowed like moonlight, her fair hair shorter than it used to be, only brushing her shoulders, and her dress more modern, but still befitting a female of her rank.

Her pale blue eyes were the same, though they too seemed honed by something he had yet to identify. She was beautiful as he knew he would be, but what he did not expect was this newfound spunk. Pushing him away like the powerful creature she was, Kaelene raised her head and changed everything he thought he knew about her with short, clipped words.

Not married. No husband. She was never married.

"I waited for you," she growled, eyes brimming with unshed tears and pain filled him at the realization.

"No, you didn't! I came back, Kae. I saw it all! The banners were hung, and the bells were ringing. I saw you in the square dressed in white, looking like a fucking angel. You did not wait for me!" Byram roared, feeling gutted.

Kaelene's eyes closed as she sank to the floor, tears pouring down her face. She laughed then, a hopeless sound. When had she become so cruel?

"Ah, so you saw me in my dress? That fucking dress," she whimpered, and her laughter turned to tears. "Father was so good at his manipulations then, you know? Remember that night we said goodbye? Well, you were right when you said they knew about us right before you left. He'd allowed me to pine for you, pretended he approved, told me you were returning soon maybe a month before," she said, and her voice took on a faraway quality. Byram listened quietly, training himself to be silent.

"I thought I was getting fitted for our wedding, you see. Father allowed me to make plans and arrangements and I was so hopeful, but it wasn't you waiting for me in the square. It was another. Dawson Kent—"

"Of the Clan Parsons?" he asked.

Byram growled, unable to stop himself as he built his kill list. Yes, he wanted to tear them limb from fucking limb. Anyone and everyone who had ever thought to take what was his.

Mine.

Shit.

He had no right to feel proprietary. Kaelene watched him, lips pursed, eyebrows furrowed. She shrugged and shook her head, and he had to wonder what she'd seen in him to make her feel confused.

"Yes. He was the first male my father tried to sell me to for the sake of alliance and wealth, power, and greed, whatever—it is all the same, isn't it? Anyway, Dawson gracefully changed his mind after I damn near broke his jaw when he spoke the first words of the bonding rites."

"You broke his jaw?" he asked, unable to contain his snort of amusement.

"Almost. Got him with a left hook you taught me, remember?" she asked, and he handed her a tissue to wipe her eyes.

"Kaelene, I didn't know—"

"I am not finished yet. There were more after Dawson, you see. My father did not give up so easily. He was the easiest to get rid of, though. Good man, Dawson," she muttered.

Kaelene tucked her feet beneath her as she leaned against the wall, and Byram hated himself a little more as he waited for her to continue. How could he have been so wrong? He'd allowed hurt pride to send him running when his sweet, beautiful Kaelene had been fighting for her freedom.

"Reginald O'Connor of the Clan Burlington was the second. He was not so kind or easily dismayed. They came for me in the middle of the night, bound and gagged me and brought me before a priest in my nightclothes, but the ceremony could not be complete without my vows, and when he pulled the gag from my lips, threatening to hurt me if I did not say them correctly, I fought anyway."

"Fuck, Kaelene. Please don't—"

"Don't what? Don't tell you how it was my father,

the very man who I depended on who had arrived late to that clandestine ceremony who stopped Reginald from killing me? Well, he did, and he was sorry then. It took me six weeks to heal completely, and, after that, father left me alone for a decade."

"How many?" growled Byram, sitting beside her on the floor of her bedroom.

She was so close, and all he wanted to do was touch her, but he did not even try. Work as he had to be worthy of the woman, Byram knew now he had failed. How did he not know any of this?

Because you did not want to know. You ran to nurse your own broken heart and left her here. Coward.

"There have been five attempted betrothals since you left. Lately, it is Morris who has been gaging my interest. He thinks I will tire of the rumors and wed him to protect my reputation," she replied and snorted.

"Rumors?"

"Yes, he thinks I do not know it was him, but my father's advisor is not as wily as he pretends to be. Morris started a smear campaign, calling me frigid, cold as ice, the virgin princess, barren even. Hell, they call me the *Rime Maiden*."

FIVE

nger filled Byram as he watched her chuckle at the names, though he knew it must hurt her. *Rime Maiden* was a cruel taunt from days of old. There was nothing worse for a female's reputation than to be called an ice queen.

Morris Blanchet. Formerly of Clan DuPont. Rose in ranks to the position of advisor to the king quickly.

The Vampire had switched Clans a few decades back and had settled himself quite nicely in the royal household. Vampire Clans were like mini empires in that they held royal titles, but the king rarely had all the power. The king's council, starting with his advisor, was who truly ruled. Something Byram was not aware of in his youth. Had he known, maybe he would have behaved differently.

Either way, Byram would have the asshole's head on a pike for the slander against Kaelene. She was so brave, so perfect, and he had been wrong. All this time he had stayed away, not looking back at his old Clan because he could not face what he thought was her betrayal, and she had been suffering.

Byram wanted to kick his own ass for his cowardice. He was an utter fucking asshole for ruining her life and it was time he confessed his sins.

"I fucked it all up, Pip. I was weak, foolish, and a coward," he murmured.

"I've been waiting so long to hear you call me that again," she whispered, ignoring his self-deprecating comments, as a fresh wave of tears flowed.

Shit.

He needed to be better than this. Better for her. Byram rose to his knees, pulling her to him. He shouldn't be doing this. He was not worthy, but nothing could stop him—*nothing except her.*

He waited for her to react—for her to hit or push him away, to give him any sign she wanted him to stop, but she didn't. Even as he cradled her to his body, his Pip exhaled a shaky sigh and threw her arms around his neck, hugging him fiercely.

Thank fuck.

"I'm sorry," he whispered. "So sorry, Pip. I am so sorry."

"Shhh," she said, shaking her head. And pressing her fingertips to his lips. "I don't know how much time we have Byram, but I know I don't want to waste any more of it hashing over the past."

"What do you want, then?"

"I want you," she replied without hesitation.

That was all he needed. Byram crashed his mouth against hers and tugged her closer. He was like a mad thing, wild and on fire with just the tiniest of kisses. He felt her sigh, swallowed it down, as he sipped heaven from her lips.

Hunger rose inside of him. It had been so long since he drank from a female—yes, there had been a handful over the last century, but that had been born of necessity and trying to put her out of his heart. It never worked, though.

She was ingrained inside of him. His Kaelene, his beautiful Pip. Still, he would not take her vein. Not unless she asked.

She moaned against his lips, and Byram pounced, tearing at clothing, until he had her smooth skin beneath his touch. Fuck, she was warm and vibrant with curves other female Vamps seemed to always be lacking. She was sweet and succulent, and so damn responsive, his head was spinning. Byram was drunk on her.

Kaelene arched her back as he pressed her down onto the carpet, his mouth never leaving hers as he plunged his tongue inside. She tasted like mulled wine and honeysuckle.

Delicious. Addicting. Perfect.

Byram reared up, pulling his shirt over his head, and unbuckling his belt. Kaelene's eyes heated as they raked over his body, and he grinned, more than happy she approved of his body.

"You've filled out," she whispered, grazing her nails down his pecs to his abs.

"As have you," he replied, eyes going straight to her large breasts, and she giggled, making them bounce perfectly under his stare.

With a growl, he climbed over her body and took one ripened cherry inside his mouth, sucking while kneading the plump globes with his hands. With his knee, he gently parted her legs, grinning as she hissed and clawed at his shoulders.

Wild cat that she was, Kaelene ran her hands all over him, and he loved the feel of her. They'd been together decades ago, were each other's firsts, and fuck, he'd missed this. Missed her. No one had ever matched him like his sweet little Pip. Always so damn sexy, calling to his most primal side with her pants and moans, and sexy little growls.

He ran his hands between them, sliding through her slick folds. So wet. She was hot and wet, and tight—*so fucking tight*—as he pressed one finger inside her.

Byram was big and needed her ready to take all of him before he could fuck her—no, *make love* to her, like he wanted. And it was love. Too soon? Maybe. But it did not feel like it. Byram had loved her for multiple lifetimes. He'd been pining for her for a hundred years, and even now, as she came apart in his arms while he worked her with his fingers, he loved her even more.

"Please," she whimpered as he placed the head of his cock at her slick entrance.

"Please what, Pip?"

"More, Byram, give me more," she begged.

"Everything, Pip. You can have everything," he growled, and pressed into her with one hard flex of his hips.

This was the most profound experience he had ever had in his life, and he owned that shit with every writhe and swivel, every thrust and withdrawal. She was his entire world, and he showed her with his body just how perfect they were together.

Kaelene rocked his universe. She made him whole, and in turn he would make sure she was safe. He was taking her from here. From her father and Morris, and anyone else with any designs to use her or manipulate her. No one would separate them again.

Not as long as he drew breath.

"Fuck Kae, tell me you're close," he growled.

He was thrusting deep inside, so he was barely coming out, pressing her clit with every swivel and grind, chasing her pleasure before he caught his own wave. His fangs descended and Byram locked eyes with her, watching her nod as she turned her head, giving him access.

"Do it, Byram. Bite me," she growled as her pussy tightened around his shaft.

Fuck. She was coming, and he wanted to bite her so damn bad. Byram growled a short, desperate sound, then he was at her throat. Her blood was like ambrosia to him, sating him down to his soul. He wanted to roar and beat his chest like a rutting fucking silverback, but he was no Shifter.

Byram was all Vampire and as her lips closed around his shoulder and she pierced him with her sharp little fangs, he had never been happier of that fucking fact. Pure, unadulterated bliss crashed into him as Kaelene staked her claim, biting him in the way of their kind. He'd been waiting his entire life for this moment, and it was better than he had ever imagined.

Byram licked the wounds he inflicted on his mate's perfect skin closed, completely unrepentant of the fact they would never fully heal. Same as his. The two of them would bear the signs of their claiming bites for always.

And fuck him if that wasn't sexy as hell. His cock was still pulsating with the last of his orgasm, and the ripples of her own bliss echoed around him. Never had Byram felt more complete than he did right at that moment.

The heat of their matebond wrapped tightly around them, searing their flesh, and Kaelene clung to him, growling with the intensity of it. Vampires claimed mates the same as other supes, with one significant difference. Blood was vital to a Vampire and could be taken from any source until said Vampire completed a claiming bond.

"Now I will be your only source of sustenance," he whispered, pride ringing in his voice.

"And I yours," she replied, smiling widely at him.

They could figure the logistics out later, all Byram cared about was that for the first time in decades, he felt grounded.

Mine.

Six

ow Kaelene had managed to have dinner with her father, King Aethelred, Morris, his advisor, and her most recent suitor, and Byram, her long lost love returned, whose bite mark she was now wearing beneath the antique choker around her neck, was beyond her.

It was a fucking magic act she had no idea she even knew until the servants came and took away the last of the dessert plates. She smiled politely as Morris stood to pull out her chair, but Byram beat him to the punch by a hair's breadth of a second.

"Thank you," she whispered, biting back her grin.

Byram smiled at her, snarled at Morris, and waited until she stepped behind him to exit the room before he moved to follow. He was jealous, protective, and she had to admit, Kaelene kind of liked that.

"Will you join us for brandy?" Byram asked casually, offering his arm.

"She does not take brandy," Morris inserted, and Kaelene frowned. "Princess, you must be tired, and we have things to discuss, Evers."

"I think I will have a brandy, thank you," she replied, as her father joined them.

"Daughter, good to see you looking so lively," the king said, patting her arm and leading the way to his study.

"With all due respect," Morris began as the king sat behind his desk and swirled his brandy in its snifter. "The princess has no place here. She should retire while we discuss our business with this Guardian," he hissed.

"Your majesty, I must beg to disagree. The princess might have valuable insight in the investigation I am conducting," Byram said, ignoring Morris and taking his concerns right to the king.

"You think a female has knowledge of the grisly murders you are looking into? Coming here with your seedy accusations, how dare you!"

"Tone it down, Morris. I've known Byram Evers

since he was a boy. Now, explain what is happening and why you suspect Vampires."

Kaelene sat stunned and listened as Byram explained why he was there. He was so unlike the boy she remembered. This Byram was wickedly intelligent, confident, and diplomatic as he proceeded with his case.

"So, you've broken Clan law then, sharing our secrets to outsiders?" Morris hissed.

"If that were true, you would have a two-ton Dragon sitting in your study, your majesty, and not me," Byram replied easily.

"A Dragon Shifter? They are back?"

"Indeed, sire," Byram replied, a small smile playing at the corners of his lips.

Vampires believed themselves to be the strongest of all supernaturals, and mostly, they were, save for one species of Shifter thought to be extinct. Dragons.

"So, your job now is to protect magic, is that it? Well, as you know, Byram, Vampires do not practice ritualistic magic. Not for a thousand years," King Aethelred said.

"I did know that, your majesty. Then I saw this," he said and withdrew his phone.

Byram handed the device to her father first, and judging from his pallor, whatever he saw was not very encouraging. Next, Morris viewed the image on the screen and hissed, until finally, Byram handed it to her.

"Stop! She has no part in this discussion. Your majesty, I insist she be ordered out," Morris demanded.

"Insisting, Morris? Really. Well, I have tried for a hundred years to insist my child do as I say to no avail," the king replied, with a sigh.

Kaelene frowned. When had she become a source of amusement for her sire?

"I insist she stay, your majesty," Byram replied quietly.

"What have you to do with our Clan politics, *Guardian*? You do not have sway here—"

"True, but Kaelene is mine," Byram hissed, and fuck, did she love the note of possession in his voice.

"Yours?" her father asked, gray eyebrows sky high.

"Yes," hissed Byram.

"Claimed?"

"Mine," he snarled.

"No! I was bringing you my suit this very night, your majesty," Morris shouted.

Kaelene's gaze bounced between the three males, and she laughed. Yes, she was claimed, but she never expected Byram to announce it without so much as a by your leave.

"Silence, female! Know your place!" Morris hissed, trembling with rage.

"Threaten my mate again, *advisor*, and I will rip your fangs from your body with my bare hands."

Morris blanched and backed up a step. Not all Vampires were fighters, and it was clear from his stance that Byram could do exactly as he promise. She stood and walked to her father, kissing his cheek before taking her place by Byram.

"Apologies, daughter, I should have listened to you earlier," the king said, nodding his goodbye. "Byram, take care of her, and good luck with your case. You have my permission to question any of our Clan and they will be compelled to answer. All I can tell you is those runes are old magic, forgotten by our kind, or not, as it would seem."

"Thank you, your majesty. I will make her happy," he vowed, bowing slightly before backing them out of the room, his body protectively shielding her from Morris' view.

Once they were in the hall, Kaelene covered her mouth to quell her laughter. Byram was facing away from her, and she wondered at his reticent to turn around. Was he regretting what he did in there? Announcing their mating that way?

But before she could drown in the avalanche of

doubts filling her mind, Byram turned and cupped the back of her neck, pulling her to him with so much strength he stole her breath.

"Breathe me," he growled in response to words she had not even uttered before his lips were on hers.

The man was a god when it came to kissing. His lips were hard, not gentle, as he staked his claim over and over with the force of his kiss. She felt their bond pulse and zing all the way through her body, from her head down to her toes.

"You ready?" he asked, when he finally ended his sensual assault.

"Ready?" she parroted.

He had her brain so damn foggy with thoughts of sex and babies and sex—*did she mention sex?* Kaelene could not even think. Her ovaries were working double time, and yes, contrary to popular belief, Vampires could make babies with other Vampires. Chubby little love babies, and she wanted to have like seventeen of Byram's right fucking now. Even more, she wanted to practice making them as soon as possible.

"Do you need to pack?" he asked again.

"Pack?"

Then it hit her. He was leaving. But this time, he was taking her with him.

"I don't need a thing but you," she replied, happiness radiating from her very soul.

Byram grinned and leaned down to kiss her again, stopping to cock his head behind him at the sound of someone clearing their throat. Kaelene giggled. It was Marguerite.

"Kae," she whispered, eyes wide and cheeks burning with the strength of her blush.

"Margie, this is Byram, my mate," she said proudly, and her companion and best friend giggled and curtsied at him.

"I know, Emil told me. Are you leaving then?" she asked, eyes big with unshed tears.

"Yeah," Kaelene said, nodding and whimpering at the loss of her friend. Margie ran and crashed into Kaelene, hugging her tight.

"We'll keep in touch. I swear it," she told her.

"I know. It's okay, you go live the life you always dreamed of, Kae. You're gonna be so great," she whispered.

Byram's cell phone buzzed, and he frowned. She felt his anxiety rise through their bond and immediately went back to him, hand on his elbow.

"We have to leave," he growled.

"I'll text you as soon as we get there," Kaelene told Margie.

"Okay. I'll have your things packed and shipped right away. I put some stuff in here for you," Margie said, whimpering but smiling as she handed her a weekender bag filled to near busting.

"Goodbye."

And with one last wave to her friend, Byram was leading Kaelene outside to a sleek gunmetal Corvette with t-tops and twenty inch tires. It was beautiful, fast, and Kaelene could not wait to get inside.

"Seatbelt," he murmured, and she acquiesced.

Difficult to kill did not mean Vampires did not get injured, and though she was confident in his skills, it was nice to know he cared.

He peeled out of the driveway like a badass bat out of hell, literally, and Kaelene had to bite her tongue to keep from squealing like that annoying little pig from the commercials. But if she had a pinwheel, damn straight her hand would be out the window to see that thing spin.

"You alright?" he asked, sparing her a glance.

"You drive like a demon," she yelled over the roar of the engine.

Byram's grin was feral, sexy, and damn, she liked it. Like really liked it. He switched gears effortlessly, driving like he was born to speed. He was not reckless, though. Every move was deliberate, calculated, like he wanted to show her a good time, but would never ever be careless with her person.

The thought made her feel warm and tingly inside, but there was another emotion that danced on the edge of those. For the first time in her life, Kaelene was free from the constraints of her Clan and tradition.

Byram was taking her some place new, where they could start over together. There would be new rules, new people, and she should be scared. Like really scared.

Kaelene grew up in a male dominated society, closed off from the world of supernaturals and humans alike. She'd been homeschooled, had no work experience. What could she offer this group of elite warrior Shifters and Witches?

The Guardians of Chaos was this larger than life organization even sheltered little Vampire princesses had heard of. What could she bring to the table?

"What's wrong?" Byram asked as he switched lanes and took an exit that would eventually lead them to the Garden State Parkway.

"Do you live with your team?" she asked.

"Yes, the Guardians live together in an old mansion in the middle of the pine barrens. We call it the Keep," he told her, his voice warm as he spoke of the place.

"Is it just a bunch of bachelors?"

"No, actually," he murmured, taking her hand. "Everyone is mated. I was the last bachelor. Was being the operative word, Pip."

Byram brought her hand, palm up, to press to his lips for a warm kiss. Gooseflesh tickled her skin as she felt the quick swipe of his tongue against her heated flesh.

Sweet, caring mate.

"Just so you know, I love you," she told him, eyes facing front, so she did not see his expression, but the slight swerve of the car and the rumble reverberating inside the close interior told her exactly what she wanted to know.

Byram Evers—*Vampire, Guardian of Chaos, and her mate*—loved her too.

SEVEN

The Keep loomed just ahead and Byram's pulse was racing. She loved him. The desire to introduce her to everyone within the walls of the magnificent magical manse warred with the need to take her to his lair and claim her against the door, the floor, the bed—*fuck yes*, the bed, and the bath, too.

It was late now, past midnight, and the Keep was quiet. As if the *manetuwak* could feel his desires, and they probably could, the first door he saw as he entered the house through the garage was his.

"Is this your room? Right off the garage?" she asked curiously.

"Yes, and no. This place is different, Pip. I will explain everything, I swear, but I need—*shit*, I am sorry. Just give me a moment," he growled, closing his eyes and swallowing back his hunger.

Shit. Shit. SHIT.

He thought claiming a mate would mean he could go for even longer periods of time without taking the vein, but his fangs were already threatening to lengthen, and he had not even touched her yet.

He heard the sounds of fabric rustling and hitting the floor, and he opened his eyes to see Kaelene biting her lower lip as she walked towards him in nothing but her skin. Fuck. She was beautiful. Pale and smooth, her blonde hair hitting her shoulders and catching the light of the moon as it shone in through the skylight above her. Stargazing was a hobby of his, but no star had ever shone as brightly as his Pip.

She was ethereal, otherworldly as she lifted her head and stalked closer. So confident, so breathtaking, owning herself like that. He did not trust himself to touch her, wanted to warn her away, but then she was there, sliding her hands up his chest, pulling on his shirt and opening his buckle.

Her mouth pressed against his chest, and Byram lost the battle for control. He took her shoulders in his hands and spun them around till her back was flat against the wall.

"I wanted to go slow for you," he growled,

claiming her mouth in a hard kiss that damn near brought him to his knees.

"I don't want slow," she gasped when he allowed her room to breathe. "I want you, Byram. Now."

He held her face in his hands, growling at the intensity of his feelings when her eyes flared, the color so intensely blue he could not look away.

"Then me is what you will have, Pip."

Careful not to break her skin yet, he placed hard, biting kisses down her chin, throat, and shoulder. His hands cupped her wonderful breasts, teasing the nipples and pulling a long moan from her lips. She was very good at this, at responding to his touch, making him feel ten feet high with her praise and lustful sounds.

Making her feel good was the only damn thing he wanted to do. That and to protect her, of course. The instincts to covet, cherish, and care for her were blinding in their intensity. He wanted to possess her, to be possessed by her. He'd never felt love so damn strong.

Those same instincts drove him to press between her thighs at just the right moment. She was slick and hot, mewling needy little noises that told him when he hit the right spot. Fuck, he loved her like this. Kaelene pulled his hair, bringing his mouth to hers.

Byram growled as he kissed her hard and deep, mimicking the pace of his body moving inside of hers. She pierced his skin with her fingernails—*naughty little Pip*, as her sex tightened around his shaft.

Byram wanted to give her time. He wanted to woo her with roses and moonlight, soft music and wine, but what she got was a Vampire half out of his mind with desire and hunger. He could not go slow if he tried, and thank fuck, she was a Vampire too and did not need him too. He bucked into her wildly, loving the way her body responded to his instinctively. So many nights he'd imagined this, imagined having her here, in his lair, wrapped around him. But this was real. She was here. His sweet Pip was not a figment of his imagination, or some fever dream come in the middle of the night to torment him.

"Mine," he growled against her lips. "Mine." As he slammed into her tight, wet heat. "Mine," he roared as the first hint of her orgasm rippled around him.

"Yours, Byram. Byram! By!" she yelled as her orgasm crested.

Byram struck quick, biting her over her claiming mark, and drinking the sweet nectar that was her blood as he pulsed deep within her channel. Her echoing bite mark on his bicep had him coming even harder.

Every pull of his blood from her lips dragged

another wave of pleasure through his body, and as he swallowed her life's essence, he knew it was the same for her. Pleasure hummed around them, a living, breathing thing pulsating through their matebond.

Kaelene was more than the mate of his heart. She was his fate. His past, present, and his future. Byram was tethered to her by every fiber of his being, and there was nowhere else he wanted to be. NO one else who would ever do.

Mate. Mine. Sweet, soft, beautiful Pip.

Without separating them, Byram lifted Kaelene in his arms. Wrapping her legs around his waist, kissing her the whole while, he walked them to his enormous king-sized bed and pressed her onto the soft mattress.

She sighed beneath him, cradling him in the soft warmth of her body and kissing him back with everything she had. He'd missed her so damn much, but even missing the girl she once was could not compare to loving her in that precise moment.

"Don't look back, By. Be in the here and now with me," she murmured, stroking her hands along his shoulders and chest, stoking the flames of his desire for her.

Would he ever not want her? The answer was simple. No. He would never not want his mate. She was everything. Neither afraid of him nor in the dark about what he was capable of. Kaelene was a Vampire too. She did not fear his hunger like the others did. Rather, she welcomed it, shared it, and satisfied it.

Sexy woman. Sweet mate. Perfect.

"Are you sure you're not a Witch, Pip?" he teased as he felt his cock harden while still buried inside of her.

This time he loved on her slow and rock steady. Never rushing or clumsy. He wanted to feel every inch of her as he loved her and he did, running his hands up and down the length of her, feeling the soft skin of her sides, her ass, her thighs, even her ankles. He crawled up the bed with her, turning them so she was astride his hips, his back against the headboard.

Kaelene moaned, arching her back and presenting her perfect tits to his mouth like an offering he was far too selfish to refuse. With every nip and suckle, her pussy tightened around him, her wetness dripping onto his thighs, and fuck, his dick was so hard, harder now that her movements grew jerky and rough.

"Byram, need," she moaned his name, begging him for something.

He gripped her hips with strong hands, taking over as he lifted her by the ass and slammed her back down, pistoning his hips up to meet each downward thrust. Together they were plummeting towards something big, something huge, and fuck, it felt good. Dangerous and edgy, larger than their other couplings, but Byram was in this now. He was not stopping, was not giving her up again. Not for anything or anyone.

They found the perfect rhythm, moving and moaning, and grinding against each other. Then, just as ecstasy loomed ahead, Byram felt Kaelene's teeth pierce his flesh, the first pull of her mouth against his vein had his cock stiffen, shooting warmth inside of her.

It was bliss. Pure. Perfect. Orgasmic. Heaven. But he was not about to go there alone. He lifted her wrist to his mouth, biting her there and sending her over the edge as he drank her blood. Their lingering release cocooned them, locking them away in a bubble that was all their own, and Byram never wanted to leave. His lair was thick with the scents of her honeysuckle sweetness, his masculine spice, the sex they'd shared, and the copper like fragrance that seemed to always cling to blood.

Byram did not mind. In fact, he loved it. Wrapping her up in his arms as she cuddled next to him and fell into sleep, Byram realized he loved her. More than he had ever thought himself capable. But with love came something else, worry.

His protective instincts were working overtime,

and it was all he could do to quiet himself down enough to sleep. She was there now, *with him*, and there was no safer place for Kaelene on the planet. He would die to protect her. Content with that knowledge, he finally allowed himself to rest beside her.

EIGHT

"So, you went to see your old Clan, and you brought home a guest? And she is a Vampire girl? I didn't even know they had those!" Furio scratched his pony-tailed head as he flicked his gaze from Kaelene to Byram and back.

"I am sorry about this," Byram whispered to Kaelene, who was staring in openmouthed horror at the Stallion Shifter.

"Uh," she replied inanely and shrugged.

He could not blame her. Byram had hoped to get her fed and relaxed before the Guardians started walking in for breakfast, but he should have known Furio and Jessenia would beat him there. Ever since their tiny bundle of joy had been born, the couple hardly slept. Not that Baby Gia wasn't worth all the fuss, of course, it was just Byram wanted a few moments to prepare Kaelene.

Oh well. Maybe food would help. He took her plate and began adding tasty morsels to it. The breakfast table was already heavily laden with tempting little pastries, souffles, fresh berries and French toast, courtesy of Furio's mate, Jessenia. She flashed a glare at her mate and shook her head as she continued to rock their new baby in her arms.

"My name is Jess, this is our baby girl, Gia, and I am so happy you are here," Jessenia smiled. "Uh, Byram? I think maybe that's enough food," Jessenia quipped, biting back her grin and failing.

Byram frowned, then noticed Kaelene was having a hard time stifling her giggle as well. When he finally looked at the dish, he understood why. It was toppling over with scoops of everything he could reach.

"Fuck. I'm sorry. Should I put some back?" he asked, feeling panicked, but Kaelene shook her head.

Shoulders shaking, she grinned wickedly and took the dish, placing it in front of her and cuddling his side with a kiss on his shoulder.

"It's fine, By. Thank you," she murmured on a shaky whisper that told her she was still giggling.

"Hey gang! Whoa, girl! You must be on some new diet I don't know about cause if you can put all that away, and still look like *that*, then, *dayum*, you need to share your secrets with Fergie here."

The redheaded dynamo and first conpar of the Guardians of Chaos, Wolf Shifter, and compulsive shopper extraordinaire with a slight shoe fetish, Fergie McAndrews Stormwolfe waltzed in on sky high stilettos and sat down right across from Byram and Kaelene. She tapped her red nails on the table and waited expectantly, and Byram just sighed.

"Um, hi. I'm Kaelene. And this is not how much I normally eat. Byram got overly excited when he was making my dish, it would seem," she muttered, grinning wickedly at the redhead.

"Byram got excited? No way. I've known him for like three years and I don't think he has shown more than one and a half emotions."

"Hey, be nice," Byram said and shook his head.

"Really? I've always known him to be quite hot tempered. Tell me more," Kaelene said, popping a strawberry into his mouth and leaning over conspiratorially.

"Oh no. This is a bad idea, bro. We need to leave the women to it," Furio mumbled, plucking his baby out of his mate's arms, and dropping a kiss on her mouth before walking away.

"Wait. What?" Byram asked, but Kaelene was busy chatting and Furio was already gone.

Jessenia, having already taken his seat, was now moving it closer to Fergie. Kaelene's eyes were wide, but she'd loosened the death grip she had had on his leg.

"Who are you? So, how do you know Byram? Why are you wearing a *Little House on the Prairie* dress? Are you aware he is a Vampire? Are you a supernatural? Wait—are you a Vampire? Are Vampires dead or undead? Do Vampires have to drink human or supernatural blood? And—*hang on, omg*—did you two boink?" Fergie asked in rapid succession, and Byram groaned his frustration.

He looked at Kaelene, fearing for her comfort. But despite her cheeks turning a bright pink color, she seemed fine. In fact, she leaned forward and replied to Fergie's questions in the same rapid fire succession as they were asked.

"My name is Kaelene. I've known Byram my whole life. We are from the same Clan. This is how all the females in the Clan dress. I am a Vampire and I know he is a Vampire. Vampires require blood to supplement their diets. We are not dead or undead. We are very much alive. We can theoretically drink from anything that has a pulse, but that doesn't mean we do. Do you eat everything alive cause it is edible? No. Right? And as for the boinking—" Kaelene cleared her throat and averted her gaze.

"Never mind, I know the answer!" Fergie yelled and clapped her hands.

That was enough. Byram stood, ready to take Kaelene back to the safety of his room, but before he could even get a word in, the rest of the females marched in. Margo and Elena, followed quickly by Holley. Kingston trailed behind with Greyson clinging to his head as the toddler shrieked with glee while sitting on his father's massive shoulders.

"Byram, you're back," he began, but the Dragon Shifter's gaze flicked to Kaelene and then to the others, and he made a complete about face.

"Kingston," Byram implored, but the male had taken one look at the interrogation that was going down and was now just shaking his head.

"Best you come with me, Byram. The female will be fine with this lot, if she is really yours," he muttered darkly.

"She is mine," Byram confirmed, hissing at the end.

Fuck.

He paused the sound, noting the wide-eyed stares of the women with concern. He rarely, if ever, forgot himself in front of them. It was easy for Shifters to go around growling and roaring, acting as their animal counterparts would. But Vampires were a different lot.

They kept to themselves, offering none of their secrets, and yet, allowing rumor to run rampant about their practices and lifestyles. He had trained himself early on to hide his strengths and weakness, his Vampiric hunger, and physical abilities from the other supes ever since he'd left his Clan.

It was not always easy, and often, Byram had felt alone. But the Clans were losing ground in this modern world, and more Vampires were branching out into mainstream society. Part of why this case was so worrying.

What if someone took information from a Clan that did not belong to the rest of the supernatural world?

Shit. Once the idea took root, he knew he had to investigate it. But what about Kaelene? He did not feel right leaving her. As if sensing his mood, she turned her blue eyes on him and reached for him with a raised hand. He caught it, and squeezed, settling when she graced him with that smile he adored.

Her smiles had seemed to only exist for him when they were younger, and now that she wore one again, he made a silent vow to ensure it never strayed far from her beautiful face.

"Will you be alright?" he whispered.

"Of course," she replied.

"Yeah, Byram. What do you think we're gonna do?" Elena asked and snorted.

The females shooed him away, and he watched her the whole while he backed out of the room before joining Kingston in the hall.

"You find anything?" the Alpha asked.

"Maybe. Call the others to your office, I think I know how we can track this ritual down."

NINE

Kaelene took a sip of the pineapple juice mimosa Jessenia handed her and tried not to laugh when Fergie continued with her story about the pros of wearing high heels when mated to a Shifter.

"So, you see, the added inches just mean I get to his mouth faster!" Fergie seemed ridiculously pleased with herself.

"But what if your mouth wants to be somewhere lower?" Jessenia asked. "Doesn't it impede your ability to get Mama some sausage?"

"Nope, you just gotta get your squats in," Fergie replied sagely, and winked. "Oh, and make sure you buy plenty of those little throw pillows to toss on the ground. Seriously, put those fuckers on everything, and make sure you have them at easy access, cause you gotta save your knees. Nothing sexy about banged up black and blue knees next time you rock a miniskirt from giving your man a primo knob job. You know what I mean?"

"That is actually a great idea," Jessenia muttered and appeared to be taking notes.

Fergie nodded, fluffing her fiery locks, obviously proud of her keen insights. Elena, Margo, and Holley were bent over laughing, Jessenia was asking which pillows were best, and Kaelene was at a total and complete loss for words.

"So, what do you think?" Fergie asked.

"About what?"

"About anything? High heels, pillows, and fellatio, for starters, I guess."

"I am sorry, Fergie. I confess, I do not understand half of what you ladies are talking about."

"Ladies? Ha! No one ever made that mistake," she replied with a snort.

"So, tell us about you and Byram," Margo, the dark-skinned beauty, asked, and Kaelene bit her lip.

She'd never done this kind of thing before, but Kaelene wanted these women, who were so important to Byram's life, to like her. She wanted to fit in here. Kaelene had to choose the past or the present, and just then, she wanted to choose the present.

What had clinging to the rules or the past ever gotten her, anyway? She loved her father, even after everything he had done, but his way of life was not good for her. Her breath stuck in her throat as she really thought about what had happened to her in the last day.

"Are you alright?" Margo asked, concern marring the otherwise smooth forehead beneath her corkscrew curls.

"I think so. I don't know," Kaelene replied, but she was panting now.

"She's hyperventilating," Elena said, and moved quickly as only a Shifter could to shove Kaelene's head forward.

Everyone stopped talking. The other females were all staring at her, concerned and a little frightened, but it was more for her than of her, and for that, Kaelene was grateful.

"Put your head between your knees. That's it, deep breaths now. Slow your breathing. Good. You alright?"

"Thanks. Sorry," she murmured, clearing her throat and downing the rest of her drink.

"It's okay. Sorry for asking so many questions. We don't mean to be nosy," Jessenia spoke up, and everyone was nodding their heads.

"I do. Ow! What? I am nosy," Fergie quipped, rubbing her arm where Jessenia had slapped her.

Kaelene giggled. Whatever home she was used to, this was home now. If she wanted to stay with Byram that was, and she did, more than anything. Bucking up her courage, she looked each one of them in the eyes before she started her tale.

"You should know, Vampires are very secretive by nature. What I am about to impart to you is something I could have been shunned for had I still been living with my old Clan."

"Is shunning bad?"

"Yes. It is banishment. It is being alone, afraid, and lost in a world that does not understand you and cannot protect you. Vampires are taught from birth that we need our Clans to feed us, to keep us hidden and safe from the rest of the world, both supernatural and human."

"But I thought Vamps were like badasses?" Fergie asked, confused.

"Indeed, and that might be true for our warriors. We are stronger than most living things, but we have one weakness, and it is that which also gives us our greatest strength. We need blood to live."

"What about garlic, sunlight, crosses, holy water?"

"What about them?"

"Can they kill you?"

"Most of what you know about Vampires is Hollywood or fiction writers. We are not dead or undead, like I said before, so the holy relic stuff does not work. Vampires are a mutation, a subspecies of a sort, though I don't really know all the science behind it. Whatever it is, our nature comprises blood and magic. We do not practice the craft as Witches do, rather, we are the result of the craft. Blood is in every living thing, and as part of our diet, it is necessary that we consume it."

"Where do you get it?" Margo asked, leaning forward with interest. Kaelene looked at her, waiting for a red flag or her inner warning system to go off. When it didn't, she continued, positive Byram's people would not harm her.

"If you are asking about human blood, that supply comes in from blood banks. A lot of our kind own and operate them. But like anyone, Vampires can be snobs. Many prefer taking the vein of other Vamps. For some reason, drinking from a blood relative does not work, and so some Clans and families have understandings."

"You get blood from others of your kind? That is interesting," Margo replied.

"Not anymore," she replied softly, her cheeks heating with the admission. "Claimed Vampires only take the vein of their mates."

"OMFG! I knew you two boinked! So, you're mated? SQUEEEEEEEEE! Congrats!" Fergie squealed and fist bumped Kaelene a little too hard, making her wince.

Still, it felt pretty fucking awesome, and she smiled and nodded as the others joined in, fist bumping, slapping hands on her shoulders, and even hugging her in celebration.

"Yes, yes, we are mated. Um, I know you all have known Byram for a long time, but I wanted to reassure you, I love him. I am not here to hurt him in any way, and I very much would like to fit in," Kaelene confessed.

"Truth," Fergie replied, her smile wide and stunning. "I am new to being a Shifter, but I will never get enough of hearing the difference between a truth and a lie. I believe you, Kaelene, and if there is anything we can do to help. We will."

"Yes, we will. Allow me to officially welcome you to the Guardians of Chaos conpars," Holley proclaimed, and her eyes glowed with powerful magic.

"What is a conpar?" Kaelene asked, unfamiliar with the term.

"*Conpar* is just another word for beloved mate. It is the official title for anyone mated to a Guardian of Chaos."

"So, you are all conpars?" Kaelene asked.

"No. Actually," Elena answered, clearing her throat, and smiling at Kaelene like the cat that got the canary. "I am a Guardian. My mate Logan is my conpar."

"Oh," Kaelene replied, shocked at the realization.

She knew she'd been told there was a female Guardian but staring at the woman in the tiny black tank top and the ripped skinny jeans, bright pink hair and matching eyes was a lot different from simply hearing about her.

Gulp.

That was when Kaelene took a serious look around the room. Every single one of these women were badass. Some were Shifters, some Witches, one smelled more human than the others, and yet she held power too. These women were not like the females she grew up with.

They were not cowed or forced into submission by males. They had not been heavily pampered, protected, or stifled under some testosterone fueled fantasy that only a male could offer them a good quality of life.

These women were strong. They were good partners to their menfolk. They were independent, yet strong enough to admit they needed their mates, wanted them, and loved them, too.

These women were her sheroes.

TEN

eart racing, Kaelene looked at all the contented faces around her. Their mate-bonds were visible to her, softly glowing, wrapping around them like warm blankets. It was obvious they were loved, and yet they seemed to have their own interests and lives.

Suddenly, Kaelene knew what she wanted. Byram was a huge part of it, of course, but she did not want to be a drain, a barnacle, on her mate. Kaelene wanted to pursue her own interests, too. She wanted to be useful and happy.

Didn't she have a right to be? Didn't everyone? First, she needed to find herself, and for a wonderfully clear moment, she knew these women could help.

"Can I ask you all a favor?"

"Shoot," Fergie replied, topping off her glass with fruity champagne goodness.

"Can you help me find some clothes that don't make me look like I am from the pioneer era?"

"*Guuurrrlllll*, you know it!"

Kaelene giggled as the women led her to a door that seemed to appear out of nowhere. Holley had leaned over and whispered the word manetuwak, which Kaelene had since been told was the name of the spirits who lived inside the Keep. They were benevolent and powerful, animating the mansion with positive energy and magic since their mission was to keep the Guardians comfortable, happy, and cared for.

"This is amazing," Kaelene whispered as she walked through the portal into a room that very closely resembled a 1950s era movie set.

It was like one of those Samuel Goldwyn films where the female lead would walk into a department store and ask to see something new. The scene would fade to a large fitting room with live models walking around, trying on the clothes for the lead.

Inside the Keep, this fitting room had perfect lighting, soft music playing in the background, a stage with a small runway, trays of snacks set up, an entire wall of mirrors, and best of all, racks of wonderful, modern clothing, accessories, makeup, and shoes.

"Wow," she whispered, and ran her hand over a soft pair of jeans. "This is exactly what I wanted."

"Yeah, the Keep does that. Go on, girl, try some stuff on and let's see if we can make a modern Vampire out of you."

It was like something out of a fairytale, only better. Okay, Kaelene loved the way the soft, clingy denim hugged her curves and lifted her ass, but even better was the freedom she felt walking around in them.

"Try the Ferragamo's," Fergie said, and she did, but truth was, she felt more at home in the motorcycle boots with the buckles and two inch heel.

"Badass," Elena murmured approvingly.

"And what about the hair?" Jessenia piped in.

"My hair?"

"Gonna leave it? Trim it? Personally, I love me a girl-hawk—"

"No. I think I am fine with the hair," Kaelene replied, and tucked her long braid inside the soft thermal she wore.

"Wow, is that your claiming mark?" Fergie asked, standing up to get a closer look.

Kaelene was quite proud of the silvered scar that resembled two tiny dots on her skin. Vampires did not like imperfections, but claiming bites were permitted in polite society, though rarely so prominently displayed.

"That's classy! Mine looks like Storm tried to rip my head off," she replied, and pulled her shirt down to show off her bite mark.

It was true, Shifters were rougher, but she could tell Fergie was still more than happy with her own claiming bite. Kaelene grinned and went back to looking herself over. The outfit was practical and comfy. Nothing like the formal dresses and ankle boots she'd been wearing most of her life.

"Why do Vampires wear dresses like that, anyway?" Jessenia asked.

"We age slowly, making us seem immortal to some, I guess. And because of that, we do not move as quickly as the times do. The old ones, like my father, who hold power and sway, prefer things to progress slowly. Females have little say in things. We are daughters, mates, and mothers. I was to be a bargaining chip for my father, Aethelred, King of the Clan Withers, but I did not exactly cooperate," she murmured.

"What did you do?"

"Well, for one thing, I fell in love with Byram, refused every suitor he threw at me, including one very nasty male who kidnapped me and tried to force me to bind myself to him according to ancient custom. After that, I kept out of his way, and he out of mine. He was riddled with guilt, you see, I was all tied up and battered when he found me. Not that I did not fight. I mean, I did—"

"Good for you, hon! And we were not judging you at all, seriously that sounds awful—" Margo said, stopping when Fergie shrieked.

"Wait a second," the redhead stood hands up like she was some kind of deranged crossing guard. "Your father is the king? Holy shit. Do you know what this means?"

"Um, no?"

"We got us a motherfucking princess in the Keep! Crown party! Hey, Keep, get us some crowns up in this bitch!"

After that, the little girls' day of trying on clothes and makeup became a full on princess party, complete with more bubbly and cute little cupcakes with pink frosting and sparkly sprinkles. By the time the male Guardians came knocking, their women were three sheets to the wind, despite some of them having supernaturally enhanced metabolism.

Even Kaelene, whose head was spinning with tales and quips from these wonderful women. Sure, she'd had Marguerite back in her former Clan, but that friendship was different. Margie had been her lady's companion before they'd started confiding in each other.

The other Vampire shared stories of her love for Emil, one of her father's guards, and passed on gossip from other servants in her father's mansion, but Kaelene had never shared her own true feelings. She'd never told her about Byram, her first and only love.

Was it crazy that she'd crashed so hard the second she'd seen him again? Maybe. Or maybe it was a hundred years' worth of longing coming to a head. The knock sounded again and a very tipsy Fergie answered it with a giggle as she stumbled off her ridiculously high heels and into her Wolf Shifter mate's waiting arms.

"Come on, *nushe*, time for bed," the big man said.

Holley was next, with Kingston waiting at the door for his willowy, tawny skinned Witch. The love in his eyes made Kaelene shiver as he picked up his woman and carried her off to the Dragon's den.

"I think someone needs a spanking," Furio whispered to Jessenia, nipping her neck between blunted teeth and squeezing her ass hard right in front of everyone and not giving a single fuck who saw.

Kaelene's mouth went dry. Vampires did not indulge in PDAs, but there was something so sexy and sweet about the Stallion and his mate whispering dirty phrases and making out like love-struck teenagers in the hallway that made her want the same.

Logan and Elena were walking hand in hand, the Panther Shifter positively goo-goo-eyed when she stared at him. Imagine seeing a fierce female warrior acting like a kitten in the arms of her mate! Kaelene was stunned. And when the beautiful, brown-skinned Margo leaped into the arms of her lover and mate, Egros, she saw sparks—actual sparks of their magical bond burning when they kissed.

By the time she was finished with her little voyeuristic escapade, Kaelene's eyes flashed to the one male remaining. Byram stood staring at her, arms crossed over his massive chest, hardly breathing—which was actually normal for their kind.

Vampires did not need quite as many breaths or heart beats as normals or Shifters, but that was not why she froze in place. It was the way his normally hazel eyes had lightened to emerald, raking up her body like green coals.

Oh. Her clothes. She forgot she was wearing the revealing tank top and ripped jeans, so unlike the dresses she normally wore. Kaelene waited for his criticism, for his judgement, but it did not come. Instead,

Byram grinned like a madman and held his hand out to her, an invitation to go to him.

How could she refuse? He was her everything. And right then she lost another chunk of her heart to the sexy male.

Mine.

Eleven

uck. Holy fuck.

A bomb could have detonated and Byram doubted very much he would have blinked at the sound. Kaelene was standing before him, wearing skintight jeans and a sexy cotton tank top, showing off every dip and curve of her luscious body.

So. Fucking. Hot.

He'd been worried about his sweet Pip, leaving her alone with the women while he discussed his plans to catch the culprits in the bloodletting murders. Would she fit in? Would she think his friends brash or uncouth?

It was difficult to gauge, being raised Vampire royalty, her lifestyle was vastly different from theirs.

Hell. It had taken him years to acclimate to modern ideas and accept the differences of living with a group of Shifters and Witches. But here she was, surprising him with her remarkable adaptability.

Hell. When Storm had knocked on the door, Byram did not know what he would find, but the sounds of glasses tinkling, and uproarious laughter was a relief. He should have never doubted Fergie, Holley, Elena, Margo, and Jessenia. They were fantastic women, all of them. And he was indebted to them for making Kaelene so damn happy.

And she *was* happy. He could tell by the sparkle in her blue eyes when the door had opened. The others had dispersed to their own rooms, and here she stood before him, looking gorgeous and sexy and a little uncertain as she waited for his reaction. He strolled towards her slowly, holding her gaze before he stopped. Byram's eyes dipped then, taking her in from head to toe. A deep rumbling growl escaped his lips as he admired her beauty.

"You look good, Pip," he murmured, transfixed by the way her hair glittered like star shine in the suddenly dim lights.

Fucking Keep. Setting the mood. As if he needed to be any more *in the mood* around her. He wanted to fuck her right now against the wall. Tear those skinny jeans off her long legs and bend her over. Images of her arching her back, pushing that gorgeous ass into him as he fucked her hard and rough made his dick swell and the growl in his throat increase.

"You think I look good?" she whispered, eyes wide, and he knew she was not fishing for compliments.

Fuucckk. Yessssss. Perfect.

But he could not talk. Not just yet. Instead, he nodded, and lifted his hands, brushing her hair off her pretty, pale shoulders. Were shoulders even sexy? Hers were. Just look at the tent he was pitching in his slacks, for fuck's sake.

"My father would have a fit if he saw me," she said, looking down with a self-deprecating laugh.

"I remember Clan life. Women here are treated differently," he murmured.

"I can tell. Your friends are incredible. They have this amazing banter, and tons of laughter. I've never seen women so happy," she mused, and fuck, that was sad.

"You had a good time, then? They didn't shock you?"

"I mean, a little," she confessed, and she was blushing now.

Fuck. She was pretty when she blushed, and Byram

was having a hard time concentrating on the conversation.

"They talk about everything, Byram. I mean *everything*. Sex and their mates, their children, and their work. It never occurred to me I could do that. I could *work*. I mean, you have a female in the Guardians. She fights alongside you," she said, shaking her head as if she still could not believe it.

"Elena is a great warrior. Is that what you want? To be a warrior?" Byram asked, curious about her desires and dreams.

Byram suddenly realized they had never really talked about her desires and wants in life. How fucking selfish of him! When they were younger, he'd gone on and on about medicine and science, wanting to study and better himself.

True, it had partially been to raise his station, so he'd be worthy of pursuing her, but that was not all of it. Byram loved being a healer. Studying chemistry and biology, magic too. Supernaturals were a puzzle, so vast and different, no group sharing everything they knew lest another have power over them.

The Guardians of Chaos were not like other Packs or Clans, their group encompassed many different species, and it was vital they could heal their own since they saw battle so frequently. Byram had a role to play here, and he fit quite nicely. But he hadn't considered Kaelene's role when he took her from her father's mansion.

He did not regret it. Not for a second. A Vampire princess was not given much opportunity for personal growth. How brave his Kaelene had been to evade her father's betrothal mechanisms for so long. But that was over now. She was his, and he was hers. There was nothing to fear from unworthy suitors.

"I don't think I could be a warrior," she replied, laughing a little at herself. "But I would like to find something, some way, to be useful. I would like to do real work."

Byram grinned, so fucking proud of her for speaking her mind. He knew it was difficult for her, and they would need to learn to be comfortable with one another outside the bedroom. But he would work on it. If it took lifetimes, he would never quit.

"So, you don't think this outfit is too much for me?" she asked, and he hated the insecurity in her voice.

Pip was a motherfucking princess. Royalty to his kind, but Vampires and their stupid fucking traditions and laws had kept their females submissive, beholden, and always questioning themselves. She'd been cowed and ruled over her whole fucking life.

No more. Not my Pip.

Okay, so he was still a possessive asshole, but it was only because he cared. Byram's chest reverberated with his snarl. He would not allow another fucking person to cow her ever again. His chest ached, filled with the desire to lift her up, to see her shine, to bolster her confidence to where she did not need him to. Her soft gasp filled his ears as Byram moved with the inhuman speed and grace of his kind and cupped both hands on her face.

"Nothing is too much for you, Pip. You're the epitome of it all. Anything you want, you go for. I'll be here rooting you on," he murmured.

"You really mean that?"

"Fuck yes, I mean it. Life is what you make it, Pip. You're gonna learn to take it by the fucking horns and own that shit, Pip. I can't wait to see you when you do," he growled before crashing his mouth into hers.

Kaelene moaned into his mouth, and he was a goner. Lifting her up, he raced down the hallway, flying with Vampiric speed to the door to his lair—*no, not his*—their lair.

He slammed the portal shut, backing her against the wall, his mouth on her neck as he sucked and bit her, not breaking the skin, not yet. Just teasing little bites that had her moaning and scratching at his shoulders.

"Fuck, Pip, want you. Want to rip these tight jeans off your perfect fucking ass and make you come screaming my name," he growled, running rough hands up the sides of her body.

Her eyes dilated with pleasure at his naughty words, and Byram's cock strained inside his pants, begging for release. His Pip liked dirty talk. Good. He made a note to increase his repertoire.

"What are you waiting for?" she asked, and fuck, his heart pounded a little harder, a little faster.

Byram walked her backward to the dresser, turning her around to face the mirror, he met her eyes in the reflective glass, taking the straps of her tank top in his hands.

"I'll get you more," he grunted before tearing the fabric from her skin easily as a sheet of paper.

Her jeans received the same treatment, and she swallowed audibly. The scent of her arousal made him dizzy as he unbuckled his belt and released his engorged shaft.

Kaelene inhaled deeply, watching as he trailed his nails down her spine, pressing her forward until her breasts smashed against the cool lacquered wood of the dresser. One hand fisted his cock while the other slid down her ass crack, then lower still, stoking her wet lips as he pushed her legs apart with his knee.

There was something so intensely erotic about having her there, splayed before him submissively, but not. The position might appear docile, but right then, Pip fucking owned him. Her body trembled and her eyes glowed with thirst as she met his stare.

"Hard, Byram, I want it hard," she growled.

He didn't wait anymore then. Still holding her neck, Byram placed his head at her entrance, and gripped her hip, then with a resounding snarl, he slammed into her. The sound of her moans was symphonic as the slap of skin against skin, the harder he pounded into her, the tighter her slick pussy gripped him.

Fuck. She was so hot. So wet. So perfect.

"I'm so deep, Pip. You feel me stretching you? Stamping myself on you?"

"Yes, Byram, more. Give me more," she ground out, and he went wild.

Pip arched her back, thrusting her ass out, taking him deeper, so deep, he went cross eyed from the pleasure alone. Byram had her pinned to the dresser as he impaled her from behind. His cock was so hard, he thought he would split her in two, but not his Pip. She was strong and every moan and growl told him she liked what he was doing to her, what she was doing to him.

Byram roared as the first wave of orgasm ripped through him. He reached around her hip, found her clit, and *tap, tap, tapped* the little beauty until her sex tightened, and she yelled his name in pleasure. Something primal inside him wanted to roar as he filled her with his cum, so much so it dripped down her thighs, marking her with his scent.

"Mine," he snarled, meeting her gaze in the mirror.

"Yours," she replied, and it was so fucking sexy to hear her say that.

After a moment, when they both could breathe easier again, Byram carried her to the bath and held her while he filled the enormous tub with scalding liquid. Once filled, he settled her down and got in behind her. The need to care for her after such a tumultuous coupling was overwhelming.

He washed her silently, loving the way she allowed him to pet and cherish her without words. Pip turned around, tender in his embrace, she lifted her legs over his thighs and snuggled close to his chest.

"Was I too rough?" he asked worriedly, hugging her tight to his body.

She shook her head, and he felt her skin tighten as

if she were smiling against his. Fuck, that felt good. Making her smile always had.

"You were perfect, By," she whispered, kissing his chest.

Whether it was her words or her lips that soothed him, Byram didn't know, but the female was working some kind of magic as she slowly moved from his chest to his neck and throat, licking, sucking, kissing. Her hands petted his arms, tracing circles up his back, working him to a frenzy with her light teasing touches.

"Feels good," he murmured, not wanting to stop.

This was the first time she had initiated physical intimacy, and he did not want to fuck it up by acting the rutting beast. It was hard. Literally. But he controlled himself.

"Is this alright?" she asked, nipping his lower lip between her sharp teeth, but not drawing blood.

His nostrils flared, but he managed to nod. Yes, it was alright. Anything she did was fucking perfect.

"And this?" she whispered, lifting herself up till she hovered over his hard length.

Again, he nodded, incapable of speech. She was tearing him to bits with her slow smile and barely there touches. He thought she would impale herself on him, but she didn't. Instead, she moved her heated pussy along his shaft, not taking him inside, just rolling her hips and sliding up and down his cock. Nothing had ever felt so fucking good.

"Fuuckk," he growled, tossing his head back as she moved again and again.

She leaned back, pulling the plug, and as the water receded from the tub, the friction felt even better. Kaelene's lips teased his, and he growled, chasing the kiss she kept denying him.

Sexy little vixen was driving him nuts. And Byram loved it. His sweet little Vampire might be timid and shy about her first time in jeans, but the sexy woman was a goddamned dynamo at this. Her lips turned up in a naughty little grin as she worked his cock, grinding her slick pussy up and down his length, teasing his mouth with her tongue.

She flicked the nubile little appendage over his fangs, and Byram lost his shit. He grabbed her by the neck, mouth fixed on hers as he took her hip with his other hand. Then Byram flexed his own. His abs bunched up, every muscle straining.

Finally, he plunged his dick and his tongue inside her simultaneously. Perfect. So fucking perfect. Pip felt beyond amazing. Warm. Hot. Wet. Safe. Heaven. Home.

Everything. She was everything. And she was finally his.

"Breakfast burritos? What's in it?" Kaelene asked, looking down at the rolled up log sitting on the plate Byram handed her as they scooped food from the makeshift buffet set up in the kitchen.

It smelled delicious, but Kaelene had never had one before. Byram grinned, adding fruit salad, a small bowl with some kind of green sauce, and a scoop of potatoes to her plate.

"It's one of Jessenia's newest specialties. When she was pregnant, she craved spicy foods like mad," he explained, holding her chair out as she sat down at the table.

Jessenia and Furio were sitting at the other end of the long table, and he was feeding her bites of food while she nursed their baby. Little Gia was only a few months old, but already she smelled of fur and magic, and Kaelene was excited for the creature she would become.

The Guardians with offspring seemed to be doubly blessed with characteristics of each parent, something that was almost unheard of in the supernatural world. At least, that was what Byram had explained to her.

He'd been sharing tidbits about his group, and that was special. That was something big and rare. Male Vampires rarely treated their women as equals, but Byram had lived away from Clan life for so long. He was different now. Better.

He was perfect, and, the truth was, Kaelene adored him. She loved him more than ever. The man Byram had become was so much better than the boy she remembered.

"Doesn't she mind cooking for everyone every day?"

"No. It's her job, actually. Jessenia runs a video blog, recording and sharing her adventures as a chef. She has sponsors and makes a pretty penny doing it."

"Wow. That is amazing."

"Come on. Take a bite," Byram coaxed, his hazel eyes flashing green as he watched her lift the strange beige log looking food to her mouth.

There was no sense in putting it off, she supposed, and Jessenia's eyes were on her now from the other side of the table. Closing hers, Kaelene took a bite. Then another. And another.

"*Ohmygods*," she moaned and Byram laughed as she took a fourth bite before swallowing. "It's like this soft, spicy, salty, sweet, bright, deliciousness wrapped up in a warm blanket of love," Kaelene groaned.

She did not even care as the rest of the Guardians who had joined them a little while ago stared while she devoured her first breakfast burrito. The women smirked as the men stared, jaws dropped, but Kaelene gave zero fucks. She and Byram had damn near set their lair on fire last night, and she must have burned like a million calories. Besides, this was the best damn thing she ever ate.

"Try it with the *salsa verde*," Byram said as she reached her last bite.

It was okay though. He was already handing her his, his eyes bright green now as he watched her chew. She should be worried about appearances, but Kaelene was completely absorbed with her meal. What the heck was wrong with her?

Uh oh. Oh shit. Could it be?

Hope, happiness, surprise, and gratitude sprang to life inside her. Kaelene dropped her half-eaten second burrito back on the plate and looked down at the hand that was now clutching her soft stomach.

"Byram," she whispered.

"What is it, love?" he asked, concerned.

"I think I'm pregnant."

The entire Keep fell silent as Kaelene whispered her news. It was rare for pregnancy to occur so quickly, but not impossible. It could happen, and they had been fucking like rabbits since she'd laid eyes on him.

"Wait, Vampires can get knocked up?" Fergie's voice pierced the haze of shock that had enveloped Kaelene and Byram.

His jaw was clenched so hard she thought he might break it. Her mate's nostrils flared, his left eye twitched, and she knew he was trying to come to terms with her suspicion.

"Yes. But it is rare and sometimes dangerous," she murmured.

"Why dangerous?"

"Fergie, we should go. Leave them to discuss it."

"Fuck that," the she-Wolf snarled at her mate. "Kae is my friend. I want to know why it's dangerous for her to be pregnant so we can help."

"Vampires live very long lives and pregnancy occurs maybe twice in all that time for a female. That is, if she survives the first time," Kaelene whispered, eyes wide as the reality set in.

Yes. She was overjoyed at the prospect of bearing Byram's young, but she did not want to lose him. Not when she'd only just found him.

"Pip, are you certain?"

"I think so. I can feel flutters," she whispered, tears threatening to fall.

"What is happening?" Fergie barked again.

Kaelene watched Byram contain his growl before he answered her. Good mate. She already knew Fergie well enough to understand the she-Wolf would not leave without getting some information first. She was fiercely protective of her friends, and Kaelene warmed at the thought she was one of them.

Lucky girl.

A baby?

Yes. A baby.

Her inner monologue was right. She was pregnant, and now her real test of fortitude would begin. Was she strong enough for this? For six months of feeding her young with her body. Of denying herself the vein to ensure the babe would not die before breathing his or her first breath.

"A Vampire cannot ingest blood before puberty. It corrupts the cells, makes aging impossible. If its mother drinks before the babe is born, the fetus will not develop. It would be stillborn, spontaneously aborted," he said, voice cracking at the end.

Kaelene whimpered at the thought. Already, she would do anything for her child. For their child. Love for Byram, for their babe, welled within her, until she felt heartbroken by the sadness in his eyes.

"But if she doesn't drink blood, what will happen?" Fergie asked, her questions tearing at Kaelene's soul.

"I will weaken. If the babe comes late, I will die," she whispered.

"No," Byram growled angrily. "No. You won't die. I won't let you. Fuck. This is my fault. My fault! I should have protected you. Fuck. Fuck. FUCK!"

His anguished roar filled the room. The power behind his cry made the dishes and glasses shake, the shelves creak, and the windows shatter outward, spraying glass everywhere. His hands cupped the back of his head as he fell to the floor, making fists, he punched the stone until it crumbled beneath his brutal assault.

Kaelene cried out, hating that he was hurting so. Pregnancy should bring joy, not this tragedy. She crumbled then, falling to her knees beside her mate where he was currently pitched forward, emotions too charged for words.

The rest of the Guardians shuffled out of the room, leaving them be, though she could hear Fergie and Jessenia question their mates on whether they should go. Gods love them, they meant well, but she needed Byram now. Needed her mate. Kaelene hugged him tight, and finally, he moved with a gut wrenching groan, wrapping her up in the steel bands that were his arms.

"I won't lose you, Pip. Not now. I can't."

"It will be okay. I'm strong, Byram. The Fates would not have brought us together to separate us now."

"Fuck the Fates, Pip. I don't trust them. Not with you. There are things I can do, as healer, I can help you and later when we have a plan, we can try later," he told her, and coldness gripped over her heart.

"No, Byram, no," she replied, shaking her head in horror as she understood what he was saying.

"This baby was created with love, Byram. The love we have that was denied for far too long. I will not give up my baby," she told him.

"Kae, please. Please, I just want to keep you safe," he whispered, his emerald gaze blazing at her.

Kaelene shook her head and stood, backing away

from him as she cradled her stomach with her arms. She was strong now. It would be difficult at the end, but right now she was strong, and it was going to suck not having his support, but he would come around. She had to believe that.

"When you are ready to be part of this, part of me and our babe, let me know. I will wait for you. I promise," she whispered just as she had a hundred years ago, only now it was so much harder to back away from his anguished scream.

She had no choice. Once upon a time, she lived for the mere sight of Byram Evers. Now, she would live to grow their child.

I will wait for you. I promise.

Days Later...

Kaelene sat still while Holley braided her hair. The *Ladies' Room*, as she later learned the magical dressing room for the females in the Keep was called, seemed especially somber that morning.

"How do you feel?" Margo asked, seemingly concerned.

"Fine," she replied, and gave her a sad little smile.

It was all Kaelene could muster at the moment. She'd been sleeping in a spare bedroom the Keep had seemed to understand she needed, providing as the manetuwak knowingly did for those in their care.

She hated being separated from Byram, but the big, dumb Vampire did not seem to understand he had hurt her with his harsh words. The very thought of getting rid of their babe made her heart hurt and her Vampire side snarl with rage.

Supernaturals thought Bear Shifters cornered the market on psychotic maternal instincts, but that was only because they knew almost nothing of Vampire females. Sure, they were treated as second-class citizens by the males, but even they knew better than to come between a Vampire mother and her young.

It was an esteemed honor, a blessing to have the ability to become pregnant. Yes, there was a risk. But anything worth anything at all came with risk.

Look at what her love for Byram had cost her. She'd been browbeaten and manipulated by her father time and time again, him always trying to break her bond to the unsuitable make who had stolen her heart. But she never broke.

Sure, she had hated Byram for a while. Hated him for leaving her and breaking his oath. But once she saw him again, it was as if all the hurt had faded away. Leaving only her love and desire in its wake. Falling into his arms had been like coming home.

"Here, hold this," Holley murmured with a smile, handing her some small hair bands the Witch would use to fasten the two long braids she'd fashioned out of Kaelene's long blonde tresses.

The Shifters here did not understand why her mate was staying away. They did not know what this meant to a Vampire male, but she knew what it cost him to be apart from her. It was costing her the same thing.

Tears welled in her eyes as she thought of the glimpse of Byram she'd gotten the night before. He'd been in pursuit of the bloodletters, trying to catch them in the act, and had started a tussle with some rogues who'd thwarted his hunt. He'd been injured in the melee, and Kaelene had wanted desperately to go to him, to help clean and dress his wounds.

One look into his haunted hazel eyes had stopped her in his tracks. Byram had not changed his mind about her pregnancy. He still wanted her to terminate their offspring, and there was no way in heaven or hell she was going to do that.

"You'll make it through this," Holley whispered, her soft hand resting on Kaelene's shoulder.

"I have to. I only hope Byram changes his mind before it's too late because I am having this baby, with or without him," She said sternly, her words a vow the gods themselves could take to the bank.

"Damn straight," Fergie said.

"No matter what the cost, little one. It's you and me," she murmured, cradling her belly.

"And me."

"And me."

"Me too."

The sentiment was repeated until there was not one dry eye left. Kaelene's shoulders sagged with relief. She might not have Byram, but she had friends here, and that was better than she'd hoped for.

Her heart might long for her mate, but these females would bolster her when she needed it. She could depend on them. And knowing that gave her the most phenomenal feeling, like a sense of belonging she had never felt before.

Fuck. Where was Byram? He should be here, she thought angrily. Her heart broke for him, but dammit, she needed him strong and present. Yes, she was determined to do it alone, but Kaelene did not want to have to. Couldn't he see that?

Please come back to me, Byram. I don't want to do this without you.

THIRTEEN

Byram felt hollow. Dead. Worse than dead. He felt the way the world thought Vampires should feel. Cold. Void of life. And why?

Why did he feel this way when everything he'd ever wanted was across the hall hanging out with the women who had come to mean as much to him as the rest of the Guardians he'd allied with all those years ago?

Because I'm a fucking coward.

A snarl of fury built in his throat, earning him the glare of his Alpha. Fuck. His Alpha. Vampires did not have Alphas. They had Kings. They did not have friends either. They had Clan.

But Byram had left all that behind a lifetime ago when he'd thought his heart would break at her betrayal. Only there hadn't been any betrayal. Kaelene, his sweet Pip, had been honest and true, enduring more hardships alone than he could have ever imagined.

She was a princess, should have been protected and taken care of by her people. Only she wasn't. She'd been the victim of her father's manipulations, almost forced to marry men she did not love, all because he had failed her.

And he was failing her again.

Fuuckk!

"Byram! Cut that growling shit out or you're gonna call my fucking Wolf," Storm snarled, and swirls of glowing blue smoke covered his body, matching the feral glint in his eyes.

Each of the Guardians, upon being mated, had received some sort of gift, a boon to their powers that helped them in battle. Byram had had several altercations since he'd found Kaelene again and claimed her as his own, but he had yet to experience anything like that.

More proof he sucked at being a Vampire, a mate, and a Guardian. No pun intended.

"Sorry," he grunted, cutting off the feral sound that seemed frozen in his throat ever since she'd started sleeping in another room.

"The Assembly is breathing down my neck for answers," Kingston growled. "Byram, I am sorry, I had to tell them about you pairing up with Kaelene."

"What?" he asked, going still at the Dragon's admission.

He smelled the man's regret, and it was like he knew what was coming before the knock sounded on the door.

"No. No. NO. NO!"

"I didn't have a choice. Neither do you," Kingston growled, power resounding in every note.

"You called me?" Kaelene's soft voice reached him, and it was like hands stroking along his skin. Fuck, he'd missed her. Missed hearing her talk to him. The scent of her. The sight.

"Thank you for coming, Kaelene," Kingston replied, a formal smile on his face.

Good. he should treat her with respect. She was important. She was a princess. Fuck that, She was his. Byram wanted to rip the Alpha's hand from hers as he shook it gently and led her to a chair. She ignored Byram, and that stung, but it afforded him the opportunity to drink her in.

She was wearing tight jeans, the kind that were more elastic than denim, and they clung lovingly to her soft curves. Her belly was slightly more pronounced, cute as fuck in the clingy little sweater she wore, outlining her voluptuous breasts. Gods, he missed them. She had the most outrageously perfect tits, fine pale skin and pink puckered nipples, always at the ready to be tweaked or suckled.

And now he was fighting a boner in a room full of supernaturals who would undoubtedly know he was horny as a fucking goat from all of two seconds of looking at her.

"She does look hot, bro," Furio whispered, as if that was fucking helpful.

Byram's lip curled as he snarled at the Stallion, who simply snorted and raised his hands as he walked away.

"Kaelene, I've discussed your situation with the Assembly. That's the body of supes who govern the Guardians of Chaos."

"Okay. What did they say?"

"Well, I won't lie. They were intrigued by us having gained a Vampire princess as conpar to one of our own."

Byram flinched at the word. Not because she was not his cherished mate, but because he had been shit at this from the beginning. Kaelene deserved better, but he had no time to go off the rails about that now. His

Alpha was saying something important, and he needed to focus.

"They believe you might be in a position to help us find the culprits who are bleeding our own, but you would have the choice to participate or not. I understand you might not want to risk anything right now—"

"You are damn fucking straight she is not putting herself at risk, Kingston. She is pregnant!"

"What do you care?" she snarled at him, and fuck, he deserved it.

"Kingston, no," Byram said, shaking his head, and ignoring the hurt he felt at her angry glare.

"You are in the unique position of being able to request access to the libraries of other Clans. Pregnant females do this, do they not? Research lineages for the sake of their young?"

Byram growled. It was true. Vampire lines could be traced back thousands of years, and since pregnancies were rare and troubled, females were known to research lineages to gauge their odds.

It seemed cold and calculating, but Byram understood the inclination. In a world where females were submissive and held menial jobs, it made sense they would try to gain some control in any way they could.

"So, you want me to announce my pregnancy and beg entry to Clan libraries? Which Clan?"

"Your old Clan, actually. Clan Withers. We understand your father allowed you to leave, but he has since disowned you, Kaelene. You are not listed as princess on the Clan Withers registry any longer."

Holy fuck. Byram had balled his hands into fists so tight he drew blood without realizing it. Only the sound of her hiss and the way her eyes blazed almost white as she scented the copper rich liquid had him stopping and rushing to the sink in the adjoined bathroom. He should know better than to do that. She would react to blood now in ways she could not control.

Fuck. He was a terrible mate. Luckily, his Vampire healing was lightning quick and already the wounds were closed. He returned to the room where the Alpha and Kaelene were still talking. Byram moved in closer until he stood directly behind her, willing her to turn around.

She didn't. Fierce little badass was ignoring him, and fuck, it stung, but he could not help being proud of her—suddenly and ridiculously so. Byram was grinning like a lunatic at the way she rubbed her tummy in gentle circles and crossed her legs, pretending she did not even know he was there.

And yes, it was all pretense. He could tell by the steadily increasing pulse at her throat. She knew he was there. Just to prove it, he growled softly, loud enough for her to hear him, to feel the vibrations on her skin. She sighed loudly, as if bored, but there it was. The subtle scent of arousal dancing on the air. Kaelene could ignore him all she wanted, but deep down, he knew she was just as affected as he.

Liar liar pants on fire.

"If I am no longer the princess, why would he let me in?"

"For the sake of his grandchild, we hope."

"Okay, I will send an inquiry today."

"Good—"

"No, she will not be put at risk, Kingston. I won't allow it!"

Uh oh. He knew he'd fucked up even before the last syllable left his lips.

"You won't *allow* it?" Kaelene asked, voice laced with barely leashed fury.

"Kae, I only meant—"

"My new friends have been teaching me some fun colloquialisms, By, and I finally figured out how to use a few of them properly—"

"Hey gang, what's doing?" Fergie asked, walking

into Kingston's office a half second before Kaelene was about to explode at Byram.

Not that he didn't deserve it. Shit.

"Kae, please, just let me—"

"Not a fucking word. You don't get to have a say in anything I do, you deadbeat, slime-licking, fang-faced, fart-breath, dickweasel!" she yelled, kicking him in the shin as she waltzed past him, head high and hips swinging.

If he wasn't on the floor, cradling his broken leg, he'd have run after her. Sexy little Pip. Gorgeous she-Vamp in her skintight jeans and belly slightly swollen with his young.

Mine.

FOURTEEN

Royal title or not, she was his queen. And she was carrying his babe. He was a total asshole, and he was going to apologize for all of it. The second he could stand again without falling.

What she was wearing on her feet, for fuck's sake?

"Steel-toed combat boots. Maybe you should wear some shin guards for the next few months, eh?" Fergie quipped as if she had heard his question.

The she-Wolf was snorting laughter as she trailed his mate. Good friend. But fuck, this was going to hurt later.

"Pip? Please, Pip, let me in," Byram cooed a few minutes later from outside her bedroom door.

He hated she was staying there, sleeping away from him. Hated it, but understood it. He had run the second things had gotten tough. Had betrayed her with words, asking her to do the unthinkable. The only thing holding him together was the knowledge she was in there, listening. Maybe.

Byram slid to the floor, leaning against the door, and did something he never expected to do. He poured out his heart to the only person in the world who had ever really mattered to him.

"The first time I saw you, I was eight years old, and you were planting flowers outside your father's mansion in Cook's herb garden. She was old and mean, but she liked me. Used to give me cookies and treats after school. That's why I was there, to collect some promised shortbread after earning top marks in math that day," Byram went on, brushing his hair back with his fingers.

"You looked at me with your pretty blue eyes and asked me who I was and where I'd been. I scoffed, called you a pipsqueak cause your voice was so high, but I thought you were a fairy or some strange creature come to bewitch me. Then Cook came out and shooed me away from you. Said you were a princess, and I was just rabble, not to trifle with my betters. She tolerated our friendship only because I wouldn't go away. You asked me questions, so many questions, about school and what my life was like, and I told you, shared it all cause I thought you were sweet and special. I didn't know, didn't understand what your life was like until I was older."

Fuck. He had thought her spoiled at first. So pretty, but what did a princess know of struggle? She had a warm house, food, blood. Everything she needed. His life had been much different. Not worse or better, just different, but he would not know that until years later.

"We shared our first kiss in that garden. You were seventeen, and I was young and bristling with hormones. Damn, Pip, you were so beautiful. I could not believe you were letting me, a low ranking nobody, touch you like I had any right. I swore then to be better, to work hard to earn that right. I tried to keep us secret, but by the time I was sent away, the king, the guards, everyone knew. I loved you so much, Pip. From the very first," he murmured.

"I still do. I love you, Pip," his voice broke, but he continued. "I made a mistake back then, returning after a couple of years, only to leave without talking to you when I thought you were marrying another. I was stupid and hurt and didn't deserve you then. Now here I am, repeating the same mistakes. This time, I thought I was strong enough to keep you. When you didn't push me away, when you claimed me too, I thought I was finally the man you deserved. Then I let you down when you needed me. I was not strong enough to face the possibility of losing you after you told me you were pregnant, and I am so sorry. I should have been stronger. I will be, I swear it. I will do everything I can to lift you up, to make you safe, please Pip. Talk to me," he murmured.

Byram could not move. Could not breathe. He waited as the seconds ticked by for any sign she might have heard him. Fuck. It would be just his luck that his woman was not even listening. His woman. Was she still? He really fucking hoped so.

Suddenly, the door opened, and he fell back clumsily. Looking ten times the fool but fuck if he cared. Pip was there, and she was smiling through tears as she jumped on him.

"*Ooof*," he grunted, not expecting that, but once she tried to move off him, but Byram tightened his grip.

"Got you now, Pip. Not letting go this time."

"You better not," she growled, kissing him hard and sighing as she softened against him.

Moving them to sitting position, Byram crushed her to him, memorizing her flavors as he kissed, kissed, and kissed her some more. She was so warm, she sizzled in his arms. And as her body pressed against his, Byram felt the flutters in her stomach, soft as butterfly wings against his own. Huffing a laugh, he moved back an inch, hand going to the slight swell there, and Pip giggled, dropping her head to his shoulder as he felt the life they had created pulsing beneath his palm.

"He's strong," he murmured.

"He?" she asked, eyebrows raised and cheeky expression on her beautiful face. "I will have you know, I am expecting a girl with light brown hair like her father's," Pip said, and the vision her words created made his chest swell with pride.

"Boy, girl, doesn't matter. I love our babe, Pip. Just as I love its mother," he told her.

"You do?" she asked, closing her eyes against the pain he'd put in hers, he kissed her again, showing her without words that he meant it.

My sweet Pip. My love. My heart. My mate.

His love for her spanned lifetimes, traveled light years, and was big enough to encompass whole universes. She clung to him, so responsive, so open and trusting. He was the luckiest man in the world, and he would make damn sure his family survived the hardships to come. Whatever he had to do, he would.

For her, he would do it all. Anything and everything for her.

"I texted my father and Morris. They offered their

congratulations. I'm allowed to use the library, but I have to go tonight. And I have to go alone."

Byram tensed. He hated the idea of her going back there, to the place where she would have been broken, bound to some man she did not love against her wishes. Her father had let her go without a fight, and Byram had taken it for the gift it was. But he'd thought it was over. Thought she would never go back there again.

Something was wrong. Something broken in that Clan, and he sure as fuck was not letting her go alone. Kaelene might be a badass finding her own footing, but she was a mated badass.

"I'm going with you."

"You can't," she told him, pressing her body against his as they sat on the floor wrapped in each other's arms.

"Why? You carry my child, they know. Why am I denied entry?"

"For that very reason. Morris has advised against allowing you into my father's territory again. He has convinced him you intend to start a coup, using me to take his crown, to take his Clan."

"But I don't want his fucking crown, Kae. I have only ever wanted you. I am a sworn Guardian now. I will never go back to Clan life. Does he intend to try to seduce you into staying with riches and servants?" he snarled, fear creeping up his throat.

"You know me better than that, I hope."

"I do, Pip. You were never one for material things."

"I've missed you, Byram," she murmured, kissing him again.

"Me too," he murmured, pressing his forehead to hers, breathing in her honeysuckle scent.

"No one else knows me like you do. Even arguing, a week in the Keep has been amazing. I am freer here than I have ever been in my life."

"Mm," he replied, brushing her soft hair from her face. Fuck, she was beautiful So much it hurt to look away. "I won't risk you. I can't, Kae."

"The other night you were asking me what I wanted to be, and I've been thinking. It's strange because I don't want to be any one thing in particular. I am afraid you'll laugh," she whispered, and he grinned at her teasing smile.

"Tell me, Pip. Tell me what you want."

"I want to be yours,"

"You are."

"And I want to be a mother."

He cupped her face with one hand, laying the other gently on her belly.

"You will be."

"I want to be a friend to you, to everyone, to Fergie and Holley, Jessenia, Elena, and Margo, and all the Guardians here."

"You're my best friend, Pip. Didn't you know?" he whispered, kissing her head when she gasped, eyes wide with shock.

"I want to help the Guardians. I am no warrior, but if looking for information in my father's library is useful. If I can somehow bridge the gap in what the supernatural world knows about Vampires to keep magic safe for the future, for our babe, then I want to do that, Byram. Help me do that."

Byram expelled a breath harshly as warring factions inside him battled. He wanted her safe. He wanted their young safe. He wanted her heart to be happy. To feel full and whole as his did when he was with her. And when he was doing his job. Shit. Kaelene was sharing her dreams with him, and devoted fool that he was, Byram wanted to help her achieve them. Even if it meant taking a risk.

"Alright, Pip. I will help you get what you want."

Sweet, good mate.

Fifteen

The pine barrens looked ominous, with the full moon leering overhead. Because the Guardians could not come to terms with who would accompany the pregnant female Vampire, the women of the group had taken command.

Margo sat beside her in the back, while Fergie manned the wheel, with Elena in the passenger seat. Holley and Jessenia stayed behind to mind the children and keep the men from rushing in and messing this up.

Logan, Elena's mate, was the only one who seemed okay with his kickass mate going off to potential danger. Not that Kae could blame him. The Panther Shifter was a seasoned warrior, and Kaelene was truly grateful for her presence.

Her father's text said nothing about having anyone

else accompany her. It just said Byram was not permitted. So, reluctantly, she'd left her mate, the father of her unborn babe, at the Keep with his Alpha literally holding him back.

She had to admit, it was kind of sexy seeing him lose his control. He'd even apologized beforehand, explaining his primal instinct to keep her safe was bound to overwhelm him the second she took off. He'd been right, but even knowing it had not prepared her for the shock of seeing a two ton Dragon basically sitting on his chest to stop him from getting to her.

Chills raced up her spin as Fergie ignored the posted speed limits and drove the few hours it took to get to her father's territory. Once out of the car, the foursome of women knocked on the door. Marguerite answered, throwing herself at Kaelene in a flurry of tears and sniffles.

"Oh, you're not alone!" the female said and hiccupped at the last word. Kaelene giggled and covered her mouth before making the introductions.

"Your father said nothing about guests," she frowned. "But I guess it's okay. Come on, you know the way to the library," she gushed, linking her arm with Kaelene's.

"Of course, Margie, I grew up here after all."

"Silly me, yes," the younger women replied. "Oh,

Emil and I have upped the date of our claiming, but not because of anything like this. Imagine, you are expecting a babe and so soon. I admit it is astonishing," she said as she pulled open the doors and ushered them inside.

"Wow," Margo whispered, her bright eyes taking in the rows of ancient tomes.

"Fascinating," Elena agreed.

"That's a lotta fucking books, Kae. I didn't know Vamps were so geeky," Fergie said, crunching her nose up in typical Fergie-style, earning a chuckle from Kaelene.

"Will Father be joining us?" Kaelene asked, suddenly wanting to see her sire.

She did not like all the ways of the Clan, but supposed it was natural for her to seek his approval regarding her pregnancy. After all, it was a rare and joyous thing for her kind.

"I don't know," Margie replied with a half shrug. "Drinks?"

"Sure," Margo returned, and Elena nodded politely.

"Great. Be right back," Marguerite smiled sweetly before she left.

"Anyone else think that Vamp is a bit freaky?" Fergie mock-whispered, and Kaelene winced.

"We have really good hearing, Ferg," she told the she-Wolf, who made an *oopsie* face as she thumbed through some open books sitting on one of the long tables in the huge library.

"So, what are we looking for?"

"Well, first, let's grab some volumes tracing lineages from that shelf," Kaelene instructed, pointing to Elena, who moved swift as her Panther allowed to get the heavy tomes.

"Margo, remember the symbol that was repeated in the ritual from the crime scenes?"

"The one shaped like a sun with rays coming out of it?"

"Yes. There is an old leather-bound book I remembered from my youth bearing the same symbol. Father used to read it all the time," she murmured, repeating the same thing she'd told Kingston and Byram after seeing the photographs.

"I'm on it," Margo replied.

Kaelene watched her new friends as they searched the shelves, working to help her find some answers to help the Guardians find the answers they'd been searching for. Images from the crime scenes replayed in her head. The death toll was up to seven now, and with each ritualistic bloodletting, the perpetrators left clues, ancient runes from Vampire Clans long since forgotten.

Kaelene was no great reader of their histories, enjoying romantic fiction instead. But she'd been born and raised in this place, and she knew more than she'd realized. Standing at her father's desk, she looked through the papers and books that sat there, carefully lifting and replacing them as she searched for the sun rune.

"I'm back," Margie sang out, entering with a rolling cart that held tea, soda, pastries, and tiny little sandwiches.

Kaelene's stomach rumbled, and she grinned, rubbing her hungry little babe, lying snug and cozy in her womb. The rest of them reached the cart first, all but Fergie, who was sitting on the sofa with a book in hand.

"Here," Margie said, bringing the she-Wolf a drink.

Her smile was a little too bright, and the pitch in her voice too high. Kaelene sniffed the cucumber sandwich she held and almost retched all over the place.

"Fergie! Stop!" she cried out as, one after the other, her companions fell to the ground.

The sickeningly sweet fragrance of Rafflesia extract filled her nostrils and the resounding snarl of Fergie's Wolf echoed in the library before a pistol fired.

"Fergie!" Kaelene cried out, trying to get to her friend's side, but steel bands wrapped around her arms and the hiss of a Vampire breathed in her ear.

"You should have come alone, princess. But I suppose I should thank you for the gifts," Morris snarled before hitting her on the head.

Kaelene did not know how much time had passed, only that the dull ache in her head where Morris had hit her felt like it was already healing. About a half hour had passed since then, she guessed.

"Ah, she joins us. Fabulous," Marguerite said cheerfully.

The petite Vampire was skipping between the bodies of Kaelene's friends where they were spread out, forming a sort of circle of flesh. The women were bound and gagged, making Kaelene grateful for the evidence that they still lived.

Marguerite and Morris would not have bothered tying them up if they were dead. She closed her eyes and strained to listen. Finally, she heard the faint sounds of heartbeats, and almost cried out with relief.

"You know, you brought us some really nifty blood bags. Shifters give the best buzz after feeding, Kae. And once Morris here perfects his little mojo, we can right the balance of magic, and bring it over to our side where it belongs," Marguerite said, unwittingly enlightening Kaelene to the reason behind all this horror.

"You two are behind the bloodletting? What about Emil, Margie? I thought you loved him."

"Love is not a luxury a female Vampire can afford, Kae. You know that," the woman said, and for the first time she sounded real.

"You give too much away, Marguerite," Morris hissed angrily, stalking towards them before ripping Margie away from where she crouched beside Kaelene.

She watched in horror as her father's advisor back-handed Kaelene's former friend. Whatever she was, seeing her hurt was not something she relished in the least. Anger fueled her as she reared back and spat at the slimy male.

"You enjoy hitting women, don't you, Morris? Big bad Vampire, beating on someone smaller, weaker. You are no man."

"I am more man than that traitorous pig you shacked up with, *princess*."

"I'm not a princess anymore."

"That's right. You aren't. You royals have been the weak link in the Vampire species, bringing us down with your ridiculous socio-political pretenses. Don't you see? Posturing amongst ourselves, playing

Monopoly on Wall street, it is all beneath us! We are the top of the food chain—"

"You're mad!" Kaelene yelled. And she saw it then, the crazy gleam in his eyes as the creaking of a door opening sounded in the dungeon-like room he held them in.

"Morris, you have the sacrifices?" a strange man asked. With him was a pair of men with eerily glowing green eyes and vertical eyelids. Shifters, but nothing like she'd ever met.

"Yes. Princess Kaelene, meet the new leader of the Loyalist Union of Logic and Order. Gregarius, this is the princess of the Clan Withers."

"Your future bride, is it? You may keep her, Morris. Now for the ritual. Perhaps you are right, draining them together will work best. Begin," the seemingly human male ordered, and Morris' lips curled up in an evil grin that made her want to cower from his stare.

But Kaelene was different now. She was made of stronger stuff than that. Tremble as she might, she glared right back at that sonovabitch, grinning when his smile faltered.

"You have no idea what hell is coming for you. I would leave now, Morris, while you can."

"Shut up! Marguerite, light the flames. I will show you what I am capable of, *princess*," he sneered, and started chanting in an ancient tongue she did not understand.

It didn't matter. He was too late. Kaelene leaned her head back and prayed to the Crimson Veil like she never had before.

Byram. Love. Mate. I will wait for you. NO matter how long it takes to reach me in the beyond. I will wait. I promise.

———

*B*ack at the Keep

"Something is wrong. They are late," Egros muttered.

The Witch had been pacing up and down Kingston's office, wearing a pattern into the stone flooring with his incessant steps. Logan appeared worried, as did the rest of them.

"Have you tried texting her?" Byram asked.

"Yes. She isn't responding, and I've tracked her location, but it appears frozen a few hundred yards from the king's mansion."

"Wait. Can you track her movement over the last hour?"

"Of course," Logan chimed in, face paling as he tracked the girls' phones. He spun his laptop around, rubbing the hair on his head as he pointed out what they'd all missed.

"Look, they reached the mansion seventy-three minutes ago. Then, twenty minutes later, they leave, going somewhere here."

"But there is nothing there. It's all woods," Byram growled, his knowledge of the area totally unfuckinghelpful.

"Alright, so I can't pinpoint an exact location, but this is where they are. The last cell tower ping leads to here within two hundred yards," Logan said, pointing to a map on the screen.

"I can track them within two hundred yards, but we gotta get there, cump," Storm growled. Blue energy swirled around his body, the Wolf Shifter anxious to find his mate.

"Get in the car," Kingston ordered, and his eyes blazed white with his Dragon.

"Driving will take too long," Furio pointed out, rubbing Jessenia's shoulder when she whimpered.

"Find them, please," she pleaded.

"We will," Furio told her, offering comfort to his mate.

"We aren't driving, I'm flying us there," the Dragon said, his smile feral as he tugged on his shirt.

"Good. You fly, it will be faster if I blink—"

"Byram," Kingston said before the Vampire could move.

"Yes?"

"Be careful. We'll be right behind you."

"Yes, Alpha." Byram bowed, dropping his hands to his side, and rolling his shoulders.

He'd never been so open with his Vampiric talents before, but the time for secrets was over. He felt eyes on him, curious and awestruck, and he could not blame them. He was about to share a part of himself with his Guardians.

Like Demons, some Vampires were capable of tapping into the shadows, of conducting themselves like light waves through space and time. That kind of travel was not possible for Shifters or Witches, which was another reason he'd hidden it. Too many questions of *hows* and *whys* he did not know the answers to.

All Byram knew was it was a shortcut to get to his mate, and he was going to take it. He just needed an anchor. His family. His group. They were it. They were everything.

Byram exhaled a breath, focusing on his mate and the babe she carried. They needed him now. His family. His mate. Byram could feel it down to his bones. Cursing himself ten times a fool for letting her get in that car without him, Byram tried to quiet his mind to prepare himself for *blinking*.

It was not easy to tap into the dark and came with great risks. Some got lost in the shadows, but Byram had a reason to stay true to his path. Two reasons.

Whatever sinister plots her father had been dealing in the dark, Byram was not about to let the man bargain his only daughter for the sake of his own greed.

Kaelene did not belong to the Clan Withers anymore. She belonged to Byram, and he to her. He only hoped he was in time. He cried out as pain lashed through his frame. Byram reached out, shocked when he saw the entire world painted red.

Seeing in black and white was one thing, but he was seeing in shades of crimson. His heart was pounding, power and energy seemed to build from within, he tossed back his head, feeling his hunger rise as he bellowed a roar unlike any other. Then he was moving, zipping through space faster than the speed of light with shades of red zooming past his eyes.

Hold on, Pip. I am coming for you.

Sixteen

The room exploded, and Byram's vision darkened around the edges. He saw figures, two of them were Shifters, another two were Vampires. All wore ridiculous red robes, though whether that was the actual color or his new *red murder vision*, he couldn't tell.

"Byram!" Kaelene cried out and struggled against the bonds that held her.

Fury engulfed him, and he loosed a roar that shook the fucking rafters. Whatever this dungeon was, he hoped Kingston was close and heard the sound of his battle cry as the robed men charged him.

These assholes did not know what he was capable of, though the two Vampires might, seeing as how they were the same. Only, those fuckers did not have

Byram's new mate magic enhanced vision. It was like he could tell where to land his deathblows with just a glance.

Fuck yes.

Fast as lightning, he plowed through one Vampire and was fighting the other when the Shifters attacked from behind. Kaelene had her hands free and was working on her legs when a crash sounded and more assholes came barreling in.

"Are you alright?" he cried out over the sounds of battle.

"Yes. Where's Storm? They shot Fergie," she yelled, right before a blast of Dragon's flame took down the door and his group of Guardians came crashing in.

Storm howled his rage, tearing enemies limb from limb until he reached his unconscious mate. Kingston was behind him as more enemies poured in.

"Fuck. Who are they?" he asked as he finally got to her, using his teeth, claws, and brute strength to free her from the bonds wrapped tight around her body.

"It's Morris! He's in league with the Loyalists. They are draining Shifters to try to harness the magic that makes them supernaturals."

"What? Impossible," he growled and helped her stand, ducking a blast of flame that flew from Kingston's maw.

"They have the ritual wrong. I was listening when Morris recited the words. It's not a bloodletting to transfer magic. The sun symbol stands for rebirth, Byram. This ritual was to allow an exchange of blood magic without the draining, I think it was used for pregnant females. We have to find that book," she told him, searching the ground for Morris' book.

Byram nodded, turning he fought two massive Shifters trying to tackle them to the ground. He didn't know where they had come from, but his *red murder vision* was back, and the startled hiss from Kaelene's lips meant she saw it, too.

"Byram, what is all the red smoke surrounding us? Your eyes! The whites are gone. They're all red," she shrieked, startled, but the smoke was good. It was sheltering her from the enemy.

"Trust me, Pip. This is good. I can protect us all now."

"Byram!" Kingston roared, the great beast morphed back into his human shape.

"Do you have everyone?"

"Yes, all but you and Kaelene," he bellowed.

"I am sending her now. Leave the second you have them. I won't be able to stop what's coming," he growled, his Fangs descending twice their normal length.

"I won't leave you," she said, clutching at his arms, but Byram needed her safe before he could put a stop to all this.

"You will be right outside, Pip. Go with Kingston. I must finish this, then I will come for you. I promise."

She straightened her shoulders, meeting his gaze and gifted him with the best damn reply he ever heard.

"Your babe and I will be waiting, By. I love you."

"I won't be long."

He watched her leave, safe in Furio's steed's flames as the enemy charged and attacked. Kingston roared, and that was his signal he had her with him. Good. Byram turned to see Morris standing at a makeshift altar.

"You stole my sacrifices. But it's not too late, there are plenty here," he hissed.

"What are you talking about, Morris? This isn't the deal!" an angry man shouted.

Byram's crimson vision was even better than his usual keen eyesight. He recognized Gregarius, new leader of the Loyalist Union of Logic and Order. Those fuckers had been trying to upset the balance of magic for way too long to be healthy for anyone.

"Strap them down," Morris ordered, and a group of Vampires grabbed the nearest Shifters, Loyalists who were now battling their supposed allies.

"You will pay, Morris," Gregarius yelled as his minions dragged him from the dungeon. Byram sincerely hoped Kingston was there to meet that sonovabitch with his beast's flame.

"The royalty has weakened us. Weaklings like your slut princess. I will make Vampires top of the food chain where we belong. Humans are naught but cattle, Shifters animals to satisfy our hunger. Once we learn the key to draining Shifters dry of their magic, we will have the upper hand. We will be back where we belong, Byram!"

"You're crazy, Morris. Give up now and I won't have to kill you."

"You can't kill me! I am the master here! You, a low ranking Vampire, can be more under my rule. Join me, Byram. Help me harness magic for the betterment of our kind," Morris shouted, arms raised, his eyes bright with madness.

"The only way you can better Vampire-kind is to die, Morris," Byram said from right behind the smaller male.

The former king's advisor had not even seen Byram move. Blinking through the shadows encased in *crimson fury*, that was what he decided to call his magical mating boon, Byram was the perfect assassin. He moved through the enemy like water through stone. He was everywhere at once, snapping necks and ripping out spines.

Morris was more than just a traitor and a murderer, he was a zealot. Crazed, irrational, and unredeemable. Ending him was the only way to ensure Kaelene's safety, and that only made Byram's job easier.

Minutes later, he walked outside, covered in blood, but uncaring of his appearance. He needed to find her. Where was she? Searching the crowd of Guardians, he saw Storm wrapping his mate's wounded thigh where she'd apparently been shot.

Fergie was sitting up and spitting mad, which was good news for her recovery. Furio had a couple of surviving enemies in cuffs, and Logan was checking Elena over for injury. The human was a genius and a doctor, to boot. He could care for the scratches and bruises already healing on Elena's arms.

Kingston was on the phone, from the angry glare in his eyes, it was the Assembly, and not his mate, on the other line. King Aethelred was standing beside him, a look of pinched sadness on his face. He smelled off. Sick? Maybe. At least he was not a traitor to all of magic, like his former advisor.

Thinking of Morris made Byram want to kill him all over again for endangering not only the entire fucking world, but Kaelene and his babe. Selfish? Maybe. But Byram could not help it. Protective instincts running rampant, he gave the older Vampire the once over. Deciding he was okay, Byram dismissed him.

Aethelred was no longer Byram's king. But he had to wonder if he too had been given the Rafflesia poison, same as the women had. The corpse flower extract induced a zombie like state that made the victim unable to move or fight back, though on some level, they were fully aware of what was happening. In other words, Morris' victims were conscious when he started draining them.

Piece. Of. Shit.

Kingston roared into the phone, and Byram felt for him. Dealing with those pencil pushers sucked balls after a battle. But Byram gave zero fucks about any of it. He needed his mate in his arms like ten minutes ago.

He blinked and his *red murder vision* was back, puffs of smoke sparked and swirled around him. Then he heard her voice, and the clouds disappeared.

"Byram! BYRAM!" Kaelene turned and vaulted over the fallen tree she'd been sitting on and charged him like the little hellion she was.

"I came for you. I told you, I would," he murmured.

"I waited. I know. I waited for you, and you came back to us," she replied, crying into his neck, and squeezing him so hard he laughed and spun her around.

"Don't do that again. Don't go off alone without me. I couldn't bear it," he said, holding her tight and crying unashamedly with the relief and joy of having her safe in his arms.

"I won't. Need you, mate."

"Need you too. I love you, Pip."

Then she smiled at him, and all the noise and the smoke, and the badness of the last few hours, all went away. Kaelene was in his arms, smiling up at him, and Byram was finally whole again.

"I love you too," she whispered, and crashed her lips to his.

SEVENTEEN

Kaelene's mouth opened in a soft moan as she stood under one of the four shower jets in hers and Byram's lair. The keep sure knew how to make a girl feel at home.

Her mate growled softly, kissing her shoulder as he massaged shampoo onto her head, washing the ugliness of the last few hours from her skin. His touch was gentle and unhurried, even though she felt the hard evidence of his arousal bumping against her back.

Her mate was blessed with a perfect physique. One she was insanely grateful for. Wide shoulders, narrow hips, flat stomach curved with muscles that roped across his abs, chest, arms, and lower still to his glutes and thighs. Damn, she loved his thighs. Was becoming quite obsessed with them, actually.

She leaned back into him when he was done rinsing and gripped her favorite muscles, loving the sexy growl that reverberated from his chest through to her back.

"Mine," he whispered, moving her hair to one shoulder, leaving the other bare for biting licks and kisses.

"Byram," she whimpered as his large hands encompassed her breasts, squeezing, molding, then pinching the tips gently.

He knew exactly how to work a female, get her all riled up. And damn, she did not want to think about how he got so good at this, but maybe some part of her was grateful.

"Hey, stay with me, Pip. It's me and you," he whispered, reading her thoughts again.

His teeth nipped her neck over the scar of the claiming bite he'd given her, and Kaelene rocked back against his erection. He was so big, so hard for her, and she could not wait until he was buried deep, making her feel things she'd only ever imagined.

Byram growled, turning her around and claiming her lips in a hard, yet tender kiss that stole her breath. Water sprayed them, but she didn't feel it. Nothing else existed in that moment. There was only Kaelene and Byram. Only their kiss, their embrace, and nothing else in the whole universe.

He slowed the passionate thrusting of his tongue, sipping from her mouth as if she were fine wine, and her heart nearly beat her to death. Byram had this way of making her feel special, like she was the only woman in the world, and she never wanted that feeling to end.

"Mine, Pip. No getting rid of me now, eh? You are finally mine," he murmured, and emotion nearly choked her.

He kissed her lips with a loud smack, grinning against her as he tugged her close, lifted her up in his arms, and stepped out of the shower. Kaelene clung to him, squealing like a lunatic. Damn, she loved this man. Even as he spun her around, making her dizzy and getting water everywhere, she loved him.

"You're crazy," she said, giggling and biting her lips as he placed her gently on the bed.

"Crazy for you," he growled, kissing the top of her foot, next her calf, then her knee.

"Fergie would call that line corny," she told him, squinting her eyes as she leaned up on her elbows, watching his powerful body as he climbed over hers, dropping nips, licks, and playful kisses as he went.

He hovered with his face over her belly, skipping the dark blonde curls of her sex, making her pout at first. Then she watched his lips tremble as he lowered his head, placing a reverent kiss on the place where their child grew, safe and sound, and Kaelene's heart exploded with love for him.

Byram's gaze flashed to her, and the tears in them had her gasping. He looked so damn beautiful, gazing at her adoringly like she hung the moon, devotion written across his face like a neon sign.

"You have given me everything, Pip. I promise to be worthy."

She cupped his cheeks and pulled him to her, claiming his lips with her own.

"You were always worthy, Byram. You're the other half of my heart, my soul. I can't breathe without you, By."

"Breathe me, Pip. Breathe me," he growled, claiming her lips with ardent passion renewed.

After fighting, Vampires usually got carried away with bloodlust, but Byram did not seem hungry. Sure, the thirst was part of him, as it was her, but as he made love to her, Byram did not give into the baser instincts. Almost as if his bond with her and her pregnancy was stopping his need for blood.

Kaelene's chest rose and fell with emotion. Could this man be any more perfect? Considerate, caring, strong, funny, and hers. All hers. Sure, he had this scary new red murder vision, but he was gentle with her.

Powerful. Sexy. Badass. Mine.

Kaelene had been raised to be submissive to a male's dominance, but Byram was a true dominant male. He did not need her to be submissive. A fact she proved by biting his lip and rolling them over until she was straddling his hips.

She loved being on top, and Byram loved letting her take the reins of their desire. Kaelene kissed him hard, licking a trail from his mouth to his ear, down his neck to his flat male nipple. She sucked on it hard, nipping it slightly and loving the way he bucked his hips beneath her, searching for her core. But not yet. Not till she was ready.

"Woman, you are making me crazy," he growled.

Kaelene loved this part. Loved teasing him into a frenzy, His body was incredible, and she wanted to memorize every inch. Byram seemed to like it as well if the way he squeezed her ass with every slip and slide of her slick pussy along the hard length of his cock was anything to go by.

Byram growled, allowing her to play, to find her rhythm, coaxing her mouth back to his. She moaned around his tongue, fascinated by the dexterity of that clever little appendage. She opened her eyes to find his blazing green, pupils narrowed as she rocked against him.

He was moving in earnest now, cock sliding ever so perfectly, hitting her clit with every move.

"Want to be inside you, Pip," he murmured, holding her neck as he kissed her mouth, panting, desperation in his glittery green gaze.

Fuck. He was so hot. And she wanted him inside her, too. Nodding her head, she angled her hips, and with a single thrust, he penetrated. Their moan echoed in the bedroom as shockwaves of pleasure sent her careening towards orgasm with just a few thrusts of her lover's body.

Kaelene was breathing like a marathon runner. Byram was no better. He held her tight, flipping her onto her back so he could get a better angle, and fuck, now she was coming. Byram growled, slamming his hips with sharp, powerful thrusts, hitting her secret spot with every move.

Sexy fierce Vampire.

Kaelene was flying then. Flying. Soaring. Skyrocketing. Shit, where was it? There! She almost had it.

So close. Close. Closer...

"Oh Gods, Byram! I'm coming," she cried out.

She was scratching his hips, embedding her nails into his flesh and he arched his back, roaring as warmth filled her—so much warmth, he emptied himself until it spilled down her thighs.

"You okay?" he asked, concerned as he lifted his body slightly, but Kaelene was having none of that.

She wrapped her legs around his waist, pulling him close, and hugged him to her body. Aftershocks trembled through her, and Byram seemed to understand. He felt them too, she could tell by the tiny shivers racing up his spine.

"Love you, Kae," he whispered, kissing her head, and her neck, her cheek, anywhere he could reach.

"Me too. I'm glad I waited," she confessed.

"You never have to wait for me again, Pip. I'm never leaving you," he said, and the smile he gifted her then felt like home.

"We're gonna be okay," she told him sternly and she meant it.

The road ahead was going to be rough, but they could make it. Together, they could do anything.

"Yours," he said, lifting up, and placing one of her hands over his heart.

"Mine," he continued, placing one of his hands over hers. Then, Byram took their remaining hands and placed them over her belly, bringing tears to her eyes as he whispered reverently.

"Ours. This is ours, Pip. And no one will ever take this away from us."

Kaelene nodded. She believed him and repeated his words back to Byram. Their matebond pulsed to life in the darkness of the room, and her mate's smoky red magic encircled them as they embraced in their lair, holding onto each other while Kaelene and Byram's child grew beneath her heart.

"Yours. Mine. Ours."

Epilogue

"So, you want one of us to let you drain our blood?" Furio asked, scratching his head.

Byram closed his eyes and sighed heavily. He'd been trying to explain the ritual he and Kaelene had translated from the book they'd recovered after the battle with Morris. Unfortunately, the Stallion Shifter had only been half listening.

"No, of course not," he growled, his patience wearing thin.

"Geez, Fur," Fergie addressed him, shaking her head. "Does your ass get jealous of all the shit that comes out of your mouth?"

"OMG! FERGIE! Not nice," Jessenia scolded her best friend, whipping her on the ass with a kitchen rag.

Byram's eyes flashed apologetically to Kaelene,

who was watching the byplay and trying not to giggle. She was failing, and the little snort that escaped her nose made Byram chuckle as well.

"Don't laugh at that. The sound was awful," she told him, but it was too late. He was laughing and walking over to nuzzle her neck, and she let him—wonderful, beautiful creature that she was.

Pip was ever ready for affection, and the more swollen she grew with their babe, the more she seemed to crave cuddles and kisses. That was fine with him.

"Ew. You guys are gross," Margo said, tossing a popcorn kernel at them, while cradling her own stomach.

The former DPCA agent was expecting her first child with Egros in another six months, but judging from her size, Byram highly suspected multiples. Not that he was stupid enough to say it.

"*Oh puhleeze*! Like it's not gross watching my sister make out with that guy all the time," Logan chimed in, hiding behind Elena when it looked like his sister was about to kick his ass.

Byram shrugged and scratched his head as he watched the insanity unfolding before them. The lights dimmed, then flared back to life when Egros almost accidentally tipped over a vase from the corner table.

"Sorry, Keep," the Witch yelled to the manetuwak who watched over them.

Fergie had been the first to talk to the manse, though Holley had been the one who'd identified the magic that seemed to run the place. It came from spirits inhabiting the dwelling. They were caretakers of those within and that was them, the Guardians of Chaos and their *conpars*. Anyway, now, she had them all talking out loud to the Keep, but in all honesty, the manetuwak seemed to like it.

The fact was, his fellow Guardians were a bunch of fucking nut jobs, and he'd brought his one true love, the fucking princess of his former Clan, there to live. He supposed that made him a nut job, too.

Sigh.

His kid was so lucky to have her as a mother. His gaze raked over her, concerned at her pallor. They were seven weeks away from the birthing, and she was growing weaker since she could not feed while pregnant.

"Am I late for the meeting?" Kingston asked, looking haggard.

"You're the Alpha," Fergie said with a duh expression on her face. "We can't have a meeting without you, so no, you aren't late. We're all just really dang early."

"Uh," he grunted, his expression uncertain.

"Come sit," Holley told her mate, eyes shining with laughter for him.

The Dragon scared the hell out of most everyone there, but Byram had only ever kept a deep respect for the man. Kingston was a good leader, a good friend, and if Kaelene's translations were correct, he might be the key to helping countless Vampires conceive.

"As you all know, Kaelene and I recovered the ancient Vampire tome Morris had been using to siphon blood from unwilling Shifters in his plan to make Vampires top of the food chain, ridiculous notion—anyway," Byram said, clearing his throat. "We think we have discovered something important."

"A gross mistranslation, actually," Kaelene informed the room. "You see, he thought this rune was the ancient sun symbol, meaning rebirth. But it isn't. It is missing a line that he added every time he performed the ritual," she explained, pausing to catch her breath.

"Are you alright?"

"Yes," she told him, turning to gift him a smile before continuing. "Morris further corrupted it by trying to use it to take magic from Shifters and give it to the Vampires, like the rebirth of a species, but that is not what this ritual is for. Thousands of years ago, there were treaties and truces between Vampires and other supernaturals."

Byram picked up his tablet and clicked a few buttons.

"Please check out the message I just sent you all. It will show you what Kaelene is talking about."

The Guardians and mates nodded, and some murmured responses, but all had the message opened and were perusing the evidence of what they'd found.

"As you can see, the runes are similar, but it isn't the sun rune as Morris thought. It is the rune that symbolizes actual birth. This ritual is not for bloodletting and stealing magic. It is to provide nourishment to pregnant Vampires from their mates alone with the help of a willing participant, usually a Shifter. There is no actual blood exchange. That's why he failed so epically. This has nothing to do with transferring power. It's a sharing of energy and sustenance without the bite."

"That's incredible," Kingston spoke first.

"Yes. And if it works, it could help all of Vampire kind. We would need to test it, though."

"And you want one of us to volunteer," Kingston murmured, reading Kaelene and Byram's matching hopeful expressions.

"Alpha, I know it is a big ask, but I have been

conferring with Egros and Logan. They do not foresee any harm coming to any of the parties, should you agree, that is," he whispered.

"Are you asking me to help you, Vampire?"

"I am, Dragon," Byram replied with a smirk, taking his alpha's outstretched hand and shaking it heartily.

"Wait a second, why does he get to help? I wanted to help," Furio grumbled.

"OMG! Are you serious? You know, sometimes I think you just need a high five. In the face. With that chair," the she-Wolf snarked.

"Fergie, that is enough picking on my mate," Jessenia growled at her bestie. "No crème brulee for you after dinner!"

"Wait, who said anything about not getting dessert? Jess? JESS! I was just kidding. Come on," Fergie yelled, chasing after her in a pair of lime green stilettos Byram could not even contemplate walking in.

"Sorry about the interruption, cump. Good luck, Kae, Byram. Better go chase my mate. She's crazy, but she's mine," Storm said, running off to catch up with his redheaded female.

"Okay, um, so what do we do?" Kingston asked.

"Please, sit down in this chair," Kaelene whispered, and she seemed to slouch a moment before rallying and gifting Byram with a smile. "You sit on his other side, By. Logan? Egros? Your turns."

"Alright," Logan jogged over and picked up what looked like a tube of lipstick.

Byram frowned. He had not been too involved with the ritual part of it. That was all Kaelene. Egros stood behind her and whispered that same ancient tongue Morris had, but his words were not heated and vile like the dead Vampire's words were.

Logan scribbled runes on Kingston's face, muttering an apology when the Alpha snarled as he touched the lipstick tube to his skin. Byram would have laughed if his entire life was not hanging in the balance. The male moved to Kaelene next and Byram last, drawing runes on his flesh with the red lipstick.

"Red is the color of blood, so this should work even better as a conduit than ash or mud. I'm going to light the candles now, and I need you all to just clear your minds as Egros chants louder. It shouldn't hurt. Probably," he said, yelping and stepping back when Byram snarled.

"Shh," Kaelene commanded, and good mate that he was, he obeyed.

Egros' voice grew louder and smoke from the candles filled the room. Wait, not the candles, it was him. The smoke came from Byram, and when he opened his eyes, his vision was stained red. Panic threatened to overwhelm him, but Kaelene was in it now. Her eyes were closed, and she was concentrating on something, and when he looked to Kingston, the big Dragon's eyes were closed tight as well.

Shit. Was he fucking this up? No. He couldn't. He wouldn't. Wind whipped at his face, flattening his hair as an immeasurable tide of magic seemed to surge. Egros' voice remained steady, and he moved among them, touching his hand to each of their heads.

The hunger that had been his constant companion since Kaelene had announced her pregnancy flared and surged, making him roar at the pain of it. Fuck. He did not think he could live with this deep, unabating thirst plaguing his being. But then Kaelene's scream reached him and Byram was beside himself.

Whatever he felt, she was feeling it, too. Worse, it would seem, and he had to remain strong. One moment more, that was all. He could feel her wavering, but she hung on. So brave, so strong.

Almost finished, Pip.

As if she heard him, her blue eyes opened, catching his gaze and burning into him like blue fire. The room seemed to spin, the thirst burning through him, then time—*or the world*—seemed to just stop.

The first thing he felt was the blissful contentment

of satisfaction, the same as if he'd just had Kaelene's vein. Panting, his gaze met hers, and he could tell from the healthy glow in her cheeks, she was feeling the same.

"Pip? You alright?" he asked, flitting over to her, and running his hands over her face, shoulders, arms—everywhere he could touch.

"Yes. Better than alright. Kingston?"

"I am good, but I have a sudden craving for steak," the Dragon replied. Everyone laughed, and Holley called out that she was going to get the grill fired up. Ribeyes for all. Kingston stood up, a little shaky at first, then slapped Byram on the back and bowed to Kaelene before joining his mate outside. He'd looked a little pale, but he was smiling, and that was a good sign.

"It worked, didn't it?" she whispered, tears pooling in her eyes.

"I think so, Pip. Come, let me see you," he murmured and helped her stand.

The last few weeks, she'd been a bit slower, a bit weaker, but right then, she seemed the epitome of health. She placed her hand on her belly, smiling through tears as he gathered her up close to his heart.

"We are going to be okay, Pip. I swear it. I love you so much."

"I love you too. Thank you, Byram. You have given

me everything. A babe, a family, you. You are my whole heart," she murmured, and she was kissing him now, and fuck, Byram had never been so happy.

The tackle hug that came from his left surprised the fuck out of him, but when he saw fiery red hair, he knew the identity of their attacker, and his protective instincts died. More arms followed, and soon he and Kaelene were being crushed by the Guardians.

"Aww! Group hug!" Fergie shouted.

"No. This is not okay," Kingston muttered, but Holley was dragging in him, and the Dragon allowed it.

"Just deal with it," the clever Witch told him.

"Guys, you are crushing us," Byram said, careful to shield her, and their young, from the weight of the insanely huge group hug Fergie had started.

Kaelene had been startled, but now she was grinning like mad, which made his heart sing. Yes, they were lunatics, but she fit right in.

Thank fuck.

"It's okay, By. Just a few more seconds," she whispered, and nuzzled his cheek.

The Guardians of Chaos were so much more to Byram than an elite group of warriors, fighting to keep magic free.

They were a Clan, a family—his family.

This battle was over, and they had won, but it would not be the last. And though the gap between supernaturals was wide, he planned to do his part to bring Vampire culture into the fold for the betterment of all. His old Clan had called him traitor, but he was not that. He was a pioneer. He and his sweet, brave Pip were going to build a life outside of the shadows and the heavy domineering laws that still governed the Clans.

They were going to be okay. More than that. They were going to learn and grow more each day, building their family with the solid foundations of love, kinship, and unwavering loyalty.

"Ready for game night?" Fergie asked before breaking the hug.

"We playing Xbox or that stupid trivia game?" Furio asked.

"We use the Xbox for the trivia game, dufus," Fergie snapped.

"What did I say? You keep snarking my man and no dessert!" Jessenia yelled as they disengaged from the hug and raced for the half dozen or so gaming controllers currently sitting in the huge living room.

"Want to play?" Byram asked.

"Only if I can have the red controller," Kaelene replied, and good mate that he was, he ran to snatch it out from the basket Fergie was currently holding over her head to keep from the griping hands of the others.

The scent of grilled steaks filled the house as Kingston set a platter of steak sandwiches on the coffee table. Laughter spilled from the open door and windows of the Keep, echoing throughout the pine barrens as the Guardians let loose with good food, fun games, and each other.

Magic was free. The bad guys had been stopped. The Guardians, their conpars, and their young, were all nestled in safe and tight, just enjoying being with one another, and all was good with the world...

The end...for now.

Thank you so much for reading the last Guardians story! Need to catch up on the rest? Grab them ALL today right HERE.

Happy Reading!

Reading on a Budget?

Hello Readers!

I am so excited to be able to offer you exclusive bundles available only on CDGORRI.COM for readers using my BUY DIRECT option.

Right now, I have several bundles available at a whopping 30% off the listed prices and there are several series bundles to choose from.

Orders will be delivered via BookFunnel email. Just download to your favorite app and READ!

Thank you for buying direct. Have an awesome day!

xoxo,

C.D. Gorri

Join the Pack!

Looking for a Paranormal Romance series that is loads of growly fun?

Welcome to the Macconwood Pack!

These stories are split into two series, the Macconwood Pack Novels Series, and the Macconwood Pack Tales. Each story features one or more Pack members their journey to their one true and fated mate. They can be read alone, though they are better read in order, as characters may show up in each other's stories.

Pack is family for the Macconwood wolves, and when you read their tales, you become family too. What are you waiting for?

Join the Pack today!

https://www.cdgorri.com/series/the-macconwood-
pack-novel-series/

No cliffhangers. Steamy PNR fun.
Go and read your next happily ever after today!

BEWARE... HERE BE DRAGONS!

The Falk Clan Tales began as my stories surrounding four dragon Brothers and how they find their one true mates, but when a long lost brother arrives on the scene, followed by a few more Shifters...what can I say? The more the merrier!

Each Dragon's chest is marked with his rose, the magical link to his heart and his magic. They each have a matching gemstone to go with it.

She's given up on love. But he's just begun.

In The Dragon's Valentine we meet the eldest Falk brother, Callius. He is on a mission to find a Castle and his one true mate, one he can trust with his diamond rose....

His heart is frozen. Can she change his mind about love?

In The Dragon's Christmas Gift our attention shifts to Alexsander, the youngest brother of the four. He has resigned himself to a life alone, until he meets *her*.

Some wounds run deep. Can a Dragon's heart be unbroken?

The Dragon's Heart is the story of Edric Falk who has vowed never to love again, but that changes when he meets his feisty mate, Joselyn Curacao.

She just wants a little fun. He's looking for a lifetime.

We finally meet Nikolai Falk and his sexy Shifter mate in The Dragon's Secret.

She doesn't believe in fairytales, until a Dragon comes knocking on her door.

Meet Castor Falk, the long lost brother of our original four Dragons, and his sassy mate Josette. The Dragon's Treasure is full of adventure and laughs.

Nothing can surprise this six hundred-year-old Dragon, except maybe her.

Devine Graystone meets his match in Sunny Daye, an irrepressible Wolf Shifter with a heart of gold. Read their story in The Dragon's Surprise.

He's a hardcore realist until she dares him to dream.

Nicholas Gravestone doesn't know what to think when he spies Minerva Lykos on the property his Dragon covets. Can this unlikely pair come to a truce? Find out in The Dragon's Dream.

Thanks for reading.

xoxo,

C.D. Gorri

*Dragon Mates & Dragon Mates 2 boxed sets are now available in hardcover, paperback, and ebook.

EXCERPT FROM MARKED BY THE DEVIL

S nap! Flash! Snap! Bang!

"Over here! The Dark Prince is by the window!"

Click! Bang! Snap!

"Oh, for fuck's sake," Avail growled. He could feel that secret part of him pushing to be released. Power pulsed through his veins, his beast demanding to be set free, but he fought the temptation.

Snap! Flash! The horde of paparazzi swarmed outside the entrance to the Leeds Foundation, snapping pictures and banging on the polished reinforced glass doors in hopes of catching a glimpse of him—*like he was their prey.*

If they only knew.

He growled aloud, eyes flashing at the throng below. The man they hunted was not the useless, spoiled playboy they took him for.

Avail Leeds was something more. A predator. Not like those uncouth vultures circling with their cameras and cheap shots.

He was the real thing. A creature humankind built into legend with stories of midnight encounters. He snorted a harsh laugh.

If only I could show them. Grrrr.

They'd been there since daybreak hoping to get a statement or a picture of him, but Avail had managed to dodge them. He was no stranger to this kind of game.

Unfortunately for me. Sigh.

They'd dubbed him the "Naughty Dark Prince" years ago, recording his exploits and reporting them with more than a touch of exaggeration, as a constant source of entertainment for *normals* the world over.

As heir to the Leeds fortune, Avail had been in the spotlight since birth. Especially after his parent's tragic death when he was an infant.

His grandparents had brought him up with the finest education and surroundings a boy could have.

So, yes, he was known to indulge in a bit of luxury

and sport in between his family's foundation and other philanthropic works.

The Leeds family was enormously wealthy. The money had come to the family at first from the land itself. Natural resources like coal and oil had started the family's legacy.

Later on, they'd dabbled in manufacturing, then real estate and development. Now the family was known for their charity.

Avail himself had increased their holdings by playing the stock market and investing in several internet start-ups. He certainly had a marvelous head for figures. The mathematical and the female kind.

He gritted his teeth at the reminder. The latter had, once again, caused him this current headache. Women would surely be the death of him, or so his grandmother promised. Often.

Oh dear. Grandmother is certain to be angry this time.

"Denise!" Avail groaned his secretary's name as he looked out his office window.

So many of them are here this time. Ugh. He slumped back in his Perigold executive chair. The exotic French walnut was highly polished and smelled of lemons. The seat was made from the leather of a sixteen-point stag that his great-grandfather had taken down himself. He remembered that day.

Hunting with Grandfather was often the best time of his life. After all, he'd taught Avail everything he knew about controlling his inner demons, so to speak. He sure missed the old man.

His darling grandmother ordered the leather made from the buck's skin to be turned into this bit of posh office furniture for Avail when he took over as president of the Leeds Foundation. Conditioned with only the best mixtures of Mink and Neatsfoot oils, the chair was fucking amazing, if he did say so himself. Soft and strong, perfect for his six-foot four-inch, two-hundred and forty-pound frame.

He was certainly grateful for it as he slunk down into the buttery depths and cradled his head in his hands. It was only seven o'clock in the morning. How did those vultures find him so quickly?

"What have you done now?" *Why does her voice have to reach that pitch?* He cringed.

"Just the usual, Denise," he answered with a grin.

His silk shirt of the night before hung open revealing a large expanse of his muscled chest, evenly covered in a dusting of black hair.

It matched the midnight dark strands atop his

head that earned him the hated moniker *"Naughty Dark Prince"*.

Of course, if he'd bothered to stay out of the public eye the name would probably be forgotten. *Fat chance.* Avail couldn't help himself. He simply loved life, women, and parties. Usually, in that order.

He didn't bother to button his shirt or his pants as Denise stomped across the floor in those ridiculous heels she wore.

The older woman had seen him in far worse shape. He could use a shower and shave, ooh, and some breakfast.

A bloody steak and half a dozen eggs should do it, but even as he thought it his stomach revolted. *Ugh. See what happens when we mix whiskey and magic!* His Devil growled inside of him and Avail groaned aloud. The magic had been a bit much, but the little Witch deserved it. Taunting him for not being interested in her obvious wiles.

The glare coming from Denise had him refocusing his attention on the motherly woman. *Ouch.* She could singe toast with that look! *So loving,* he thought. His secretary of seven years cared about him. That was nice.

"Well, Denise, I suppose you want to know what happened."

"Oh, a night of wining and dining the little trust fund baby? What's to know? Did *little pookie* not like getting kicked out of bed at 3AM?"

Denise Reynolds stood over Avail with a large, steaming mug of his favorite French roast, served black, in one hand. In the other was a large cup of tomato juice and six aspirin. Otherwise, he might have growled at her insolence. *As if.* He loved the crotchety older woman.

Her white hair was sprayed straight up like spindles guarding a castle. The sight was a bit harsh on his poor bloodshot eyes.

Yes, he'd had far too good a time last night, but it wasn't with *little pookie* as much as it was with the whiskey he'd imbibed.

And the magic he'd wielded.

It was nearing the last quarter moon and Avail's beastie had been up for some good old-fashioned debauchery. As was the little Witch he'd brought along for the ride.

Bambi was a trust fund baby and a Witch. He'd met her at *The Thirsty Dog* where he'd gone to partake in some booze and dancing, perhaps a little nookie with a stranger.

He thought he'd found the perfect partner for the evening in the wicked Bambi. The woman had been down for just about anything. Including skinny dipping in the frigid Blue Hole which was just a few miles from his home.

He'd used a few tricks with some ancient runes and conjured a little light show while they swam. He'd even allowed his Devil to play a little bit as well. Hoping for a little suck and blow afterwards.

Not the card game.

And then it had all gone wrong. Bambi had wanted promises with her sex. That was a serious no in his book. Then the taunting came and out she went.

Like a light.

"Well?"

"Oh Denise, what can I say? She wanted more than an evening's entertainment. I simply didn't see us headed that way."

"Well, normally I'd say the girl had standards, but uh, I don't think so."

He stretched as he swallowed his aspirin and downed the tomato juice. Avail held his hot coffee carefully. Denise had a sadistic side and he'd caught her trying to burn his Devil once or twice over the years.

"Humph. How is *that* too hot for you?" She rolled her eyes and gathered the empty glass as he continued to wait for his coffee to cool down.

"I told you before, I'm not that kind of Devil,

Denise," he murmured and sipped the brew as it reached the perfect temperature.

Heaven.

He continued to sip with his eyes closed ignoring everything but the smooth warm liquid as it slid down his throat.

"Really, Avail? You took *that* silicone doll to the Blue Hole! Your grandmother is going to be furious with you."

"Yes, yes, I know. Wait, how did you know?" He frowned.

The swimming spot had been shunned by locals for decades, but the Leeds family still enjoyed the crystal-clear waters.

They were fed by an underground glacier though some still claim to be baffled by its existence. *Whatever.*

Still, he knew better than to take a normal to one of his family's private haunts. He also knew better than to use magic in front of anyone. But he'd figured it was alright since Bambi was in fact a Witch.

Even better, she had her own money. So, he didn't need to worry about her motives. Ideally, she'd been looking for a little light fun on a Friday night. That was all!

How wrong he'd been.

"Avail, you need to see this."

"Hmm? What?" He turned and looked at the older woman who was staring at the television with her mouth hanging open.

"Pookie took pictures! *Ha!* Looks like you've finally did it this time. And look, an interview too!"

"Oh fuck! Turn it up!"

"Leedsy is a very naughty boy! Mmm hmm. He fed me whiskey and oysters on a silk sheet by the pool...

I tell you the truth I didn't mind spanking him, but the ball and gag was where I drew the line. I like it when my men talk dirty, you know?...

Of course, that's true!...

Well, he insisted on wearing my thong as a choker...

Yes, I'd be willing to go out with him again. He is a big boy after all, and his endurance is divine...

I found his size to be more than adequate though his oral skills were slightly exaggerated...

but that is nothing compared to what happened afterwards...

yeah we both saw him...

the actual Jersey Devil..."

For fucks sake...

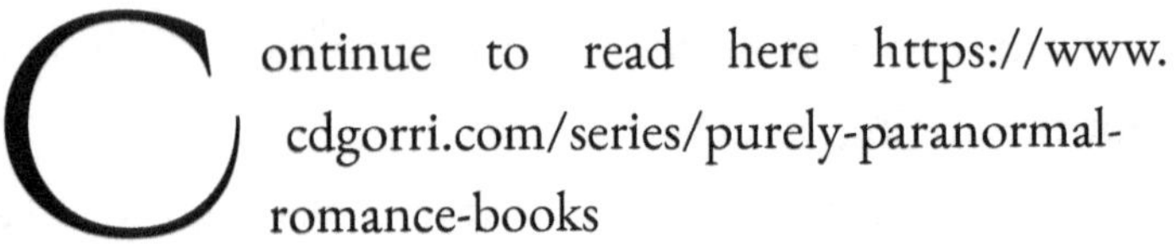

Continue to read here https://www.cdgorri.com/series/purely-paranormal-romance-books

The Maverick Pride Tales:

Dire Wolf Mates:

Wyvern Protection Unit:

Jersey Sure Shifters/EveL Worlds:

The Guardians of Chaos:

Twice Mated Tales

Hearts of Stone Series

Moongate Island Tales

Mated in Hope Falls

Speed Dating with the Denizens of the Underworld

Hungry Fur Love

Island Stripe Pride

NYC Shifter Tales

A Howlin' Good Fairytale Retelling

Standalones:

Witch Shifter Clan

Young Adult/Urban Fantasy Books

The Grazi Kelly Novel Series

The Angela Tanner Files

G'Witches Magical Mysteries Series

Co-written with P. Mattern

Witches of Westwood Academy

with Gina Kincade

<u>Blackthorn Academy For Supernaturals</u>

*<u>*Be sure to check out my BUY DIRECT BUNDLES</u> and get 30% off when you buy available only my website.*

USA Today Bestselling author C.D. Gorri writes paranormal and contemporary romance and urban fantasy books with plenty of steam and humor.

Join her mailing list here: https://www.cdgorri.com/newsletter

An avid reader with a profound love for books and literature, she is usually found with a book in hand. C.D. lives in her home state, New Jersey, where many of her characters and stories are based. Her tales are fast-paced yet detailed with satisfying conclusions. If you enjoy powerful heroines and loyal heroes who face relatable problems in supernatural settings, journey into the Grazi Kelly Universe today.

You will find sassy, curvy heroines and sexy, love-driven heroes who find their HEAs between the pages.

Wolves, Bears, Dragons, Tigers, Witches, Vampires, and tons more Shifters and supernatural creatures dwell within her paranormal works. The most important thing is every mate in this universe is fated, loyal, and true lovers always get their happily-ever-afters.

In her contemporary works, you will find fiercely possessive men and the smart, confident, curvy women they are crazy about. As always, the HEA is between the pages.

Thank you and happy reading!
del mare alla stella,
C.D. Gorri

http://www.cdgorri.com
https://www.facebook.com/Cdgorribooks
https://www.bookbub.com/authors/c-d-gorri
https://twitter.com/cgor22
https://instagram.com/cdgorri/
https://www.goodreads.com/cdgorri
https://www.tiktok.com/@cdgorriauthor